SAINT LIVRAQUE

Saint Livraque

Copyright © 2025 by Alastair Rudra Sharp. All rights reserved.

No part of this publication may be reproduced, stored in a retrieval system, or transmitted in any form or by any means, digital, electronic, mechanical, photocopying, recording, or otherwise, or conveyed via the Internet or a website without prior written permission of the publisher, except in the case of brief quotations embodied in critical articles and reviews.

ISBN: (hardcover)
            (paperback)
            (ebook)

Printed in the United States of America

Saint Livraque

Alastair Rudra Sharp

OTHER NOVELS:

The Crooked Wings Trilogy:
Crooked Wings
Spreading Wings
Ocean House

There's a Way
and its sequel: Devil Whisperer

Up from the Bottom

The Book of Consequences

Taking Care

Alone (a pandemic novel)

Forword

While this is entirely a work of fiction, the denizens of a certain hilltop bastide in the Lot et Garonne department in South West France may recognise some similarities, perhaps some slight misrepresentations and more than a few wilful flights of fancy.

It is to them, who after all were the impetus, that I dedicate this work. Thank you one and all, even the bats and their fleas.

Saint Livraque

That Wednesday was quite a day.
Things crashed.
We officially went bust and closed the café.
Sally's uncle crashed down stairs in his dilapidated five storey hotel in France and broke his leg.

This pandemic seems to have turned everything upside down. We were doing pretty well before they brought in the lockdowns. Our little café, «The Crooked Nook», in a narrow lane on the edge of the central business district in Melbourne, was attracting a dedicated following. We did some fancy variations of coffee, six different kinds of «milk» and Sally was making fabulous one-of-a-kind pastries that sold out like «hot cakes», if you will excuse the expression.
However.
There is always debt
There is rent to be paid.
There is the burden of insurance.
And then there is a myriad of little expenses that running a small café requires.
Why are teaspoons so expensive and why do otherwise law-abiding citizens steal them?

Although we were doing a quietly roaring trade, we weren't exactly getting rich. On a good day, when the sun shone, we would be packed out, all our little tables out in the laneway well occupied. But even then, we discovered that making enough to get ahead was challenging. We were eking out an existence, an enjoyable existence for sure, but that was all.

At the time, we were both coming off failed marriages.

Mine just fell apart from disuse, a kind of mutual apathy. Gigi and I never had an argument in our whole relationship, it was just that we weren't very interested in each other any more. I barely remember what attracted us in the first place. We stuck it out for a while, then we agreed to do something different. We sold the house, thanked each other for not having produced any children and split the proceeds. She went to live in the Northern Rivers, where she met a lady farmer, fell in love and has a much better relationship than we ever had. She has baby goats.

Sally's marriage was different. She married the man of her dreams, a well-known footballer, a physical he-man who seemed to have no fear of anything. At first he was a very loving husband, they were a picturesque pair on sports award nights, but it was all a front. He was very good at football, but after a couple of concussions, which forced his early retirement, he rapidly deteriorated into a monster and beat her up almost constantly. He took all his pent up rage and poured it onto her. She stuck it out for way too long, because she really loved him. Finally, black and blue, she got a restraining order against him. She got the divorce on the strength of it and that same day he drove his Lotus Elan off a railway bridge. They were on the front page of the papers again but for a very different reason. Sometimes Sally ruefully wonders whether she should call herself a widow or a divorcee.

We met in the local amateur theatre group.

Although I had always harboured a desire to be an actor, I never took the plunge to try to do it seriously. As they say, ninety-nine percent of actors are out of work ninety-nine percent of the time. I got a proper, as they say, day job. My mid-level position in the Department of Veterans Affairs never excited me at all but kept me respectable, satisfied my parents' worries for their son's wellbeing, paid me regularly, and diligently contributed to my superannuation. So instead of grovelling in actors' agents' waiting rooms and doing underpaid ads for sugary drinks, I joined the local amateur theatre. Gigi hated the theatre, so that was another reason why our marriage had no juice in it. I spent my nights and weekends as a part time thespian and she watched American soap operas.

The theatre group was auditioning for the Importance of Being Ernest. I was of course expecting to be cast in the lead rôle of Mr Worthing and, as the director was my old buddy David, it was pretty much guaranteed.

Sally came, albeit reluctantly, to the audition. She had no experience in the theatre at all, but had been dragged there by her bestie Annabelle who was auditioning to play the ingenue Cecily. Annabelle aced it. She could put on an eloquent English plummy accent and had quite a sexy delivery, so she was perfect. Sally did her best to read for a small part, but she was as nervous as a titmouse and tended to fall over the lines. She was close to tears by the end of it.

After the audition we had afternoon tea in the foyer of our little theatre. I took pity on Sally and sat with her. She admitted that this was her first ever experience at this kind of thing. There was something about her that made me lean in and listen to her with care. She had an honesty, a sweetness that I found quite charming.

After my marriage floated away I moved into a small flat, walking distance from the office and close to the theatre. I lived a quiet, static, almost celibate kind of existence. The theatre was the most important thing in my life. I was attracted to different women, on and off, but nothing of any substance came of it. I think maybe I had convinced myself that this kind of non-commitment was the kind of life I liked. It was trouble free. I think I was playing the leading man in my own domestic comedy.

I don't really know why, but at the end of the afternoon tea, I asked Sally if she would like to join me for an evening meal that night. She was still shaky from the audition and not all that keen, but Annabelle pushed her and she reluctantly accepted. Annabelle claimed she couldn't join us because she was meeting her boyfriend. Maybe she was.

We went to a little Vietnamese place which I went to quite often and it turned out she liked Asian food as much as I did. It was a pleasant evening and our conversation stayed carefully neutral but friendly. When I suggested we exchange numbers, she was willing.

As it turned out, David's stage manager had a bust up with her assistant, who instantly quit. By then we were well into rehearsals and Annabelle suggested that Sally might be a good replacement. Sally was managing a bistro in one of the big hotels, so her times were a bit challenging, but she took it on. We quickly saw that she was a skilled manager. She had a great head for details, calm under pressure, worked fast, and was perfect in the ASM rôle. The stage manager adored her. It turned out that being behind the scenes suited her much better.

The play went well, we got some nice reviews, especially Annabelle, and we closed to a full house. And by then I knew that I really liked Sally. We had seen a lot of each other in the course of the play, but we also managed to find time to be on our own. She shared her marriage story with me and I shared mine. Neither of us was at all interested in trying it again.

Life went on for a while, and we found ourselves gravitating towards each other quite a lot.

Then there was one afternoon down at the Fairfield Boathouse with the froth on our cappuccinos silently popping in the sun when somehow we were holding hands and gazing into each other's eyes. Without even thinking about it, I asked her if she would like to come and live with me. I suppose that I should admit that our relationship had become gently physical, very tentative at first but very sweet.

Her response was not what I expected.

She began to cry.

Then she admitted that she had a terrible fear that she had fallen in love with another «leading man», like her husband, and that terrified her. That she said she had fallen in love took my breath away, because I knew I was pretty much the same.

So we went on holding hands and the froth on our cappuccinos evaporated.

She stayed a few nights with me in my little flat and it was wonderful to wake up and find her beside me, but it was way too small for two people. Her flat was not much better.

So, in a way, the first thing we did as a «formal» couple was to co-sign a lease on a bigger one.

That was a few years ago now.

Then as we both crossed into our forties, we talked about doing something different.

Sally's Uncle Kurt is a self-made eccentric. He trained as a mechanic, but never worked in mainstream automotive establishments. Instead he set up a garage where he customised all sorts of vehicles. Several wild-west kind of car films used and abused some of his modified monsters out in the desert and wealthy car collectors came to him to create expensive one-offs. He was minorly famous and made pots of money.

Then a few years back he sold his business to an American software executive for a massive sum, including his impressive collection of his own inventions, and took off overseas.

Kurt was the youngest of three boys, never married and never admitting to having fathered any children. I wondered if maybe he was gay but Sally doesn't think so, because he doesn't use eau de cologne. Anyway, she says, now and then she would meet certain women when she went out to stay with him, but none of them seemed to last very long. I suspect he was not all that easy to live with.

He is probably approaching sixty but never says anything about his age. He's a big fellow and muscled, although I never saw him work out nor did he seem to be interested in sport. He likes to laugh and he has that deep big man's voice that booms.

Kurt was very fond of Sally, mainly because she was an only child and the youngest of the extended family. Her father had been, as she describes him, a distant presence in her life, working long hours in a highrise city office and saying little to anyone at home. She always thought that he didn't think much of her, and she wondered if she was a disappointment to him because she was a girl and he had no other children. She never broached the subject with him. Her mother was the power in her household, according to Sally. Her mother is a wonderful woman, warm and generous, and once her husband died, he retired and died in quick succession, she seemed to find a new energy to her life. She went back to Latrobe University as a mature-age student and now runs a charity for single Mums.

Kurt was the most important male in Sally's early life and she adored hanging out with him. He taught her to drive by taking her out to his private testing ground, behind his big workshop, buckling her into an incredibly powerful souped-up Corvette and letting her go round and round the circuit by herself till she perfected it. She was twelve at the time. She didn't hit anything and is still is an incredibly skilled driver.

I met him several times and he would clap me on the shoulder and tell me if I treated his Sally properly I would be his friend for life. I promised I would.

I think he used Old Spice.

After he took off, from time to time Sally would hear from him as he described roaming around Europe. In Italy, he bought a massive red Ducati and put a matching trailer on the back. He holed up in the Austrian Alps and we wondered who with. It always sounded a little like he was looking to settle down somewhere, telling her about some gorgeous village above the snow line, or a beachfront cabin on the Adriatic, but then, after a while, he moved on. He stayed in a Gothic château perched above the Rhine and seemed to be leading a kind of monastic life, before he moved into a communal yurt in Amsterdam. I don't really know what he was doing in all these places.

Then one day he phoned up and told her he'd bought a disused five storey hotel in a small village in South West France. When she asked him why, he said he was going to do it up. She asked him what he thought he would use it for and he chuckled.

«Gonna fill it with all me favourite toys.»

We weren't sure what that meant.

He promised he'd keep a room ready for us to visit.

I felt quite honoured to be included.

It was about the time Kurt sold his business that we had decided to quit our jobs and do something together.

Sally had always wanted to have her own café, where she could design everything herself. It was a friend of Annabelle's who told her about a lane project where a row of old warehouses was being renovated and expressions of interest were being canvassed for small businesses to set up, particularly in the food line. We went and had a look and she loved the whole idea. She got a glowing reference from her Hotel boss, and with a smallish bank loan we were seen to be viable so we were given a lease.

What we leased was an empty elbow-shaped box about the size of a double garage. The warehouses had been an old bike factory at one time but why our particular one was shaped the way it was we never found out. It gave us the name «The Crooked Nook» and we liked it. It was a coffee nook and it was not straight.

The project developer had put in basic electrics, plumbing and insulation and the lessees would be expected to do the rest. No rent would be paid until the business opened.

The bank loan covered all the lease pre-payments with enough left to do the development of the café. Neither of us had been great savers, and what we had from the sales of our two flats soon disappeared.

I have to say the six months we spent on it were the happiest I have ever spent. Sally designed it: the little kitchen at the back, then a serving counter behind the open space for cute little tables and benches round the edge. We found most of the furniture in an opshop in Gembrook. They had a nice 1950's mismatched look about them. Our tables and chairs could be set both sides of the laneway in decent weather. I did as much of the physical work as I could. I am OK with my hands and I learnt lots by visiting the other guys all doing their renovations either side of us.

There was a community spirit to it as we formed a kind of club, sharing tools, solving challenges, and planning our big opening. We were an eclectic lot. An Italian family creating a Sicilian bistro, an older Vietnamese couple looking to do traditional cuisine, two vegan ladies who were monsters with power tools and had a fondness for root vegetables, and a blonde Swedish chocolate maker who was also a body builder and sang opera as he worked. Together we were creating a small international hub of good things to eat and drink.

The idea was to get everyone's shop ready at the same time for a grand opening.

The Council offered a moderately generous grant for the inauguration which allowed for a bit of pre-publicity. We got interviewed on local community radio and our little enterprise was featured in a glossy brochure. There was even enough money to fund a street band. They did super loud Pearl Jam songs. It was a great day, a local Councillor gave a short and pointless speech into a microphone that sporadically cooperated and hordes of people streamed in.

After the euphoria of the opening, of course as we got going we made mistakes, made messes, laughed a lot and finished up exhausted, but we were happily up and running.

Things started off pretty well. Sally was out the back cooking fabulous things. I got to be a more than passable barista and played front-of-house to my heart's content.

Then Covid struck.

We had to close for the lockdown and lane life died. The laneway had no chairs and tables. It was forlornly bleak.

There was a gentleman's agreement on the rent to be greatly reduced and we bunkered down and held our breath. We spent miserable days at home, watching the news on TV for way too long which was depressing. The theatre was closed. At one point there was a brief opening for while, with face masks and all that and the rent quickly went back to normal.

Then we closed down again as the second wave came in.

By the time it looked like the lane might come back to life it was too late. We'd simply run out of money. Literally. We had used up all we had. The bank, who had been so friendly when we started up, was now stone-cold business.

We were done.

So that was a distinctly odd Wednesday.

In the morning we signed the papers and closed the shop. A couple of gay guys were negotiating to take it over and we would recoup a little something from the sale of the contents.

Then Kurt called Sally.

He was in hospital, dealing with medicos who only spoke French. Evidently he had scant French. He had fallen down a flight of stairs and broken his leg. He was asking if Sally could come and take care of things.

Sally told him what had happened so far that day, and to her complete shock he started laughing.

«Perfect!» he yelled. I could hear him across the room. «Nothing to hold you two back!» Then he told her he would buy our tickets right away. He said he thought we could get a flight to London, as they were just starting to reopen international travel.

Although we had hummed and haa-ed a lot about getting the jab, we knew we had to if we were to keep the café going. We even got double jabbed. Of course that turned out to be a waste of time from the point of view of the café. We had a general ambivalence to the jabs, having spent too much time on the internet reading opinions of scientists on both sides, but at least now we could travel with our health passes.

Sally put down the phone and stared at me.

«Do you want to go to France?»

«Pourquoi pas?» I said dredging up the best of my high school French.

She called him back and told him we were willing to come.

I spent the rest of the afternoon checking in with the contacts I still had in the public service about travel and health cards. They were great and showed us shortcut ways to get the documents we would need. For once I was happy that I had spent all those years in the Department.

For the following week we were in a flurry of activity, closing up the flat, renting a storage bin for its contents, finishing handing over the café and its contents, buying suitcases and telling our bemused families where we were going.

Most everyone thought we were nuts to be travelling with all this covid in the air. Kurt's folk already thought he was nuts.

Sally's Mum was the only enthusiast. «Go on,» she'd said, «be a devil, two devils.» Then she smiled. «Maybe I'll come and visit.»

We talked to Kurt every day. He was bored stupid stuck in the hospital until they hobbled him with a full leg plaster and he could go back to his village. He complained in very fruity language, but at the same time he never seemed to be out of good humour. He was looking forward to seeing us and he had great plans for the hotel.

Back in the village he told us that, as he couldn't climb his stairs, he was living in the spare room of his English friend Patrick, whose wife, he said, when she was out of earshot, was something of a harridan.

Our tickets arrived and they would take us through Heathrow, round London to Gatwick by bus and then backtrack to Bordeaux.

Kurt promised that Patrick would be there to pick us up.

So just a week later our pre-flight Covid tests showing negative, we were on one of the first Qantas flights to London where we would connect with the short hop back to France. Uncle Kurt was a generous spender of money and so we flew business. I had never done that, never even imagined I would ever do something so extravagant.

They treated us like royalty the whole way. I think the crew were just so happy to be on the job again. The business lounge in Singapore was sumptuous and we were only sorry that our lay-over was so short.

At Heathrow we went through the landing process of lines and documents, but our health cards worked and business class passengers got priority. Quite frankly everyone seemed rather overjoyed that people were starting to travel again and we were treated like minor VIPs. Maybe it was the euphoria of reopening after the pandemic or maybe we were so euphoric ourselves that we just imagined that everyone else was too. Maybe it was the champagne.

To make the quick flight to Bordeaux meant a change of airports. Being business class got us onto the first bus that tootled halfway round London on a busy freeway to Gatwick airport and into another business lounge. We probably drank more complimentary champagne than was good for us, but I reasoned it would help our immune systems. Certainly by the time we boarded the British Airways flight for the final leg, Sally was distinctly giggly.

And then, almost before we knew it, there we were on French soil.

It's a two hour drive from Bordeaux to Saint Livraque.

Patrick is a wiry little man, in his sixties, with a thin wispy moustache and threads of brown hair wandering aimlessly across his scalp. He was standing outside the big glass doors with a chunk of cardboard with «Sally and Greg» written in black paint. Obviously he'd done it in a hurry as the paint had run. It wasn't such a bad bit of artwork, in a way.

When we waved he was all smiles. As soon as we emerged with our shiny new suitcases, he started talking a mile a minute and I have to say I did not understand a word he said. Turns out he's from Shropshire and he has an accent, kind of like Welsh.

He led us to his car, a very old model right-hand drive Rover from England. For the next two hours, because I was sitting in the front, I nearly had heart failure as we plunged into the traffic on the wrong side of the road from what I was used to, sitting where the steering wheel should have been, hurtling through rural France. Obviously he'd been in France long enough that it didn't bother him at all. He chattered away the whole time as I gradually worked out how to understand his accent.

We sailed off down an immaculately neat freeway, paying a toll at the end. I offered to pay the toll, but Patrick assured me that Kurt had taken care of that.

Once we left the freeway we snaked through winding back roads only wide enough for one car. Patrick barreled along and the aging suspension on the Rover let us know the conditions of the road surface as we went. The country roads were not cared for like the freeway. We had a few near misses as all the drivers coming towards us seemed to think they were on their own private road, blithely expecting that no-one would be coming the other way. Miraculously we didn't hit anyone or get driven into a ditch. We crossed canals a few times on tiny bridges that were strictly one lane wide and negotiated a couple of villages where the streets were narrow and had blind corners. It was all exotic and fascinating but the champagne finally hit Sally and she passed out on the back seat.

The last part of the journey was a steep uphill.

The Rover roared away as we climbed a twisting and turning road above a wonderfully fertile valley that stretched off into the distance, following the bends of the river. Here and there wide swathes of sunflowers made the valley look like a green and yellow quilt.

At the top of the climb, the walls of the village are the first thing you see. The road runs up underneath a steep, thickly vegetated slope, then loops sharply round to go in through what had been the arched defensive entrance back in the middle ages.

«Welcome to Saint Livraque.» shouted Patrick over the revving Rover, and Sally sat up.

2.

Kurt was sitting on a cane chaise longue in the late afternoon sun when we pulled up.

He swung his plastered leg sideways and lurched to his feet. Sally staggered out of the Rover and they gave each other a bear hug. Kurt is a big boy, solid in every direction and he enfolded her in his big arms with great affection.

He looked over her head at me and grinned.

«Bienvenue mon pote!» he bellowed. His French had an awful Aussie accent.

Patrick's wife came out to greet us and I was surprised to see that she was a head taller than Patrick and much younger. She didn't look like a harridan to me. She did have an accent as strong as her husband, and she was in fact Welsh.

The Browns had bought their little house about fifteen years ago, paying not much more than the price of a mid-sized Renault for it. The previous owner had died, a French war widow, and her family, all of whom had moved to big cities for work, just wanted to get rid of it. It had seen no physical improvements, probably since the 1970's. Living on Patrick's pension, they had done it up themselves, bit by bit, and it was now a cosy little place full of handmade home comforts.

It only had the one spare bedroom now dominated by Kurt, so we were to be housed in the village «gite» next door. A gite is a self-catering house you can rent for a day or a month, where almost everything is supplied. Kurt had booked us in for a week. The Mairie, the village council, owned the gite, and village residents got a discount if they rented it. Kurt had just qualified. The gite house was very nicely renovated, with a modern kitchen fully equipped and quite a fancy bathroom, while keeping the old big exposed beams and the classic paneglass windows.

Although we had been fed and alcoholed prodigiously for the whole journey, the Browns had prepared a welcome feast. We installed our suitcases next door and came back for home-made soup, a generous gratin of home-grown veggies and a rich rum-infused English trifle.

We both tried our best to stay awake while our hosts plied us with questions about our journey, our life in Australia, including how we dealt with Covid. Obviously not too much happens in this little village so they were hungry for fresh stories.

We finally excused ourselves and stumbled off to bed next door, utterly exhausted and totally unable to work out what time it was.

We woke to banging on the front door, having no sense of what hemisphere we were in or even what day it was.

Kurt wanted to show us his hotel.

We moaned and groaned but there was no curbing his enthusiasm. We dragged ourselves next door and had breakfast with Kurt and Gwyn. Patrick had gone off down the hill to the nearest bigger town that actually still had working shops. He came back with warm croissants and a baguette. It was a bit sad that Saint Livraque had lost its bakery a few years back. A French town without a «boulanger» isn't a real French town any more.

They were the best croissants we had ever tasted, steeped in butter with a fine slightly crunchy crust and a lightly moist inside that melted in your mouth. Evidently, in France, a good croissant must please all five senses.

These ones certainly did.

Once we had gorged ourselves on several of what could have been prize-winning croissants, Kurt was on his one good foot ready to go.

We walked beside him, slowly, up the street, and took in the village. Most of the houses are joined together and there is a pleasing architectural style that they share. They are not identical but variations on the local look, many with layers of thin horizontal red bricks between wooden cross beams, some of them diagonal.

When we reached it, Kurt's hotel was only impressive because of its size. It is the biggest building in the village if not quite the tallest, being only slightly shorter than the top of the spire of the Catholic church. It probably had a nice original facade of stone at one time, but in years gone by the facade had been plastered over with what is now very crumbly grey stucco. The French word for it is «crepi», which to my ear sounded very appropriate.

At first glance, the building looked like a sad candidate for demolition, but as Kurt made his crutch-inhibited way towards it, he cautioned us not to be fooled by the outward appearance.

«A hidden gem!» he crowed, «about to be brought back to life.»

Our first impressions were not enhanced by the rusty iron sign tilting dangerously over the rotting canvas awning with the name of the hotel in barely decipherable letters: «Hotel des Chauves Souris».

«Bats.» explained Kurt, when I asked why the hotel was named after bald mice. My schoolboy French was still functioning enough for me to know the word for «bald» (chauve) and the word for «mice» (souris). I didn't need to ask why bats were called bald mice, because it sort of made sense.

Sally asked a better question. «Why would you want to call your hotel a bat hotel?»

Kurt laughed. «Well you could say that towards the end of its commercial life, it did welcome lots of what you might call human bats, but that's not the historic reason. No, our little village, at one time, so I am told, was a bit famous for its bat caves. There's a whole row of them under the ramparts. Full of bats.»

By then we were standing out in front of the building looking up.

«Why did people like bats?» asked Sally.

«Search me.» he shrugged.

«What did you mean by human bats?» I asked.

«Well,» he said, «not to put too fine a point on it, this hotel, which was quite fancy, once upon a time, ended up as, well, not much more than a bit of a whore house.»

He pushed open the wide wooden door at the centre of the front, not needing a key to get in. He had to lean on it to get it fully open. He reached around and switched on the light. A long fly-specked fluorescent light hung down from the ceiling and, once it had stopped flickering, we found ourselves in a large room with quite an ornate fireplace in one corner. The room was littered with piles of rubble and building materials.

«Fancy restaurant in its day.» said Kurt. «Big kitchen out the back.»

He pointed to a pile of what I thought were toilets. «Bet you've never seen one of those.»

Sally took a closer look. «Wash basins?»

«Nah,» he grinned, «bidets.»

Neither of us knew what he was talking about.

«A very French invention for lady's hygiene. Two floors up, there were ten tiny little rooms with paper thin walls between them. Each room had one single bed, a wash basin and one of these. One shared toilet at the end of the corridor but no showers.»

«It was a brothel.» I said, just to be certain what we were talking about.

«It was.»

Sally smiled. «I hope you are not going to continue in that line of business.»

«Not my style,» he said. «Anyway first thing I did up there was knock down all the walls and pull out everything on that floor. I didn't like the vibe. I have different plans for that level.»

He led us into the back of the building and the kitchen was indeed big but in no condition to cook anything any more. Huge black stoves and a vast walk-in coolroom suggested a previously prosperous outfit. There were spider webs everywhere. It could have been the set for a film about ghosts or a halloween horror flick.

«This all has to go.» he said.

Then beyond the kitchen was another building with a small rotting wooden door, threatening to fall apart. He pushed it open to reveal a big open space with massive wooden doors at the other end which would lead to the street behind.

«This was the grange, back in the day.» said Kurt. «They would have kept their animals in here. Half the houses in the village have granges like this. Back in the middle ages your animals were your wealth.»

There were no cattle of course but car bodies instead. His shiny Ducati sat with its trailer amongst a collection of old vehicles, none of them shiny. They were all coated in layers of neglect. More props for the horror movie.

Sally grinned. «These came with the property?»

«Yep.» He put his arm round his niece, «When I saw them, I knew this was my spot.»

He introduced us to each one, like they were his pets. He had plans to do them all up. I had never heard of some of them. One was a pale blue Simca Aronde, which he had decided would be the regular vehicle for getting around. Another one was a little red Deux Chevaux with a saggy soft top and headlamps that made it look like a frog. He managed to prise the door open and it was full of cobwebs. «I have plans for this little baby.» said Kurt looking at Sally, «I reckon she'll be your petite amie.».

She poked her head in and said, «That won't be soon.»

Lurking in the shadows was a big black Panhard which looked like something from an old French film about funerals. When I asked Kurt if he had a plan for it, he patted it, which raised a cloud of dust. «Not yet.» he said.

There was a dark green Peugeot 203 and I had to admit I had heard of them, but as it had no wheels and sat on wooden blocks, I didn't think it would be doing anything too exciting for a while.

Then there was a big old grey van with a snub nose.

«Classic Citroen this is.» said Kurt running his hand lovingly along its cobwebbed flank. «Gonna be my work horse.»

«Are you going to start up a garage business?» asked Sally.

«Doubt it.» he muttered. «Bloody French bureaucracy would drive me nuts.»

«So all these cars are your toys?»

«Yep. Gonna dig a pit, put in a hoist, and renovate these babies.» he said, and you could hear the relish in his voice.

Patrick joined us as we stood there.

«Loads of potential, don't you think?» he said.

«For what?» I asked.

«Could be anything.» he said. «Look at the size of it.»

«The question is,» said Sally, gazing around her, «what would be viable in a little village like this on top of a hill?»

«Oh you'd have to use your imagination for that,» Patrick said. «I grant you IKEA won't be opening a branch up here.»

«Wait till you see upstairs.» said Kurt. «It will blow your mind.»

«I can't see you going upstairs anytime soon.» said Sally.

«You are not wrong.» he grunted. «Bloody stairs. I should've fixed them, soon as I bought it.»

«Planning to put in a lift?» I thought I was making a joke but he lowered his considerable eyebrows and glowered at me.

«Nah.» Then he clumped his way back towards the front door. «Patrick'll take you up. Watch out for the rotten steps here and there.»

«I think I just hurt his feelings.» I said.

«He is a bit sensitive.» said Patrick.

The stairs going up were narrow, dark, creaky and treacherous. Patrick guided us past the worst bits, although there was a string of pale yellow bulbs hanging over the stairs to slightly diminish the gloom. Between them ran fine filigrees of spider's web forming a kind of lace ceiling,

The next floor up had a corridor running down the centre with rooms off it on either side. There was junky furniture in all of them.

At the far end, Kurt had decided that was his bedroom. He'd rigged up a sort of temporary ensuite, if you could call it that, bare pipes running along the wall to a toilet that wasn't attached to anything yet, a shower base that also seemed to be just sitting on the floor.

«Very basic plumbing at this point.» said Patrick. «No hot water yet.»

It certainly wasn't legal, seeing that the effluent from everything seemed to run down one pipe. I wondered where it all went but I wasn't going to ask.

The bedroom itself was not much more than a big mattress on the floor, surrounded by piles of boxes and a few clothes, mostly motor cycle leathers, hanging on nails along the walls.

«He was living in this?» Sally asked, looking around her.

«Uhuh.» nodded Patrick. «It's a bit rough but he thought he'd get onto fixing things up pretty fast. Won't happen quite so fast now.»

We went carefully up to the next level where the ten brothel rooms had been. Sure enough he had really cleaned it out. It was completely bare. You could see the marks on the exterior walls and across the wooden floors, showing where the rooms would have been and the holes where pipes from all the bidets and wash basins would have drained. Here and there on the floor were buckets to catch the leaks from above.

There were small windows looking out to the street and then, being higher than the row of houses opposite, beyond the walls to the hills on the far side of the valley.

«It's got a lovely view.» remarked Sally.

«He's planning to make this his living space and put in big windows.» said Patrick.

I nodded. «I can see why.»

«And one more level.» said Patrick, leading us to a narrow set of dangerously shaky stairs at the back of the space.

«Can't actually use the stairs, too far gone.» he said, then he moved a wooden ladder across to lay on the stairs. He was quite an agile man for his age and scooted up the ladder and expected us to follow.

We managed, despite our jetlag and champagne hangovers but it was worth it. The top of the stairs ended in a little wooden shed with a half rotten door, opening to a flat roof terrace with a brick parapet round it. The floor was made of cement with quite a few cracks in it. I could only imagine what would happen in a major downpour, hence the buckets on the floor below. When I mentioned this to Patrick, he nodded.

«A bit like a sieve really.» he said. «It's all got to get a good reno. We've got a roofer living round the corner. He happens to be our Mayor»

If we ignored the state of the floor though, there was a lot to be admired. The outlook was spectacular. Apart from the church spire, it had an uninterrupted panoramic view of the whole area. Beyond the river valley, running from east to west, below the village walls, there were ranges of green and yellow hills undulating further and further away. Some of the hills had little villages perched on the top. It looked like the French had defence in their minds when it came to village placement.

«On a really good day, maybe three times a year, when the snow is on them and the sun is setting, you can see the Pyrenees.» said Patrick. «They're two hundred K's away but they can be as clear as day.»

«I can imagine magical meals up here in the summer.» said Sally.

«Maybe Kurt will install a dumb waiter.» I said. I knew why I kept thinking about lifts. This building had a hell of a lot of stairs

As we gazed at the French countryside, I felt a little shiver of excitement. This could be quite a fun adventure. I looked at Sally and she smiled. I think she was feeling the same.

«Romantic isn't it?» I said.

«Well it's certainly a change from our flat and the Crooked Nook.»

As we carefully descended, Sally said: «Kurt told us this was a five storey hotel but there's only three floors and the flat roof.»

«He's counting the cellar.» replied Patrick. «I can't show you that yet because the steps are not safe.»

«Is there wine in it?» I asked hopefully.

He shook his head. «Bottles yes, but none with anything in them worth drinking.»

«So how long ago was it a working hotel?» Sally asked.

«Quite a long time in one form or another. Back in the days of the French Revolution it was a Republican stronghold, anti-royalists. Then it was different things at different times. I suppose it became whatever worked according to what France was going through at the time. It stopped being a going concern before we got here. The story goes that the owners were a couple of gay guys who were running all sorts of barely legal or not at all legal activities, like hourly rent for the rooms upstairs, and supplying various substances that you can't buy at a pharmacy. As I heard it, the local gendarmerie were tolerant of it as long as they were offered incentives, a freebee at the bar, for example, maybe the occasional dalliance upstairs, but a new superintendent in the district came in. The way I heard it, he was a «by-the-book» kind of man and the boys had to do a midnight runner.»

«I suppose that's why there's all that stuff everywhere, no time to pack.» I thought.

«So who owned it after they ran away?» asked Sally.

«That I never knew, but in France, if you don't pay your «Taxe Foncière» and your «Taxe Habitation», then after a while the building gets taken over and sold off.»

«That's when my Uncle bought it?»

«Yep. No other bidders. He turned up with that massive bike of his and pitched his little tent in the caravan park under the eastern wall. I heard him come. Hard to miss that huge bike of his. So as it happened, it was the day before they did the auction. When I met him, walking Brian, my little doggie friend, he was just wandering round having a look. He'd expected there would be somewhere to eat or get a coffee. I had to disappoint him. When we passed this place, he saw the old Hotel sign and then the «A vendre» For Sale sign on the door announcing the auction. The door was not locked so we took a look inside. I had never bothered up until then, expecting that it was not worth the effort. Walking in that day it confirmed my impression. Too far gone I thought. He stood there for a long time and I had to wonder what he was thinking. He didn't say anything.

Anyway, he came back to our place for breakfast and then wandered off to explore the village. I suspect he went right back and had another look. He would have found the cars out the back.

Anyway, the next morning I went over for the auction, like just about everyone in the village. I was a bit surprised to find Kurt was there in the Mairie. Not much happens in this village so there were quite a few folk, but I knew none of them had any interest in bidding for this wreck. They were just there for the entertainment. So anyway the Mayor welcomed everyone and opened the auction.

The auctioneer named the starting price.

A few people chuckled but nothing else happened. Then when it was obvious no-one seemed interested, they opened up to any offers. I really don't think Kurt understood any of it to be honest, not being much of a French speaker, but when he saw that no-one else bid, he named a figure. He wrote it on a piece of paper and yelled. Someone else translated what he wrote. How he chose that figure I have no idea. The whole room seemed to freeze with shock and everyone stared at this new person.»

«Was it close to the starting price?» I asked.

«Less than half.»

«And they accepted his bid?»

He nodded.

«The way it works is, if they reach the amount that covers the arrears, then off it goes. He must have come in thereabouts or a bit above it. The auctioneer, who was obviously not too hopeful of getting any bids at all, was kind of relieved I think.»

«Did Kurt really know what he was buying?»

«Turns out he'd had another look that morning. Far as I can tell he wandered into the back, saw the cars, and ended up in the Mairie with his finger up. It's funny, they were happy that someone had bid but there was a bit of a reaction when he said his name, but they sorted that out. Quite frankly I think they were a bit amazed anyone wanted it.»

«That's Kurt.» said Sally. «He never did things the way normal people do.»

When we got back to Patrick's house, Kurt was talking to a heavily built bald Englishman with a thick cockney accent. What struck me was his ears. It looked like he had two raw hamburgers on either side of his head.

«This is Raymond.» said Kurt. «Gonna fix ma stairs.»

«That's good.» said Sally. «They're a mess.»

«You're a carpenter?» I asked.

«I can do anyfink.» he replied.

I couldn't resist asking: «What happened to your ears?»

He put his hands up to them as if he had just remembered he had them.

«I'm a prop.» he said.

He could see that meant nothing to me, so he added: «Rugby. I'm one of the chaps in the middle of the scrum. The old lugs get a bit of a bashin' in there.»

He was expecting, seeing we were Aussies, that we would know all about that. The Wallabies were among the best international Rugby team, if you don't count the All Blacks. Sadly we come from a part of Australia that favours a different brand of football.

He was not impressed.

While Kurt hobbled back up the street to his folly with Raymond, Patrick took us on a tour of the village.

He took his little dog Brian, a woolly little white pooch of indistinct heritage with a permanently bent tail. Patrick said he was the only dog he ever knew who couldn't wag his tail but he did do a kind of rear-end shimmy when he was happy. He did this when Patrick told him we were going for a walk.

Saint Livraque is more or less square, with a few curves and corners here and there. As we would soon find out, nothing in this village is exactly square, horizontal or vertical. I was soon thinking about it as the natural extension of the Crooked Nook. It was a whole crooked village.

On three sides the defensive walls are still there. Towering above the river they are very impressive, massively thick dark grey stone at the base to buttress the height. On the other two sides, the walls are not as thick but each shows where the other entrances to the village once stood. On the fourth side, to the east, which does not slope away as steeply, there is a wide moat outside the wall, still filled with water «and carp and frogs» said Patrick when we walked past. The caravan park sits on its bank.

«The walls are still in good shape.» I observed.

«The European Union paid to get them all restored.» Patrick told us, as we gazed down at them.

«How old are they?» asked Sally.

«Late thirteenth century.» he said. «The uncle of the French King Louis something decided to create a whole string of defensive positions in the valley. They're called Bastides.»

«Who were they defending against?»

«Sometimes the English, sometimes other French. Depends on the era.»

«So this village has quite some history?»

«It does. We will have to get our village historian to do a proper tour.»

«You have a village historian?»

«Government approved she is. Charges the set fee of four Euros per person for a tour.»

«That's all?» asked Sally.

«Government regulation.»

As we walked, we met our first Saint Livraquais or Saint Livraquaises if they were female. It was immediately clear that protocol required that you said «Bonjour» to everyone you met. If they were children you were required to kiss them on both cheeks. The children would tilt up with their heads to one side expecting it. I wondered about a fear of Covid but no-one in this village seemed to be worried about that. No-one wore masks and everyone seemed quite happy to do the «bises», cheek kisses, to people they knew, handshakes for people they didn't.

Quite a few of them were out walking their dogs.

«The best way to meet the locals is with your dog.» said Patrick. «Dogs overcome all language barriers.»

Patrick's French was basic but he seemed to manage. The locals were obviously used to him and some could even manage a bit of English.

It seemed that almost everyone in the village of a certain age had a double-barrelled name, the men had «Jean» before the next name, Jean-Claude, Jean-François, Jean-Jacques, and the women had «Marie», Marie-Christine, Marie-France, Marie-Hélène. It was unusual to find anyone with just one name, except the younger generation. There weren't too many of them in the village. Once they finished high school, it seemed that the village was no longer where they wanted to be. It is the same, so I am told, all over France. The young head for the cities.

The architecture of the village is quite homogeneous in style. The bastide is roughly square with a grid of streets, running the full width and length of the village. Behind each street there is a narrow alley. The design of bastides evidently is much the same wherever you go. There is a central square, usually with a church in it and often a covered market place. Saint Livraque has both although there is no market anymore. The streets and alleys are designed in a grid so that the Bastide defenders could run quickly from one side of the village to the other when attacks were mounted on more than one side.

Most of the houses are made of stone and most of them are attached to the others on either side with shared walls. The walls are up to a metre thick and are composed of different sized local stones all held together with a mix of mud, chalk and straw. The roof tiles are terra cotta, a universal dark red. Maybe a third of the houses are unoccupied, although some are in the process of renovation, mostly, according to Patrick, by foreigners. A few are very close to falling in on themselves.

«We are an international village.» Patrick told us as we strolled along. He would point out a house and tell us the nationality of the occupants. Some of the houses were «maisons secondaires», holiday homes for Belgians and the Dutch, who mostly only appeared in the summer. The half dozen English and Irish tended to be more permanent like Patrick and Gwyn. The newest phenomenon was the post-Brexit English who were planning to become French. Many of the other houses were rentals, with most of the renters being Portuguese farm workers.

«The one kind of European you won't find here is German.» he said, as we approached an enclosure with a stone wall at the back. Six photos of people were implanted in the stonework of the wall. In front of each photo was a stone vase with plastic flowers in it.

«The resistance was pretty strong here during the war.» he said. «These six people were shot by the SS against the church wall towards the end of the war. So even to this day Germans are not really welcome.»

«Even now?» I was a bit surprised. That was more than seventy years ago.

«Oh sure.» Then he smiled. «They were not so happy about Kurt when he said his name buying the hotel.»

«He's not German.» said Sally.

«But he sounded like one. Kurt Eissen sounds German.»

Sally nodded. «I'm an Eissen, but we are third generation Aussies.»

«Yeah, they sorted it out. But the first impulse was hackles raised.»

We stood in front of the memorial wall and looked at the photos. Each one had the name and age. Five young men, all under thirty, two of them brothers, and one woman.

«The story goes that the Brits dropped a cache of weapons in the woods for the Resistance, but someone spilled the beans. As you will find out, if you stick around in this village there are distinct factions.

Have been for centuries and the war made people take sides. Anyway when these Resistance kids went out to collect the weapons, the Bosch were sitting there. Marched them back into the square, stood them up against the church and that was that. You can still see the bullet marks. The woman was different. The Bosch were driving back in their armoured vehicles when she was on the road, taking bread to her kids. She ran when she saw them and one of them shot her just in case she was one of the resistance.»

We stood and stared at the wall.

They were all younger than us.

Hard to imagine.

It was a sunny day and when we got back, Gwyn had carried a lush green salad out to their back courtyard under a big market seller's umbrella. Evidently Gwyn had tried her luck as a market stall holder selling organic grains and seeds in the markets of different towns up and down the valley. Every day there is a market somewhere, but her business never took off. All she got from it in the end was the umbrella and barrels of unsold chick peas. Her salad was heavy on the chick peas.

Kurt had hobbled back from his folly and was sunning himself.

«So how do you like our little Bastide?» he asked when we came back.

«It's so full of history.» remarked Sally.

«Yeah. History and blood.»

«You mean what happened during the war?» I asked, as I found a very comfy cane chair to enjoy the sun.

«Which war?» he snorted. «Hundred Years War, Wars of Religion, attacks of the French crusaders on the Cathars. A thousand years of bad blood flows in the veins of every village in this region.»

«You're a history buff now.» laughed Sally.

«Nah. I just did the four euro tour with Agathe. She can do it in English, well her kind of English, but you can follow it. It's worth every centime. I'll set you guys up if you like. It takes three hours.»

«Three hours just to tour this village?»

«Three hours of history. She starts with prehistoric times, then the Romans. It's an old place.»

Gwyn served up the salad and Patrick opened a local bottle of white wine. It was that classic picture of what you always imagined life in France would be like. Sun, chicken salad and wine.

«So what's the plan?» I asked once we were pretty replete with lunch.

Kurt shrugged. «Well, I don't have one exactly.»

«Well right now you mend. You do nothing.» said Gwyn. She glared at Kurt like he was a naughty boy.

It was funny. Kurt is a pretty confident sort of bloke, a self-starter, but under her stern gaze he seemed to cringe.

«Yeah, well, that comes first.»

Sally nodded. «I can't see you living in the midst of all that rubble, even if you had two good legs.»

«I was fine before this.» he muttered, tapping his cast.

«But even then,» she said, glancing at Gwyn, «you were sleeping on a mattress on the floor, you had the most amateur plumbing I have ever seen.»

«Temporary, that's all.»

«So apart from the fact that you are a short-term cripple,» I said, «why did you want us to come?»

«You were broke, no work, no prospects. I saved your arses.»

I frowned. «You didn't know that when you called.»

He grinned and tapped the side of his nose. «Not as thick as I look.» he said.

Sally shook her head. «I reckon you called us because you freaked out. Broken leg in a foreign country. You needed help. Of course you did.

«Quite right,» said Gwyn. «Don't listen to his bullshit.»

The two women exchanged looks and I could see they were going to be a team. Kurt was in trouble. Two harridans.

«Who cares,» said Kurt. «The universe has decreed that you are supposed to live in France with me and bring the bat hotel back to glory.»

«You want to run it as a hotel?»

«Hell no. Why would I want to do that?»

«Why did you buy it then?»

«It needed rescuing. It was calling me.»

«OK. So you answered the call, bought a five storey derelict hotel. You want to bring it back to glory. How's that going to look?»

It seemed just short of total craziness to me.

«I don't know yet.» he said, scratching with his finger under his leg plaster. «It'll come to me, as we go along.»

«I still don't see how we fit in.» said Sally. «We did our little café back home, but we're not exactly renovaters.»

«It'll work out.» he said.

3.

Our jetlag wore off and the after effects of all that champagne.
We began to find our feet.
It was early in September with balmy autumn days and crisp mornings.

A short walk from the gite was a lookout that had been built into the top of the defensive wall and gave a sweeping view of the valley below. As the sun rose, we would take our cups of tea and go down there to watch the sunrise. We never saw the Pyrenees, but the rolls of green hills across the valley were just as picturesque. The sun would highlight little villages here and there while the valley itelf was full of orchards, fields of ripe sunflowers and tall crops of corn, winnowing in the breeze. It was all very green and yellow, and fertile. Sadly, quite a few farms now looked like sheets of plastic as lots of the strawberry and tomato growers had huge hot houses. It was a patchwork quilt of textures and colours.

Sometimes the valley would be blanketed in fog drawn down by the river. Some mornings it was as if we were looking out across a puffy white lake of cloud with the far hills as the lake shore. Then, as the morning began to warm, the fog would rise and dissipate completely before it reached the walls of Saint Livraque.

Hobbling maybe, but Kurt was unstoppable in his quest to get the renovation of the Bat Hotel on the go. He still had no idea what the end product would be, but that didn't seem to faze him in the slightest. At the very least he wanted to have all the old and rotten vestiges of the hotel's past infamy removed and replaced. Nothing rotten would be tolerated. Nothing should let in water, neither roof nor cellar.

The plumbing and the electrics had to be completely new. He even toyed with the idea of solar panels till he discovered that they would be illegal because he lived less than two hundred metres from an historically significant installation. This turned out to be the old market building, called the «Halle» which was nothing more than an open pavilion, but what was significant was that the roof beams, built some three hundred years ago, were all held together with wooden nails and the beams had carved joints to fit into each other. It was impressive to look at. So no solar panels.

Kurt, having established a bank account in the nearest big town, now brandished a local credit card and was flush with ready funds. I could never work out just how much money he had, but it seemed to just keep flowing. I have to say I wasn't complaining. After our near penury, thanks to the pandemic, now we were being buoyed along in great style. It wasn't that he was ostentatious in his spending, but he didn't hold back on whatever he wanted to do. He hadn't said anything about paying us, but he did say he would cover whatever we needed.

He knew what our lack of resources amounted to.

It was strange, in a way, to be out of work, not earning anything, but taken care of. Any kind of money worries seemed irrelevant, at least for now.

For the hotel renovations, most of the artisans he needed were right there in the village. The electrician lived round the corner, the plumber was the electrician's brother-in-law. The village also seemed to be populated by a small army of very willing workers, mostly on the black. («Noir» means they don't declare it.) These were locals, most of them retired, who were drawing their very comfortable French pensions but who were still illicitly plying their trades. Everyone seemed to be in on it and everyone knew who could do what. You need a man with a trailer, give him ten euros and the pile of bidets goes off to the «decheterie», the local recycle centre.

They try to recycle everything in France and the supervisor at the decheterie is very strict. Everything has to go in the correct container or you get yelled at. I doubt there is a market for second hand bidets, but you never know. All the old kitchen fittings and the furniture went the same way. Every now and then Patrick and Kurt would go off with the borrowed trailer and come back with souvenirs from other people's throw aways. Patrick loved rescuing old things. They did score some impressive old doors that Kurt intended to use, somewhere.

A week after we arrived, the place was a hive of activity. There were workers tearing out anything that was rotten, which was probably half the building's interiors. Kurt stumped painfully and loudly up and down the stairs while Raymond tried to fix them. I quickly recognised that Raymond was more bluff than skill, and I wondered just how secure those stairs were going to be. He seemed mostly to be driving in a lot of nails, ignoring the possibility that he was simply covering up the rot. Meanwhile Kurt went on yelling his instructions and having whoever was around translate them into French for the locals. The only French words he seemed to be fluent with were the swear words. He was «putain» this and «merde» that, almost every sentence. The standard Aussie swear words seemed to work just as well alongside the new ones.

I helped out here and there, but mostly I felt a bit superfluous as a workman. So with lots of time on our hands, Sally and I settled into discovering life as new Saint Livraquais. That's how the French say it when there are two genders involved. French is a very gender-conscious language, where everything has to be either male or female. Some of it is obvious but much makes no logical sense at all. A car is feminine, a boat is masculine. If you ask why, they shrug and say «C'est comme ça», that 's the way it is. If it's a group of different things or people then it is always male.

As he promised, Kurt lined us up the village historian for the four euro tour. I should say «historienne», seeing as Agathe was a woman.

Her English was workable with a strong accent but she was full of history and proved to be excellent value for our combined eight euros. We started at the lookout, gazing out into the valley and imagining neanderthals tromping about with clubs or creating cave galleries of ice-age grafitti. Further up the river there are caves that were occupied by troglodytes, so they say, thousands of years go. In more modern times, the Romans built a road heading towards Spain a few valleys across and in this valley they established outposts, at least one with a stone bath house. In several small villages along the river, traces of them can still be seen, although in France there are so many relics that nobody takes too much notice of them. Coming from our ridiculously infant country, at least as judged by European occupation, anything older than three hundred years was a marvel to us.

In more recent times by local standards, the eighth century, there was a big battle somewhere in the valley, Agathe was sure it was right below where we were standing, between the Frankish King Charlemagne and the Saracens. The Franks won.

It was fascinating to imagine the battles and the comings and goings of different civilisations over centuries. Of course we had to overlook the big sixteen-wheeled trucks barrelling along the main road in the valley below while Agathe described cavalry charges and siege engines. Almost every century something dramatic happened.

In the middle of all this I asked about how the village got its name. Was there in fact a real Saint Livraque?

Like the answer to so many questions, it came with the Gallic shrug. There is a story of course but whether it is based on fact or fantasy, according to Agathe, no-one is too sure. Historians, she insisted, like to be certain of their facts, and she was not certain. Nonetheless she was more than happy to share the story, whether it was nothing more than a myth or not.

The story goes that Saint Livraque was a young man, from a semi-noble family, who managed the household of a medieval Lord in some province in the north of France. She thought it might have been in Alsace. So one year, there was a terrible drought creating a wide-spread famine, which meant the peasants were starving. One night, according to the story, this young man had a vision of an angel who told him to open the granaries of the Lord to feed the people. Even knowing his Lord would throw a fit, he obeyed the angel and did it. The grateful peasants thought he was a saint while the Lord put a price on his head. He became a saintly fugitive. According to legend he fled to the far end of France, our end, and took up residence in the caves below the walls of our village. This all happened long before the walls were there. So even if it is just a legend, it makes a good story.

I asked if there was a shrine to this saint, but she shook her head. They don't seem to know when exactly he lived, when he died, or where he was interred. If in fact he had existed at all. Agathe said she had done some research on Saint Livraque but she never found anything that confirmed whether he was real or not. I asked her if she believed in the story and she wavered, maybe, maybe not.

Then she took us off round the village. We did a circumambulation so she could describe the history of the walls and the moat. There are quarries not far off down in the valley where they got all the stones. It was hard to imagine the work it must have taken to drag all that rock up the steep climb, but I suppose back in the thirteenth century labour was cheap. Sadly none of the barbicans, the guard-houses at the entrances, are still there. They used to have draw-bridges on them according to Agathe.

Once we had heard the history of creating the defences, as ordered by the King, Agathe described how the village was then termed a bastide. There was plenty of defending to be done.

I have to admit I never really knew what the Hundred Years War was all about, but she was very forthcoming. In the fourteenth century all the villages in this valley were faithful to the English crown. The whole region from here to the Atlantic bent the knee to the English, although they were really Normans, men from the north, who had added England to their collection. This all took place after the French King called Jean the Good, lost a battle in Poitiers, so he wasn't all that good. Consequently, the territory all went to the English/Norman Crown. There was a local skirmish which Agathe claims was the start of the whole hundred year long spectacle. A monastery in English-controlled territory built a wall that a local Lord, who was faithful to the French king, claimed was an infringement on his land. His forces attacked and the monks called in the English. Start of a hundred years of war. They obviously didn't believe in arbitration or negotiation in those days. The English won that first battle and went on to years of raiding and pillaging the French, mostly using fast horses to mount lightning attacks on unsuspecting towns, raping and slaughtering the locals and carrying off the nobles for ransom. Naturally the English would have been having their way with the local maidens. Agathe seemed to be particularly interested in that, saying that there was probably a lot of English DNA in this region. These raids were called «Chevauchés», because they were rapid horse-mounted campaigns and they enabled a lot of English soldiers to become rather wealthy.

Nothing lasts forever of course, and in 1370 the gloriously named Duc D'Anjou et Du Guesclin took it all back. Then of course the English fought back and held it for a bit, then lost it again. You can imagine what happened to the locals. It must have been hell trying to work out whose side to be on. Agathe relished telling us a gory tale that in one of the oldest houses in the village, not that long ago, someone demolished an interior wall to reveal a hidden chamber behind it, full of human skeletons. Forensic archeologists tested them and said they were burnt alive by the English. The archeologists were French, so how biased they were I was not willing to ask.

Anyway, finally the English left Saint Livraque in peace. Not really. Agathe, who I am sure must love horror films, regaled us with what happened over the next several hundred years. The English left and it was a quiet backwater for a hundred years before the French decimated each other in the name of Jesus. Calvinists controlled the village at first, but the Catholics attacked unmercifully. Huguenots got slaughtered in different parts of the region and she claims that in a château on a nearby hill the Protestants barricaded themselves inside against attack. The château must have been made of wood because the Catholics burnt it to the ground, incinerating the Protestants.

When Sally finally protested that all this burning and killing was a terrible thing, Agathe lifted her hands in the French gesture of «What can you do?»

«C'est notre histoire.» she said.

She seemed to love all the mayhem. Maybe she lives a dull everyday life, so the juiciest thing is to relive the wild history that surrounds her.

To make us feel better about the current epidemic, I suppose, she told us that the population of the village was almost totally wiped out by a pandemic in the middle of the seventeenth century. Our old friend Covid was benign by comparison. No vaccines back then.

That all happened in the middle of a war when the village supported the young King Louis XIV. It was amazing how she kept all these dates straight in her head.

Not everything in the history was that dark, although she did tend to enjoy those bits more than the others. During the French Revolution there were four republican cafés in Saint Livraque where social philosophy and political rhetoric was fiercely debated. At that time it was quite an intellectual hotspot. Sadly now, each one of those establishments is just another village house. A mildly famous poet was born here in the nineteenth century but the name was not familiar to us. His house has a worn brass plaque on it, now almost totally illegible and host to pigeon poo. I half promised myself I would find a copy of his poems and see if I could read them.

The church, which dominates the centre of the village, is solid stone with a spire that houses the bell tower from which the town hears the hours and the half hours rung out. These days the church only opens for religious services once a month when the district priest, who now serves half a dozen parishes, comes up the hill in his little Renault and takes care of an ageing and diminishing congregation. Its other openings are for funerals and now and then a wedding and not so often a baptism.

Agathe had no qualms about revealing where the huge iron key is cached. One of the stones at the base of the buttress beside the big wooden door is moveable. Inside the church is very austere by Catholic standards, almost as if it is pretending to be Calvinistic. Rows of wooden chairs face a simple altar above which hangs a crucifix painted in fading colours that would do well in a horror movie. There is one stained glass window with the figure of a bearded saint with sheep.

«Is that Saint Livraque?» asked Sally.

«Perhaps.» Agathe shrugged. «I don't think anyone knows what he looked like.»

As we gazed up at it, the sun came out and illuminated the colours.

«Maybe that's a sign.» I said, and waving up to the image I said: «Bonjour Saint Livraque.»

She proudly showed us the Halle, the market pavilion with its impressive beamwork but of otherwise dubious historical importance. She readily admitted that as far as she knew nothing historic ever happened in it. The brotherhood of French Architects just liked the beams.

We stopped at the memorial erected to commemorate the First World War which stands at the Western entrance to the village. The names of the «Sons of France» who died were inscribed alphabetically, one on top of the other, on the tall grey stone pillar. They represented more than thirty percent of the total adult male population of the village at the time. Agathe hoped we would still be there in November when on the eleventh day of the eleventh month at the eleventh hour the village honours the fallen.

We passed quickly over the atrocities of the Second World War, but she insisted that we stop at the memorial wall nonetheless. The most interesting thing she said was that in fact during the war the village split itself into three factions. One was the resistance, the Maquis, who were mostly communists and Protestants. They blew up local bridges and laid landmines wherever Germans would congregate. Many of the Catholics tended to side with the Germans and formed what was called the Milice, a kind of local vigilante police. They got reviled and hunted from the village after the war. The third group were the non-aligned, mostly atheists and old folk, who refused to take sides. What was fascinating was that, as she admitted, these three groups had always existed, long before the war, in one form or another and to this day they still do. It's a three-way family feud, lasting centuries. Evidently after the war the village emptied of almost anyone who had an active rôle in the war. There was guilt to be had on all sides.

From the end of the war till now not much else happened. Agathe had nothing much to add, except the village got smaller and smaller, as one after another the shops went out of business, the schools closed and the bus no longer came up the hill. The most important recent significant events were when the Tour de France climbed the hill on three different occasions. The climb was credited as difficult.

These days, Agathe lamented, it is very quiet, except for the occasional arrival of foreigners coming to renovate the houses. The Mayor jokes that the English are coming back to make reparations for the rape and pillage of centuries ago. I think Agathe rather enjoyed the tales of rape and pillage, although I might be exaggerating her sangfroid.

As the village population dropped away, so did the commerce. Agathe showed us where the shops used to be, once some dozen of them, now dead-eyed buildings with dusty interiors. At its height it had not only the Bat Hotel but several guest houses, two cafés, two bakers, a butcher, an epicerie and two beauty salons. Agathe explained that the existence of two of everything was indicative of the town's split factions. The other split was by gender. The girls' school at one end of the town was now used for an old folks club house and the boys' school at the other had become a storage place for the town equipment.

Apart from the post-agency, a kind of sub-branch of the post office which is staffed by a reputedly unreliable lady, (Agathe's assessment) the only shop left is the bookshop. We were surprised there was one as we hadn't seen it as we walked around. She took us up a small alley, an impasse, and there it was, nothing more than a hole in the wall with a sign out front that said: «Livres Vracs». Neither of us got the joke till Agathe explained it. It was a word-play on the name of the town, but «Livres Vracs» means Books in Bulk. Inside there was indeed a bulk lot of books. Piles and piles of old books stacked on tables and sagging bookshelves. At the far end of the dimly lit garage-sized space sat an old man in a black beret, surrounded by several cats nestled in cat baskets on the floor. The smell was distinctly feline.

The old man looked up as we came in and Agathe introduced us. His name was Jean-Pierre and his family had been Saint Livraquais for centuries. He was a retired school teacher who had collected books all his life. He spoke reasonable English and he did have lots of English books. When I asked him if this was a viable business in a village with no other shops he took off his glasses so he could look at me with more focus.

«I offer my books to the world for the upliftment of the human mind. Commerce has no place in the intellect,» All this was spoken carefully in rounded English tones.

I didn't venture to ask how many customers he saw in a day. I suspect we might have been the only ones for a while. However, Agathe informed us that he opens every day from ten to twelve except public holidays.

I asked if he had a copy of the poetry of the village's most famous literary son and of course he did. I offered to pay for it, but he shook his head. «I give you this as a welcome to our village,» and handed me a dusty, thin little volume. I opened it and tried to read something. It was old French and I could not make any sense of it.

«Ah,» he said when I shook my head. «He writes in literary French, passé simple. It has a very different conjugation.»

To do the local poet justice he read one of the poems. He had a resonant voice and I sensed the beauty in the writing even if I could not catch the meaning.

Sally asked him what it was about.

«He speaks of the terrible burden of history even in a small village like ours. The burden of long existence and human misdeeds. He says that we who live here carry the burdens of our history the way dogs have fleas.»

Agathe chuckled as he explained this. «Our poor local poet did not have such a robust sense of history. He is after all a poet not a historian. Poets are, by their very nature, sad people.»

I didn't think it was wise to comment on her rather bloody enjoyment of the history as she saw it.

The poetry of the words sounded quite beautiful, but seemed at odds with the subject matter. However I didn't want to spoil Jean-Pierre's obvious reverence for the local literary hero.

I promised to brush up on my conjugations so I could take advantage of his generosity. I suspect he was happy to see it go as there would not be any other requests for it, seeing how much dust it had gathered.

Sally, who is a real bookworm, picked through some of the English books. There were many of the classics. She found one of Charles Dickens that she had never read, Bleak House. It had no price on it. When she asked how much, he moved his head from side to side. «Ah, what is a book like that worth?» Then he said: «If you bring it back when you are finished then it can be a «cadeau»».

Obviously this was less a commercial enterprise than a labour of love.

We promised to come and visit him often.

4.

Naturally enough, our one week in the gite turned into two and then three. Although there was an absolute ant-heap of activity in the hotel, it wasn't going to be livable for quite a while. Even Kurt accepted that and given that he still had one leg incarcerated in plaster, his narrow stairs were something he could deal with maybe once a day to inspect the works. Bit by bit, he let us become his work supervisors, language barriers notwithstanding. Our apprenticeship with 'The Crooked Nook» was put to good use.

In the meantime we also got to know the village more and more. We found those folk who had some English and we embarked on a rapid course of basic French. Often our conversations in the street were «Franglais» plus gestures. The French have a terrific range of facial expressions that are so much more evocative than words. The way they use their lips and the corners of their mouths is very expressive. Maybe their dexterity with their mouths explains the excellence of French cuisine.

While going up the stairs was still a trial for Kurt, he turned his attention instead to the garage and put his considerable mechanic skills to work on the vehicles he had acquired with the property. He started right away on the old Citroen van, his future workhorse.

«This is a compact work of art, this baby,» he said with his head under the hood.

It was built in 1956 and was called an H class. The engine is crammed into the small snubbed nose front and as Kurt is a big boy it was not easy for him to get into it, but he soon had the engine out and in pieces all over the floor. His plaster rapidly took on a good coat of grease smears. I wondered if he was able to find manuals to fix the Citroen, but he seemed to know what he was doing without one. Apart from anything else it would be in French.

He went off with Patrick every now and then to a car-wrecking yard further up the valley and would come back crowing with triumph that he found the part he needed. He didn't need words because he took the broken part to show the junkyard dealers. It turns out there are dozens of old vans like that lying about, so parts were never a problem, even if they weren't exactly in great condition. I loved discovering the word for van in French, a «fourgon», a bit like a foregone conclusion.

The day Kurt finally started it up, it choked and spat, but eventually he had it running. It rocked gently in place as the engine got going, as if it was really keen to get back out on the road. Kind of like a dog wagging its tail when you say the word «walk».

Once the engine was back in, with newish parts, and going to his liking, he worked on the gears, the brakes and the suspension all of which had not moved in years. It was a day of celebration when he had Patrick start the motor and actually move it a few feet back and forth to test the gears. Finding tyres the right size was not easy, they were the classic skinny tyres of bygone days, but he and Patrick found some in barely usable condition and once they were on and inflated, then at last he had Patrick back the old van out into the daylight. His right leg being rigid, there was no way he was going to drive it just yet.

The two high wooden doors to the grange opened up to the street behind the hotel. It took two of us, me and Patrick to haul them open. Patrick backed the van out into the street, where it hiccuped a few times, as if it was blinking in the sunlight after long years of hibernation. A bit of pumping on the accelerator seemed to cheer it up, and eventually Patrick got some reasonable momentum for a short run up and back along the street. Then Kurt heaved himself on board for a second run, sitting with the biggest grin on his face.

Meanwhile the plumbers and the electricians began the task of re-wiring and replumbing the whole place, which meant that we had various discussions with Kurt about what he wanted with the different areas. Where to put bathrooms, how many bathrooms, where to put light switches and wall plugs? We learnt about «va et viens» light switches. It means «come and go» which refers to switches at more than one place for the same light. We chose an open space at the back of the first floor to be our «suite», and Kurt insisted we would have our own «ensuite». The big space where the ten bedrooms used to be on the second floor would become a lounge and dining area with a kitchen at one end. We all went off with Patrick to a showroom in an expansive box-shaped store on the outskirts of the biggest town in the valley. Every town in France is like this. The centre of the town, usually featuring a church and a market place, is medieval or even older, often with remnants of the old walled defences still surviving. Around the core, with its inevitably narrow little streets, there are the houses from the later centuries, often outside the earliest defences. Most of the houses inside the towns are closely packed with shared walls, while others are a little grander and have courtyards and enclosed small gardens. Here and there, the streets fanning out from the centre had the little shops that were the domains of commerce in the middle ages, now mostly shuttered and cobwebbed. Then beyond that, in what were previously goat farms or potato fields, there are huge warehouse-sized modern glass structures of appallingly bland ugliness, being supermarkets, hardware stores, car dealers, and all the other modes of contemporary commerce lining the major roads into the town. The bigger the town, the more big box stores there are. The French call them «grand surfaces». So every town of any size consists of concentric circles of the history of merchandising.

The «grand surface» we went to had about a dozen display kitchens ranging from the basic plastic, resin and stainless steel to the high-end marble and oak, to what they called «La Cuisine Americaine» which meant double door fridges and fancy German appliances. You can design your own kitchen using their software and then they collect the pieces for the whole kitchen, appliances and all. They deliver it in boxes ready to assemble.

Raymond had managed to replace the most rotten of the stairs within a few days after some terse conversations with Kurt who quickly recognised an obvious lack of skill. Even with one leg, Kurt would stand over the work till he was satisfied. Raymond looked a bit shamefaced as it progressed. In the end we got ourselves a reasonably secure set of stairs and we found ourselves going up and down with new confidence. The stairs were now a mixture of new and old wood, kind of like a patchwork of pine and poplar, oak and elm.

Raymond insisted on being paid in cash as he completed each set of stairs. We suspected he was perilously short of money. It also turned out he had no papers to show his, if any, qualifications. He admitted, under quite some pressure from Gwyn, that he was not actually insured either, which is illegal in France. With Raymond, you paid for what you got, because there was no way he could be sued for malpractice. The illegality didn't seem to worry Kurt as long as he got the stairs done properly. Once all the stairs were done, including totally replacing the ones that went up to the flat roof, Raymond kept begging Kurt to let him do other jobs. This confirmed our suspicions that he was barely scratching out a living. He probably saw Kurt as his lifeline, or at least a short term cashcow.

Later we did discover that Raymond had a gorgeous-looking Cockney wife, much younger than him, who he absolutely adored, but who treated him like a servant. She demanded fancy things that he could not afford, and if he didn't come through she would threaten to leave him. Evidently now and then she did skip, which terrified him. Then after a few days of torturing him, she would come back and taunt him with stories of finding a new man. Although it is not exactly history, we heard all this from Agathe, told with quite some relish. We met the wife once, in the market of a town further up the valley. She was indeed very striking and dressed to impress. I almost felt sorry for Raymond.

I think Kurt did too, so more out of pity than need, Kurt let him begin to work on the front of the building. There wasn't much skill in the first phase. Kurt had decided that all the «crepi», the crumbling stucco, had to be chipped off so we could see what was underneath. Raymond assured Kurt he was just the man for the job. He certainly had the muscles.

Before the crepi could come off there were two old signs to deal with. The rusty iron sign tilting dangerously over the rotting canvas awning with the name of the hotel in barely decipherable letters, «Hotel des Chauves Souris», was desperately in need of demolition. There was also a rotting hard plastic sign with holes i it, advertising Kronenberg beer. It was hanging by one perilous metal spike. That came down first, falling apart the minute he touched it. Then when Raymond got up on a ladder to see what condition the awning was in, he gave it a good shake which disturbed a family of chauves souris, the bats it advertised. They had been nesting inside the folds of the awning and when he pulled at it, out they came. We were standing underneath and got showered in dry bat shit. They were tiny little black creatures, squealing in fright before darting away.

«The hotel had the right name.» laughed Kurt. He was actually happy that they were real bats.

Raymond was cursing in Cockney as the rotten awning had collapsed onto his bald head.

As we brushed off the bat shit, Sally wondered: «Do people really like bats?»

«Maybe it depends if you read Marvel comics.» I said.

To my amazement that meant nothing to her and she looked at me blankly.

«Batman and the bat cave?»

«Oh.» Then she said «but honestly why would this town be famous for bats?»

We decided to ask Agathe next time we saw her.

Later in the afternoon she drove past in her little Renault Cleo and we waved her down.

She looked up at the damaged wall where the canopy had hung. Some of the «crepi» had come down with the canopy. Raymond was up a long ladder attacking the stucco with a mallet. We stood well back.

«Ah yes, the bats.» Agathe said with a big smile. «Before the war the bats were quite a thing in this village.»

«Why?»

«It is because Saint Livraque himself became thought of as the patron saint of bats.»

When we looked puzzled she said: «Well every saint is the patron saint of something.»

«There must be a story attached to that.» Sally said.

«Oh yes, there is.» Agathe parked the Cleo well clear of the falling debris and came to join us in front of the remnants of the awning. «The story goes that a woman, who had a very sick child, had a dream in which she saw Saint Livraque.»

«Someone in the village?»

«No, she lived further up the valley, but in this dream he came to her, told her who he was and that the bats, he said they were his bats, they could save her child.»

«She believed it?»

«I think she was at the point of desperation. So she came up here and took her child into one of the caves under the walls.»

«The bat caves?»

«Exactly. So inside the cave there is no light so she had a candle and as she held it up, the bats all began to fly around her head. She held the child up and some of the bats came and landed on it.»

«Oh my God,» shivered Sally «that would have freaked me out.»

«But the child got cured, I assume.» I said more fascinated than horrified.

Agathe nodded. «The bats have fleas. The fleas like to suck the blood of bats but they also like to suck the blood of humans.»

«This gets worse and worse.» squirmed Sally.

I think Agathe was rather enjoying Sally's discomfort.

«No, no,» she said, «it gets better. The fleas landed on the child and sucked its blood. Whatever the child was sick with, and I think it was some kind of fever, it was gone. When the woman came out of the cave, her child was cured.»

«And people really believe that?»

«Why not? Here in France we have a long history of saints performing miracles. It is quite normal.»

«So after that Saint Livraque became famous?»

«Yes and no.» said Agathe with that classic French gesture of the hands, suggesting ambiguity. «The Catholic church refused to take up the case, because there was no real relationship to Saint Livraque, and anyway it was only one example of a supposed miracle. The Catholics need more evidence than that.»

«But the locals believed it?» I asked.

«Of course. Soon lots of people were taking their sick relatives into the cave to be bitten by bat fleas.»

«Did they get cured?»

«Who knows? Some people claim it worked and others said it did not.»

«So our little village was famous as a bat cure?»

«For nearly a century, but the Second World War seemed to put an end to it.»

«Nobody goes there any more?»

«I don't think so. Maybe some do. But there are still the fleas, and also bats are thought of as carrying lots of diseases so many people are scared of them.

«Me for one.» said Sally. «Look at the Corona virus. That came from bats.»

«So they say. It may not be true.» said Agathe.

Then I asked her «Do you believe that the bats or their fleas can cure people?»

«Who knows? Maybe.»

«Have you been into the caves?»

«I have. My Father took me when I was a child. We wore cloth like bee-keepers so that the fleas could not bite us.»

«You saw the bats?»

«Oh yes, there were hundreds of them. But I have to say that I have not been in there for a long time. As far as I know they are still there. It is not interesting.»

«And do you think Saint Livraque really is the patron saint of bats?» asked Sally.

Agathe smiled. «I like to think so. I think our village needs to have a real saint. If a village has a saint name then it should have a saint story to go with it. History demands it.»

«But there have been no recent miracles?»

She shook her head. «I haven't heard of any.»

«So now nobody comes to our village for the bats?» I asked

«It is true. It is just a part of our history that nobody is interested in any more.»

«Maybe if Kurt opens the Bat Hotel, something might happen.»

«Maybe so.»

And off she went in her little Cleo.

By the end of the afternoon Rayond had managed to remove the most dangerous of the «crepi».

The wall still looked horrible.

As Sally and I walked back to the gite at the end of the afternoon, we couldn't stop thinking about the bats and their fleas.

What would it be like if we could somehow bring the whole bats and saints story back to life? The theatre man in me was very excited. If the story could be recreated into something active, then the village itself might come back to life. It was an entertaining thought.

We had dinner that night thanks to Gwyn and her solid Welsh cooking skills and we talked about bats. They had heard the story of the cure but thought of it as a quaint old piece of folklore but nothing more.

Kurt however was more like us and he was tickled by the idea of bat tourism.

«We ought to go into the bat caves and check them out.» he said.

«Not with that leg you won't.» said Gwyn.

«Plaster's coming off soon. I'll be as good as new.»

«So even if we do go into the caves and let's say there are lots of bats, then what?»

«Stir up a story.» said Kurt.

«Pretend to get cured?» I suggested «Maybe your leg magically heals!»

We laughed but Kurt shook his head

«Get publicity.» he said, «Get people intrigued.»

«Then what?» asked Sally.

«Well then we'd have to re-open the Bat Hotel as a restaurant or at least as a cafe. This town needs something like that. Like it used to have.»

«Wait a minute.» said Sally. «Are you seriously considering going into business with your five storey monster?»

He sat back in his chair and stretched out his incarcerated right leg.
«Oh I don't know, but it's a fun idea.»

It was and a seed was sown.

All of us kept thinking about it and talking about it.

And somehow, someone must have talked to someone, because within a couple of days the whole village seemed to be interested in this new and intriguing idea. We were pretty sure Agathe might have been behind it. People kept turning up as the work went on in the hotel and asking what the plan was.

This got a little more serious when Kurt got a visit from the Mayor.

The Mayor of Saint Livraque is a direct descendant of the family that had command of the defences when it first became a bastide. Their names are inscribed on a marble plaque in the Mairie. Gérard Gaspard became the Mayor when his elderly cousin got too sick to stay in the rôle. There are municipal elections for the Council every six years and the rule seems to be that a team puts itself up for election as the Councillors. If there is more than one team standing, then elections are held. If there is only one team, then that team, unopposed, gets to choose who is the Mayor. There has only ever been one team in Saint Livraque since the war and even then, if we understand it correctly, they have trouble persuading enough locals to be on the team. So Mayor Gaspard had to be leaned on by his family but now he plays the rôle with a certain taciturn dignity. His family has been in the building trade for generations, so as well as the town Mayor he is also one of the main town artisans. He specialises in roofing.

He has almost no English so when he wants to talk to Kurt he brings his teenage son who seems to have learnt to speak English from American rap music and he speaks sort of like a resident of Chicago or somewhere. He is quite fluent nonetheless. When he is not translating he spends his time in his father's restored barn screaming amplified lyrics to rap music. The whole village gets to hear it, if not enjoy it. Who do you complain to? The Mayor?

There had been early conversations about what Kurt intended with the old hotel. At first there was a faint hope that Kurt would become some kind of hotelier. There is a liqueur licence that was held by the hotel when it was running, but in the absence of an establishment to sell alcohol, the Mairie kept the licence alive by holding it itself. They were hoping Kurt would take it on. Some of the locals, especially the older ones, hankered for the days when you could drop in at the end of the working day for a convivial glass of Lillet or Pastis. Disappointment set in pretty rapidly when Kurt showed no signs of being interested in restarting the hotel as a bar.

As there was no building construction being planned, the Mayor had not much to say to Kurt anyway. He didn't do internal renovations. However when the idea of a return to bat fame began to float about, the Mayor appeared with his son in tow.

Kurt was caught off guard a bit by the visit. The Mayor seemed to think this was a business strategy in the making and he wanted to add his enthusiastic support. Although Kurt quite liked the idea as an idea, he was certainly not ready to be too specific.

They talked about fixing the roof, meaning the floor of the terrace, but nothing else.

The Mayor left, feeling, as far as I could make out, that the whole thing was a bit of local gossip that had been whipped up for village entertainment and had no future.

The desire to explore the caves however did not go away. The whole story of the woman and the child, the old myth of the saint, it all touched the dramatic side of my nature. I wanted to take a look.

The threat however of being covered in bat fleas had to be taken seriously.

When we started talking about going into the caves, and how to protect ourselves, it was no surprise that Gwyn had the best solution. She is quite a whizz with a sewing machine so she sent Patrick off up the valley to one of those big stores that sell everything made in China and he came back with yards of mosquito netting. Sally had no intention of going anywhere near the bat caves, and Kurt was not going to make it down the steep decline to get to the caves under the walls, so it was just me and Patrick.

Patrick was dead keen. He seems to like a bit of adventure.

Within a day Gwyn had our supposedly flea-proof outfits done. She had built them around two straw hats and then sewed in drawstrings at the waist. To protect our arms and legs she had us wearing long sleeves, garden gloves and good boots.

I suppose we did look a bit like anarchic apiarists.

We decided to be a bit discreet so we carried the outfits down to a spot just above the caves and then with Kurt and Sally watching and Gwyn helping to dress us, we got togged up.

To get to the caves we followed a barely visible tangled path down a steep and rocky set of old stone steps covered in moss and sludge, so it was not easy. Patrick had armed himself up with equipment he decided might be required: a rope, a big torch, bug spray, a machete and a hammer, all hanging from a belt at his waist. Now he looked like a rock climbing apiarist. I just took my phone for photos.

At first we couldn't even see the caves at all because of the thick mass of laurel saplings, spindly sumac trees and wild figs hugging the rocks under the walls, but we eventually found an opening, and wedging ourselves between the brambles and thin tree trunks we squeezed in, carefully protecting our flea-proofing. The opening was not much bigger than one mid-sized man could fit in. At first, when we stood up inside it, we thought it was a very small cave with nothing in it, but off to one side, barely visible from the entrance was an opening that revealed a rocky kind of corridor, leading back further into the interior. The rocks are chalky limestone, light grey in colour, but quite jagged. We had to watch ourselves not to get snagged as we inched forward.

Then surprisingly it opened out into a much bigger chamber with an inward downslope, going back deeper under the village. And there they were. There were dozens of little bats, like the ones that had lived in the hotel awning, about the size of a mouse. They were hanging upside down from crags of rock, but had become agitated by our approach. Some began to fly around us, strangely silent and a bit scary.

All those horror films with bats came to my mind.

Patrick shone his big industrial flashlight up into the far reaches of the cave. It revealed other colonies, or maybe they were family groups. And then at the very back of this cave there was a spring, a small runnel of water coming from a rock fissure high up on one wall then running across the floor and then disappearing into a crevice.

I didn't see any fleas, although I suppose they are so little that they might not be visible, especially in the dark, but I did make sure my outfit stayed intact.

We looked around, although I am not sure really what we expected to find. There was nothing there except the bats and the spring. We stood there for a while and the bats seemed to settle. We were about to make our way back out again when Patrick noticed another kind of corridor going off to one side. It was very narrow and after a few metres started to slope sharply downwards.

Patrick decided to use his rope to hold us together in case there was an unseen decline. He's a very prudent man, because as he inched his way forward with me holding the rope, he nearly disappeared into a steeper drop. He worked his way carefully down and I stayed at the top to be his anchor. When he reached the bottom which was not too far, he said I didn't really need the rope and I carefully followed.

Now we were really deep under the village.

It was in this much deeper chamber that we found the signs of previous visitors, human ones. The chamber opened out as we worked deeper into it and the water from the chamber above reappeared, now running along one side and forming a pool in the middle. There were no bats here.

However it was clear that people had lived here at some point. There was a pile of broken terracotta pots and remnants of a fireplace. We looked up, using the big flashlight to see where the smoke would have gone. Certainly much of the ceiling of the cave had charcoal coating on it, but as there were various crevices going up it was impossible to tell where the smoke would have gone.

«Who would have lived here?» I asked Patrick, and my voice bounced off the roof.

«Maybe it was Saint Livraque himself!» he chuckled.

It was impossible to tell how old any of this was. Maybe Agathe would know. I took some photos.

As far as we could tell there were no more corridors going deeper into the substrata of the rock, nor was there any other entrance to this cave except the one we had slithered down.

Why would someone want to live this deep inside the hill? Who were they?

We scrambled back up the slope to the bat cave and they registered their dismay by circling us. I tried photographing them too but they were just blurs.

Again we worked our way around the walls of this cave to see if there were any other corridors or openings but we didn't find any.

At last we edged out into the sun again and took off our anti-flea armour.

5.

Agathe was very keen to find out what we had discovered.

«But there are four caves,» she said, «but you only went into one?» Then she described where the other three were and we realised we hadn't gone far enough, both along the walls and, for one of them, lower down the slope. We would have to return.

What excited her most, being of an historical bent, was the pile of shards of pottery. I showed her some photos, which were a bit dark and not very clear and she frowned. «I have not seen those before.»

When I told her where they were, she was surprised. It sounded like it was an extension of the first cave she hadn't known was there.

«So you must go back.» she said. «Get samples and we will have them analysed. Maybe they are Roman.»

«There you go.» said Kurt. «Could put our little village on the map!»

Sally had to laugh «We might have to turn your ground floor into an historic museum.»

He grinned. «You never know.»

A day later Patrick and I donned our gear and went back. We had two missions. One was to find the other three caves, and the other was to collect samples of the clay pot shards.

We started with the other three caves and quite frankly nothing much came of it. Two were quite small and did not go deep into the hillside. There were signs that people had been there, some food wrappers, cigarette butts, some dog turds. People and dogs.

The third one lower down had other caves off a fairly wide opening, and there were many signs that this had been visited often. There was a Coke tin and some shreds of paper, a baby's plastic disposable nappie and a potato chip bag. Nothing historic or worth analysing. It showed someone had been there, at least fairly recently. All of the caves had bats, but not as many as the first cave and none had running water or interesting artifacts.

We came out a bit disappointed.

Then when we went back to the first cave and made it down into the lower chamber, we had a bag to collect stuff. I knelt down and picked up a few pieces of the terra cotta and then my hand landed on something I was not expecting. A cigarette lighter. A Bic, like the pens.

«Definitely not Roman.» laughed Patrick through his flea-proof netting.

We took some of the pot shards anyway just in case.

Although Agathe was disappointed that the cigarette lighter had been with the pottery shards, nonetheless she took them. She had a friend who was a retired archaeologist. He had been the one who trained her to be the local «historienne». The way she talked about him, I wondered if he might have been a bit more than a mentor.

She went off in her Cleo to consult her friend Jacques.

I kept the Bic lighter as a souvenir.

6.

Kurt went off to get his leg checked out. When he came back he was grumpy, having expected to hear that he could get rid of the plaster.

Instead, the doctor yelled at him for not taking care of himself, especially as the cast was filthy and covered in car grease. The old cast came off and the leg was X-rayed. The bones were mending, according to the doc, but not as fast as he had hoped. He told Kurt that if he stopped stumping up and down stairs it would mend faster. Nonetheless, he was in for six more weeks on one leg.

Kurt's new clean plaster was as big and heavy as the old one and he cursed and swore.

Gwyn smirked as he railed against all things medical.

«Take things easy, what a load of crap.» he growled to anyone who would listen.

«Doesn't take a physician to tell you that.» she said tapping his new plaster with a spoon. «You are your own worst enemy.»

Meanwhile the work on the hotel went on at quite a pace and we were getting close to giving up the gite and moving into the Bat Hotel ourselves. Kurt took us back up the valley, pushing us to buy some very nice French bedroom furniture for our suite. His generosity was quite touching. It felt in a way like he had acquired us as his new family and was expressing his love in the form of gifts.

A big tough guy he might be, but inside somewhere was a good heart.

We were at the point where finishing structural work on the big salon upstairs and to the bedrooms and bathrooms on the second floor was done. The local painter and decorator had given his «devi», his quote, and now brought in his girlfriend to help him, and the two of them yelled at each other all day in Portuguese.

While the renovations were humming nicely, Patrick took Kurt off to get the van registered which was perhaps the happiest day Kurt had had for quite a while. He still couldn't drive it himself, but just sitting next to Patrick with the new seat belts on, he was all smiles.

I had to curb my inclination to wonder at the wisdom of an old truck as a workhorse, but he obviously loved the thing.

«Gonna give this old girl a good coat of paint soon and we can take her to vintage car rallies.» There was no choice about colours as all vans of that era were grey.

Sally began to spend a lot of time in the «Livres Vracs» and she and Jean-Pierre became good buddies. I think he was basically quite lonely and when she showed an interest in learning a bit more French and asking him to tell her stories about his life, he really took a shine to her.

When I gently mentioned that she seemed to be spending a lot of time round there, she grinned.

«Feeling jealous are we?»

I assured her that I was not. And anyway I liked his company just as much as she did. If nothing else, my french was really coming on.

Agathe came back with some good news. Some of the shards from the cave were quite old.

«Probably that cave has been used by different people at different times.»

«So how old?»

«A few centuries at least. One of them had part of a branding underneath from a pottery in Fumelle that has not been in business for more than a century. Jacques has kept it to show his friends.»

That seemed to be the end of our interest in the bat caves and we didn't feel any impulse to go back.

That was until the early morning when Kurt started screaming.

We heard all about it when we went over to Gwyn and Patrick's for breakfast.

At some ungodly hour of the morning, Kurt had sat up in bed yelling his head off. When they raced in to see what was happening, he was yelling at the wall opposite his bed.

When they came in, it broke whatever was happening and he stared at them, white faced, like he had seen a ghost.

He had.

«That bloody saint was right there.»

«A bad dream?»

«Who was it?»

«It was him. Livraque.»

«Who?»

«The bloody saint. The one who lived under the walls.»

«How do you know it was him?»

«He told me.»

«What did he say?»

«He reckoned he had called me.»

«He spoke in English?»

Kurt had frowned. «He must've because I understood him perfectly.»

«What did he mean, he called you?»

«Here. This village. He told me I am supposed to work for him. He reckoned he threw me down the stairs to wake me up.»

«You believe that?»

He shook his head. «Buggered if I know. It was bloody real.»

«What kind of work?»

«No idea. He didn' t say.»

«So how come you were yelling? The whole village must have heard you.»

«I dunno. I think he just freaked me out.»

So we had to chew on this at breakfast.

Kurt kept going back over it, trying to make some sense out of it.

Sally ventured to suggest it was probably the pork roast from the night before and the whole thing was just a nightmare.

You could see he rather wanted to believe that, but it was obvious he couldn't shake it.

After breakfast we went up to the hotel. The kitchen had been installed the day before and the guy who oversaw it was coming back to check that Kurt was happy with it.

We spent the morning on the finishing touches, but by lunchtime Kurt seemed to be short of breath and looking pale. Getting up the stairs was still tough. Getting to the salon was three flights.

He signed the papers, told the man what a great kitchen it was, with me doing the translation, and the man was happy.

However walking back to Gwyn's he started swaying on his feet, at least the good foot. I had to catch him from falling. He is a big bloke and I nearly dropped him.

«What's up?» I asked, as I helped him along.

«Dizzy. That bloody dream.»

He went to lie down and we started lunch in the back courtyard without him.

It wasn't ten minutes before he was yelling again.

We raced in and he was sitting up on his bed staring at the wall.

«He came back?» I asked.

He nodded. «He's getting shitty with me for not believing him.»

«What did he say?»

«He says he's going to prove it to me.»

«How?»

«If I go into his cave he will cure my leg.»

Gwyn couldn't control herself and she burst out laughing.

«Get bitten by fleas and it'll fix a broken leg? You have to be kidding.»

He looked at her, with a slightly wobbly grin, like he agreed with her, but then he shook his head.

«That's what he said. I don't know if it's the fleas or what. He just said I had to go into his cave and he would heal the leg.»

«That's ridiculous.» snorted Gwyn.

« I wouldn't be too sure. I think it's worth a try.» said Patrick. When we all stared at him in disbelief, he shrugged «I mean why not? What have you got to lose?»

«I think I might be losing me marbles.» Kurt muttered.

«What did he look like?» asked Sally.

Kurt frowned. «Well,» he said. «He was not all that old, maybe my age. He had quite long hair and a beard, wore a robe kind of thing.»

«Like Jesus?» I asked.

He shrugged. «Kinda.»

«And he spoke English?» asked Sally.

«He must've.»

«And you talked to him, so that was in English?»

He shook his head. «I don't know. Maybe I did.»

«You better tell Agathe.» I said. «You're adding to the history.»

«No way.» said Kurt. «The whole village'd think I was a fruitcake.»

I refrained from mentioning that the village already had its doubts about Kurt.

He joined us in the courtyard and we spent the rest of lunch talking about it, until it was clear Kurt needed to lie down again. Sally offered to sit with him and to everyone's surprise he accepted her offer.

«Maybe I'll get some rest if you're there.» he muttered. It was clear the whole episode had frightened him, but he was also exhausted.

Sally went and got her Charles Dickens and Kurt went back to bed.

We stayed around just in case anything happened but the whole afternoon wore on without any disturbance. I took the opportunity to ask Patrick and Gwyn about how they ended up in this little village. They were a bit coy about it and I was intrigued. Finally Gwyn shrugged and said: «Might as well tell him, he'll find out soon enough.»

Patrick sat back and let her talk.

It turns out they aren't technically married. Patrick still has a wife back in Shropshire somewhere. Gwyn was entangled with a man who made pornographic films. She appeared in several of them. I have to say my eyebrows shot up and I looked at her with new eyes. Well in truth, when she was a bit younger she must have been a good-looking lady and well-built in all the right places. These days, in this village, she hides it all behind messy hair and frumpy clothes. She saw my look when she talked about her short film career and she grinned a quite sexy grin. She didn't go into the gory details.

So their story goes that there was some kind of fight going on in a pub on the Welsh border, and Patrick just happened to wander into the middle of it all and, according to Gwyn, was quite a hero and saved her from serious harm. Then they had to hide from the nasty guy, the one who made the porn. At the same time Patrick was already living in a trailer behind a butcher's shop because his wife had thrown him out. So they took refuge in each other and escaped their destinies together. They have been an item ever since. They are an odd couple, but as they spoke you could see they were actually genuinely fond of each other. They decided it was time to leave England behind and in the same old Rover they still have, they crossed the Channel and followed their noses.

They started in Brittany but it rained too much and they headed south. And just like Kurt, they stumbled across this village and saw their little house. The for sale sign evidently was a bit battered and it looked like no-one was interested. No-one was, so when they approached the agent, she was so excited that they could more or less name their price. They bought the house because nobody else wanted it.

I couldn't wait to share the story with Sally.

Late in the day Kurt emerged with Sally. He seemed to have got some colour back in his face and was more cheerful.

«No saintly visions?» asked Gwyn, who was clearly rather enjoying the whole thing.

«Nuthin'.» said Kurt.

Then Sally said something that was very surprising. «He wanted to give you a break, so you can get used to the idea that he is real.»

«Probably.» nodded Kurt.

«No, that's what he said.»

«What?»

We were all stunned.

«You saw him?» I asked.

«No. Well not really. I just got a bit drowsy when you were asleep and I think maybe I just picked up a thought.»

«I hope it's not contagious.» said Gwyn, although with a wink.

«Well it seems we might have a resident ghost.» I said.

«At least he's a saint so that's probably a good thing.» said Patrick. «Maybe even a blessing.»

Patrick is a lapsed Catholic, so I suppose the idea of saintly presence wasn't all that alien to him.

Then Sally had an interesting thought.

«Did he look like the saint in the stained glass window in the church? The one with the sheep?»

«Maybe.» answered Kurt. «I don't think I ever really took a good look at that window.»

Knowing where the key was, we went over to the church to have a look. It was late afternoon and the sun was behind the window which really lit it up.

Kurt gazed up at it.

«Yeah, that's him.» he said.

7.

A couple of days went by without any further saintly visitations and Kurt seemed to get over the initial shock of it.

We talked about it, on and off, and it seemed like he was beginning to think of it as nothng more than a bad dream.

Then one morning, when we came over for coffee, Kurt was sitting in the courtyard with Patrick.

«He's back.» said Kurt as we came in.

«Our resident saint?»

He nodded.

Sally smiled. «I thought he would.»

«I was hoping it was just a passing freak out, but it's not.»

It was hard to tell how Kurt felt about it, maybe a mix of intrigue and intimidation.

«At least you weren't yelling this time.» said Gwyn.

«Nah. It was different. Kind of like he turned down the heat a bit.»

«What did he say?»

«Not much. It was like he just wanted me to know he was there, kind of get a bit more used to having him around.».

«No instructions?»

«Just one. Go to the cave.»

«Which one?»

«The one with the water running in it. It's his he said.»

I had to chuckle. «Maybe he left his Bic lighter there.»

«Why does he want you to go down there?» asked Patrick. «There's nothing there.»

«Fix this.» said Kurt tapping his plaster-cast.

«What?»

I think we all said it at once, a choir of disbelief.

«How's he going to do that?» asked Sally.

«He didn't say.»

Gwyn shook her head. «How are you going to get down there with this leg?»

«Slowly.» answered Kurt «But I think I have to do it.»

«You believe he can mend a broken leg?» Patrick was half convinced.

«What the hell do I know.» muttered Kurt. «But that's what he said.»

«Won't hurt to give it a try.» said Patrick. «Greg and me could carry you I suppose.»

«Well,» said Gwyn, «if you're serious, I'd better make another flea-proof outfit.»

«No thanks.» Kurt said. «If I'm going to go down there, I am going without any armour and let him do whatever he wants to do, fleas and all.»

«You really believe he's going to cure your leg?» Sally was almost laughing at the idea.

«Dunno, but I've got to give it a shot.» said Kurt. « He'll most likely give me hell if I don't.»

«How about we all go?» said Patrick.

Neither Sally nor Gwyn had any desire to go.

«I'll be happy to wait here till you walk in with two good legs.» said Gwyn.

So Patrick and I put our flea-proof outfits back on. Kurt stumped along unprotected and off we went.

Gwyn and Sally came as far as the descent down the stone steps and then watched us from the top of the wall.

It was tricky getting Kurt down, as the steps are narrow and overgrown with moss and underbrush covering some of them. We are both much smaller and lighter than Kurt so it took a lot of effort and a few near crashes. Kurt's good leg did all the work as he swung the cast out and round on each step. When we got to the entrance we were all out of breath.

Kurt lowered himself onto a rock and sat looking at the entrance.

«Am I turning into a nutcase?» he muttered, mostly to himself.
Patrick and I put on the netting to protect our faces and waited.

At last he hauled himself to his good foot and nodded.
«Better get in there.»
Knowing how narrow the entrance was Patrick had brought a handsaw and he hacked away at the Sumac bushes. Then with Patrick in front and me behind, we worked Kurt through the opening and into the first cave. Patrick shone his big torch towards the cave corridor leading deeper under the hill.

Patrick led the way into the larger cave further back where all the bats had been.

When we had come the last two times the bats had been disturbed and flew all round us, now, nothing moved. The bats were there, hundreds of them, but they hung there as if they had all been told to sit still. Their little black eyes blinked at us when the torch picked them out, but they didn't budge.

Kurt stood in the middle and looked around him.
«Plenty of bats.»
«Now what?» asked Patrick.
«This isn't it.» Kurt said.
«Why not? It's got the water.» said Patrick.
Kurt turned slowly, looking around the cave. «He kinda showed it to me. There was like a pond or something.»
«That's the other one then, down there.» and Patrick shone his torch towards the partially hidden opening that we had found the first time. «It's a big drop, though.»
We went over to the opening and shone the torch down there.
«Shit.» said Kurt.
«Maybe you don't need to go down there.» said Patrick.
«Nah. Gotta do it.»
Patrick and I looked at each other. There was no turning back. It was going to have to be attempted.

Prudently, Patrick had brought his rope so we hooked it to Kurt's belt. With his weight it was going to take both of us to hold it while he lowered himself down. The descent wasn't vertical so an able-bodied person could get down easily enough, as we had the first time.

Kurt slowly made his way down the slope, feet first, using his hands to steady himself. He let the plaster-cast leg swing out and down like a useless anchor on a deserted ship, using the other leg as a brace. He got about halfway, with us letting out the rope, hand over hand to take his weight.

Suddenly there was no weight anymore as the rope came away from his belt and he crashed down the slope to the bottom with a shower of rocks and rubble going with him.

The noise of it reverberated through the cave.

He made no sound and lay still.

We rushed down as fast as we could, dislodging a few small stones ourselves as we went. He was lying there on his back staring up at us.

«You OK?» I asked frantically.

He seemed to be stunned but his eyes were open.

Then he moved his head a bit, then his arms, then his good leg.

«Mmm.» he murmured. «Nothing broken.»

He hadn't tried to move the leg in the cast.

I knelt next to him and gently lifted the cast.

It came away in my hands. The plaster had been shattered by the fall and was now just loose pieces.

And then he moved the leg.

«The bastard.» growled Kurt.

Patrick and I looked at each other in the torch light. Then we watched as Kurt flexed his broken leg.

«Careful,» I said «You might make it worse.»

«Nah.» said Kurt.

Then to our amazement, he scrambled to his feet, both of them. He gingerly put his weight on the right leg, now unencumbered.

«Yeah.» said Kurt. «He did it.»

He took a few steps and he seemed to have no pain at all.

Then he turned to look at us.

«I felt him do that. He undid the bloody rope. He did that.»

«I tied it pretty well.» said Patrick.

«Not your fault, mate.»

«So you really think it's fixed?» I asked.

«What do I know.» said Kurt. «This is all way too weird.»

«It doesn't hurt?» asked Patrick.

«Nuthin'.»

He took a few steps, moving towards the pool of water from the stream running from higher up. He limped but maybe that was simply because he hadn't used his leg for all those weeks. When he got to the pool, he looked down into it. We came up beside him and we could see our reflections in the water by the light of the torch. The water was still and dark and our reflections looked ghostly in the torchlight.

«What the hell is this?» he said, mostly to himself I think.

«If I had stayed a good Catholic I would have said it was a miracle.» said Patrick.

«Never believed in miracles.» said Kurt. «Mechanics are realists.»

«Maybe,» I said, not sure why, «this is your Saint Paul on the road to Damascus moment.»

Patrick laughed. «Look what happened to him.»

«Won't happen.» said Kurt.

«So what now?» I said. «Are you getting any inner messages?»

Kurt looked down at our reflections in the water as if he was checking to see if there was any kind of message, then he shook his head.

«Nah. I got what I came for.»

With Patrick on one side and me on the other, we made it back up the slope. Kurt could put weight on his newly unplastered leg so we were just there as insurance. We certainly didn't want him to fall back down and maybe break the other one.

However by the time we made it back to Patrick's house, the girls having given up waiting for us, Kurt was white-faced and exhausted. Nonetheless he insisted that he should walk in unaided. I carried the bits of his leg plaster as souvenirs.

Gwyn and Sally were sitting at the kitchen table drinking tea, when he came in. They looked up and he stood there like King Kong with his arms out and his legs apart.

«All fixed.» he growled.

Sally jumped up and gave him a big hug but Gwyn eyed him with suspicion.

«Really?» she said. «Or did you just cut your plaster off down there?»

«You don't believe in miracles?» he grinned at her. «Ask the boys what happened.» Then he sank into a chair with Sally hovering over him.

She looked over at me. «So what happened?»

I told them what happened and Patrick backed me up.

«So you really believe that a dead saint healed your broken leg?» said Gwyn, clearly not at all convinced.

«What do I know?» said Kurt, now obviously very tired and ready to drop. «Like Greg just told you, I went down the slope with the rope tight. How it got undone beats me but I felt it go. I hit the bottom, the plaster hit first as I recall it and that was that. Two good legs. Look I am not complaining, saint or not, I've got me pins back and I am happy.»

Then he closed his eyes. «But right now I gotta have a lie down. I am buggered.»

We helped him to his room and he sank onto the bed and closed his eyes.

We got out of our flea-proof gear and joined the girls for a cuppa.

«What do you think?» asked Sally.

I really didn't know what to say about that. «Well either it was an incredible fluke, or it was the work of a dead saint. His leg is fixed as far as I can tell.»

«Doesn't make much sense to me.» said Gwyn. «Why the hell would a dead saint want to heal a nearly mended broken leg on a very unsaintly Aussie mechanic? What's the point?»

She was right I suppose.

What was it all about?

8.

Kurt slept for the rest of the day and every now and then Sally would pop her head in to see if he was OK but he didn't budge. Even when we made dinner, he showed no signs of getting up.

The next morning, when we went round, he was up.

«Leg still working?» I asked.

He got to his feet and did a little sort of jig.

«Good as new.» he said.

«The saint didn't come to visit? asked Sally.

He shook his head. «Left me in peace. I suppose he thought he'd done enough for one day.»

Just to be sure, Patrick took Kurt back to the doctor and we came along for the ride. Kurt was keen to drive himself now he could use a clutch, but we all prevailed. Plenty of time for driving when we were sure he had two good legs. He sat grumpily as Patrick drove in his old Rover.

«This is such a shit of a car.» Kurt muttered «A bloody disgrace to British engineering.» Sally and I sat in the back seat and neither of us could hide our smiles.

At the hospital, they did the x-rays and sure enough, as the doctor scratched his head, holding up the previous x-rays to compare with the new ones, the break was gone. Kurt couldn't resist a bit of a smirk and told the doc it was a miracle.

With the distinct limitations of language, the doctor just nodded and let it pass.

So that afternoon Kurt happily moved out of Patrick's house and into the Bat Hotel.

By that time we had overseen quite a lot of work to the point where he now had a proper bedroom with furniture and a working ensuite bathroom with legal plumbing. It still needed the finishing touches like tiles on the walls and a coat of paint, but all the essentials were there including a spectacular triangular spa bath with jets in each corner. It was his indulgence, big enough for three people but we declined his invitation to join him.

That spa bath was the first thing he made good use of, now that he no longer had plaster on one leg. He hadn't had a decent immersion in water for months and he spent the entire afternoon refreshing the hot water and running the jets, with a stack of motor cycle magazines to keep him company. The village plumber had done a sterling job of replacing everything to do with water, so the new gas-fired hotwater service was put to very good use.

We had already made several visits to the big box furniture store up the valley to see what they had so when we went back to get Kurt's bedroom set up, he decided to splash out on a massive lounge suite, a fancy dining table and eight teak chairs. The girl who served us in the store, who spoke tolerable English, couldn't believe her luck as he wandered about the store, saying, «I'll take that» many times. We ended up getting such a significant truckload that the girl was able to get us free delivery. I suspect we were probably the best customers she had ever seen.

When the store truck turned up, most of the things were manhandled up the stairs with the help of all the local workers, but the lounge suite was so big it was never going to make it up the narrow stairs. The only solution was to elevate it from street level and in through one of the newly expanded front windows. Kurt had all the pokey little square windows pulled out and replaced them with double glazed floor length windows that opened up to let in the air. I think some people call them french windows.

Luckily the village had access to the Mayor's Manitou, a huge red machine with an extendable arm and a rotatable platform on the end. Mayor Gaspard was very generous when we asked him, even driving the monster himself. The lounge suite came in two parts so each went up on its own and was angled to squeeze in through the window. Graciously refusing any payment for the job, the Mayor said: «aperitif», meaning that when we have an evening of wine and cheese, we invite him.

Now the hotel was beginning to feel habitable, it was time for us to leave the gite and we moved in too. Not that we had much stuff to move.
The first night we slept there, it was a bit eery.
In the silence of the night the building seemed to very quietly groan and moan to itself. Things moved. Little creaks and cracks could be heard. Heaven knows what ghosts were lurking in that place. We lay in our new luxurious king size bed, Sally and me, rather keen to initiate it but the strange feeling in the air killed that. Most of the night we lay there, listening to the Bat Hotel sing its strange night songs.
Kurt didn't seem to notice any of this and he slept in peace.

Within a day or two the three of us began to establish ourselves into a new routine, although we still found ourselves going round to Gwyn and Patrick's pretty often.
It fell to Sally and me to be the cooks, the shoppers and the general house bodies while Kurt threw himself into finishing off supervising the renovations and resuscitating his toys in the garage. The Citroen van was up and running and he had the engine in the Simca chugging but not yet purring as he assured us it should.
Neither of us had been brave enough to try driving on the other side of the road just yet.
After a few days, it felt like we had come to a comfortable modus vivendi, while both Sally and I wondered if we were really needed any more. A quiet life in an empty hotel seemed to be what we were facing and we wondered if Kurt really needed us.

The saint took care of that question.
Maybe the third or fourth day after the visit to the cave and the miraculous cure, we were deeply asleep when we heard Kurt yelling.
When we appeared at his newly constructed bedroom door he was sitting up in his new kingside bed, white-faced.

«Are you OK?»
«No, I am not. That bloody saint is torturing me.»
«He was in your dream?»
«Fucking nightmare.»
«What did he say?»
«I owe him.»
«What does that mean?»
« He says he brought me here for a purpose.»
«Saint Livraque, the village you mean?»
«He reckons I have a debt to pay, so he gave me this hotel.»
«But you bought it at the auction, didn't you?»
«Of course I did, but he reckons he made it happen. No-one else bid.»

It sounded vaguely plausible.
«So what does he want?»
Kurt shook his head in disgust. «Work.»
«What does that mean? How do you work for a dead saint?»
«I have no idea.»
«You'd better ask him.»
«How the hell do I do that when he turns up when he feels like it and ruins my sleep?»

We had no answer to that.

There was no going back to sleep so we put together a breakfast.
As we were sitting there, in the predawn silence, Kurt shook his head. «I forgot one thing. He's sending me someone to help.»
«Who is it?»
«Buggered if I know. He didn't say.»

Patrick turned up a bit later to let us know that he and Gwyn were off for a few days to stay with the people who owned Brian's Mother, Brian being the Brown's scrawny little tail-challenged dog. He was not exactly a thoroughbred, as Patrick almost proudly boasted, but Brian loved to go and see his Mum. They'd be gone a couple of days. Evidently the couple owned a canal barge and tootled up and down the Canal de Midi at a leisurely pace. Patrick and Gwyn would join them for a few days to explore the River Tarn. Kurt still had keys to their place, so we promised to water their indoor plants.

The day went on, but once we had waved goodbye to the Browns you could see the saintly intrusion had totally thrown Kurt. He worked on tuning the engine of the old Simca, muttering to himself trying to make some kind of sense out of it. It didn't want to sing and tended to blow nasty smoke. The Simca was not cooperating and Kurt was grumpy.

Sally and I did some housework but we too seemed to be listless and out of sorts.

That was until a very welcome distraction turned up in the form of loud motorbike engines.

Kurt heard them, well the whole village would have heard them, and he went out to see what it was. Three massive bikes had pulled up outside the church, so he walked down to see who they were. Bike riders camaraderie I suppose.

Sally and I were up on the roof by then, reading books, thanks to the generosity of Jean-Pierre, so we peered over the parapet and watched.

The three riders, all in heavy leather outfits, took their helmets off, and from where we were we could see that at least one of them was a woman, as she shook out her long blonde hair.

A second one who also appeared to be a woman was busy rolling herself a cigarette.

We watched as Kurt started talking to them. He ran his hands over one of the bikes, nodding with satisfaction.

After a while they all walked back towards the grange and we lost sight of them. It was all too intriguing not to miss so we went downstairs. When we walked into the garage, Kurt was showing them his Ducati.

Only then did we realise that they were all women. They were French and luckily, for Kurt, one of them spoke English.

When he saw us, he grinned. «A bit of company.» he said. «My favourite kind of company.»

It turns out they were all from somewhere in Alsace and had been touring the southwest together. The one who spoke English, her name was Christelle, introduced the other two, Laetitia and Yvette. They were a fascinating threesome. Yvette was petite, although solidly armoured in thick bike leathers. She was maybe in her late twenties, with long blonde hair and huge leather boots with heels. When she took her big gloves off, she had delicate manicured red nails. Laetitia was a solid bike lady, maybe forty. She was the smoker, with short greying hair and tattoos. Christelle was perhaps forty as well, with serious dark eyes and short brown hair. She explained that they belonged to a woman-only bike club based in Haguenau and had known each other for years. Each year they would choose a part of France to explore together.

The part of their history that really attracted Kurt was that Laetitia was in fact a trained mechanic. She kept the other two girls' bikes in good shape. Laetitia didn't have much English, but she really wanted to tell Kurt what she could do and how good she was, which pushed Christelle into a long and complex translation exercise. Laetitia explained that she and her brother ran a bike shop that sold and repaired bikes. Her loving speciality was Harley Davidsons. Hers was the biggest you can get, called «Fat Bob». She'd had it imported because she wanted a green one. In France, she sneered, they only sell black. The other two girls had blue Kawasakis which were both high powered.

Kurt was obviously impressed with all this, except for his inbuilt dislike of Harleys but he kept that to himself, and he invited them upstairs. All thoughts about dead saints were banished. They went back to the church and revved up their bikes to park them next to the Ducati in the garage.

We went upstairs and made tea. Sally had been flexing her baking skills that morning and had made a really excellent fruit cake.

As we sat together in the newly uplifted lounge suite, and the girls shed their leathers, we found out more about them.

Christelle taught English in a senior high school and was using her two weeks school holidays to visit a part of France she had never been to before. Yvette was a hairdresser, which she called an esthetician, who was divorcing her husband and had stolen, as far as we could tell, his bike. They each had a pup tent and sleeping bag in their saddle bags and were exploring the South West, staying at camp grounds, and following the canals.

They wanted to know our story. We were the first Australians they had met. They were fascinated as Kurt told them about his life as a mechanic in Australia. They had seen the famous movie of the souped-up cars doing battle in the desert, so they were suitably impressed that he had a rôle in it. When he told them he had quit everything and decided to tour around Europe, they quizzed him about how and why he ended up in Saint Livraque. He glanced at us and then said it all happened by accident. When they found out he was the new owner of the Bat Hotel, they wanted to know what he planned to do with it. He hadn't decided yet, but let dangle the possibility of having a cafe or maybe starting a mechanic workshop.

He was enjoying himself.

By the end of the afternoon, after he had taken them on a tour of the five levels, even including the cellar that had nothing done to it yet and had to be approached by still rather dangerous stone steps, he was inviting them to make use of the guest bedroom that was not yet finished.

That was going to be our next trip up the valley. The room was just an empty space but the girls each had blow-up mattresses for their sleeping bags so they were well equipped. The third bathroom on that floor was also not entirely ready for use including not having a door but the plumbing was done, had hot water and the toilet worked. They were very happy to accept Kurt 's offer.

Once they had moved their things into the spare room and Sally had hung a sheet over the doorway of the guest bathroom, we adjourned upstairs and Sally and I cooked up what we called «Cuisine Australienne». Laetitia disappeared up onto the roof to roll a smoke but was soon back. They had no idea what Australians ate so it didn't really matter what we made. Kurt broke open a bottle of red wine from the Duras which was positively critiqued and quickly disappeared.

After dinner, Christelle brought out a bottle of Armagnac that they had purchased earlier that day when they visited the town of Nerac in the region famous for the brew. Christelle's skill at translation began to deteriorate as the contents of the Armagnac bottle diminished and the night wore on, and by the end we were all a bit non compos.

We staggered off to bed after a most entertaining evening.

Sally and I lay there listening to the three French girls laughing hysterically as they got ready for bed. Sally whispered: «Do you think one of them might be Kurt's assistant sent by the saint?»

«Which one?»

«I bet it's Yvette. After all if she is getting divorced then she will need something new in her life.»

«Free haircuts for Kurt.» Not that Kurt had ever shown any interest in tonsorial elegance.

«Not Christelle.» said Sally after a long pause when I thought she had already gone off to sleep. «She's going back to school.»

«But she's the only one who speaks English.»

«Doesn't matter.»

«Hey then maybe it's Laetitia!» Which made us both laugh as that was the least likely.

When I thought about it, I doubted any of those ladies were sent by the saint, unless maybe as a short term distraction.

Who knows what saints do?

The girls woke early and we could hear them chattering away. Sally invited them up for breakfast and when Kurt arrived he proposed a bike tour of the area. Now he was two-legged again, he had already run his Ducati up and down the back street, lovingly tuning it to perfection, but had not gone any further. He suggested, as we had a whole herd of bikes, that we go for an outing. Other than visiting shops up the valley Sally and I hadn't seen anything much of the region since we got here.

Kurt threw us a challenge. Were we up for riding pillion? Sally had no problem with that as she had ridden with Kurt back in Australia. I had never done that and bikes were not exactly my favourite mode of transport. I didn't want to be a spoilsport though, so I said OK.

Kurt proposed that Laetitia would take Sally on her Harley and I would ride behind him.

One of Kurt's neighbors, Jérome, another brother-in-law of the plumber, had a couple of Honda mid-sized bikes for his teenaged sons and a trail bike, so he and Kurt had already struck up a bikers' friendship.

Kurt went off to borrow two helmets and came back with leather jackets as well.

The four bikes were wheeled outside the grange and Sally happily hopped up behind Laetitia. I gingerly climbed aboard the monstrous Ducati and couldn't decide where to put my arms. I was not inclined to hug Kurt. «Grab there.» he muttered, not bothering to disguise his disgust at my obvious discomfort. Luckily under the pillion passenger's seat there are chrome handles you can grip. I took the firmest of grips and I think my jaw did the same.

I was not far short of terrified as we roared off to the end of the town. Then going down the hill, with all its bends, meant the bike would tilt inwards or outwards at each turn. I was horribly disinclined to lean anywhere. Kurt yelled «Lean!».

Somehow we got to the bottom way faster than I would have liked and arrived at the less terrifying rises and falls of the road in the valley. The three girls had kept their bikes right on Kurt's tail.

Kurt pulled up where the road crosses the river and the other three bikes pulled in beside us.

«Scared the shit out of you, did I?» grinned Kurt, lifting his helmet.

«I'll get used to it.» I muttered.

The day was warming up and beside the bridge there is a long strip of greyish sand, being the local beach. A couple of kids were already in the water.

«Fancy a dip?» yelled Kurt, as he stood the Ducati back on its stand.

The girls did. What shocked us was when they shed their leathers, off came most of their other clothes and they raced into the water in their undies.

«Must be a French thing.» said Kurt, leering just a little at Sally. «Care to join them?»

«No swim you?» yelled Laetitia from the water.

«'Course I do. I'm an Aussie.» he yelled back, and stripped down to his jocks. He certainly had one leg a lot thinner and whiter than the other one.

We took our leathers off but that was it. We sat on the grey sand while they splashed about. It didn't seem to bother the French kids who took no notice of the bathing attire of the newcomers.

After a while they all came out and we sat on the sand while they dried in the warm sun.

Laetitia rolled herself a smoke.

«Gonna find us a great French lunch.» announced Kurt after a while, as they started to put their clothes back on.

On one of our previous trips up the valley to buy furniture we had passed a sign for a château that was both a hotel and restaurant. Kurt had promised us we would check it out one day, so now we roared off and the girls followed until we turned into the long poplar-lined driveway.

It's not all that fancy a château as it turns out, one of hundreds dotted all over the French country-side, but it was still an impressive midsized edifice of solid stone with two slate-roofed towers. The restaurant, however, was spectacularly impressive. It had been established in a renovated horse stables retaining the massive oak beams and exposed brickwork. The renovation must have cost a fortune.

As it happened, being a week day, we were the only clients. The owner himself came out when he heard the bikes, standing in the stone archway that led to the restaurant. At first he looked a bit stern, maybe worrying that he was about to be invaded by a bikie gang, but once he saw helmets come off to reveal female hairdos he started to smile.

«Déjeuner?» yelled Kurt in his awful Aussie accent.

The owner gave a little bow and gestured to invite us in.

«You are English?» he asked, in English.

«No mate. Aus-tra-lee.» said Kurt, trying to imitate the way the French say it.

Once the girls had shrugged off their leathers, stowed their helmets and said «Bonjour», the owner happily reverted to French.

Inside there were maybe twenty tables all set up with folded red cloth serviettes, quite expensive looking silverware and wine glasses of different sizes. It was all quite fancy but a bit sad to see it unoccupied. The owner rearranged two tables to make a six-person setting and brought us menus.

This was our first proper French meal and it was pretty good. There is a tradition in the more respectable French restaurants to offer a little something while the clients peruse the menu. It's called «amuse bouche», literally to entertain your mouth.

Ours was a multi-coloured, multi-layered work of art in a small glass, like a sherry glass. It had avocado, salmon, sundried tomato with goat's cheese and was deliciously spiced.

Another tradition in France is the «Formule», a discount if you follow the chef's suggestions for two or three courses.

Kurt announced it was his «shout» which Christelle could not translate until it was explained that he was offering to pay for everyone. We all ended up following the formule because it sounded so good.

And it was.

We had prawns in little handbags called «Aumoniers» made of crispy filo pastry for the entree, then a superb white fish called «Aiglefin», in a wine sauce and delicately diced veggies for the «plat principal», the main course. Kurt invited Christelle to choose the wine and, as we were all having fish, she insisted that we should have white wine from her home region, so a bottle of Riesling from where she was born just happened to be on the wine list. It sat in a bucket of ice on a little stand by the table and halfway through the lunch had to be replaced with a second one, it was so good. We ended up with the most fragile but delicious profiteroles in dark chocolate followed by tiny espresso coffees.

Our host was so happy with us that he brought out an extra dessert to go with the coffee, which he said his wife, who was the chef, had made specially. These were tiny little round cakes of many different colours which she called «Financiers». She brought them out herself, and when we asked why they were called that she shrugged. «That's their name.» she said.

It felt like a private banquet and by the time we staggered up from the table, half the afternoon was gone and we all agreed we needed a nap. I caught sight of the bill, as Kurt paid it and was shocked at how little it actually was. We would have paid three times that much for a meal like that in Melbourne.

The bikes roared back up the hill to the village and with all that wine in me, I happily leaned whichever way the bike went.

We all retired and as the workers preparing the ground floor for new concrete had finished for the day, there was a long period of late afternoon peace in the Bat Hotel.

Sally and I both fell deeply asleep.

It must have been around six o'clock in the evening when we heard laughing coming from Kurt's bedroom. We got up and went to see what was going on.

The girls had discovered Kurt's spa bath.

When we looked in, there they were, one girl in each corner with the spa jets running and Kurt enjoying the spectacle sitting on the toilet, with the lid closed I should add.

«Baptising me bath!» he crowed when he saw us.

The girls starting yelling at him to come in.

«Nah.» he smiled, «I'm too big.»

The girls had other ideas and the three of them jumped up and grabbed him. We watched, maybe a bit in horror as three naked French women, dripping wet, managed to overpower their host and dump him, fully clothed, in his own bath.

We tactfully withdrew in case they turned on us and we left them to it, all of them laughing hysterically.

We went up onto the roof and Sally said: «I wonder where this is going to end.»

«I don't think this is the kind of assistant the saint had in mind.» I added.

Sally smiled. «Patrick and Gwyn are going to be sorry they missed all the fun.»

Finally they all emerged, dried off, and we put together a simple evening meal and polished off the rest of the Armagnac. Several times Laetitia disappeared up onto the roof for a smoke. Kurt had told her he didn't mind her smoking, but she still insisted. She said that the other girls were not smokers.

It seemed like the three girls were having just the best time and they laughed and joked the whole time. They were planning to begin the return journey to Alsace the next day so that Christelle would be there in good time for the start of the next semester.

They said this had been by far the best part of their trip and they would take home great memories of Saint Livraque. We said we were honoured that they were the first guests in the Bat Hotel.

By the time we tumbled into bed we had had quite a wild day.

Then the saint came back.

In the middle of the night we heard yelling but this time it was not Kurt, nor was it laughing, but it came from the guest bedroom. Kurt was on his feet and we joined him at the door of the guest bedroom.

Laetitia was doing the yelling and it took a moment for Christelle to get her to calm down enough to tell us what she was upset about.

Laetitia had woken to see a man in a robe standing in the middle of the room, she said. When we asked if the other two had seen the man, they shook their heads. Only Laetitia had seen him.

«Must've been the Armagnac.» said Kurt.

When this was translated, Laetitia turned on Kurt. She was a head shorter than him but stood in front of him glaring and angry. She was poking him in the chest as she yelled. Kurt evidently does not sleep with clothes on and he had grabbed a sheet to wrap round himself. Now he was in danger of losing it as he fended her off.

Christelle was doing her best to translate. Laetitia blamed Kurt because the man had said she had been guided to this village because she had to work with Kurt. She wanted to know who he was and why she had to work with Kurt.

Sally tried to calm things down by asking what the man looked like. We knew in an instant who it was.

How were we going to explain this?

Sally somehow seemed to have taken charge. She told them that we had seen the vision of the man before and that he was not a real man. The girls, especially Laetitia, were not convinced.

As we were all wide awake, Sally suggested that we go upstairs and have a cup of tea and we would tell them what we knew. It was only then that I realised I was standing in a room with three more or less naked women, so we hastily backed out.

Kurt put on a tracksuit, the girls grabbed some clothes, and Sally put on the kettle.

Laetitia forgot her personally imposed discipline and rolled herself a smoke and lit it right there. Her hands shook as she made it.

Poor Christelle was then put to work at three o'clock in the morning. Sally did the talking which I think was wise, as the intrusion of a strange man into their room had scared the girls, even if two of them hadn't seen him.

Sally told them about Saint Livraque and that Kurt had been having visitations.

The girls looked at him, sceptical at first, but certainly with interest, although Laetitia still had a dark look. Sally said we would go to the church in the morning so Laetitia could see the stained glass window to verify if it was in fact our saint. Sally did her best to recall the history of the village saint. The girls all sat up with a start when she got to the point where Saint Livraque was said to be from Alsace.

When she got to the part about the bats and their fleas and the fact that Kurt had had a broken leg, their eyes widened, especially when she described how the leg got fixed. Their scepticism faded. Kurt had to show them his very white leg which had lost some of its muscle so was quite different from his good leg. Although they had seen him more or less naked, they hadn't noticed the difference in his legs.

We asked Laetitia what she thought the saint had said to her. She frowned. Basically there were two things, very clear. He claimed he had brought her to this village and that she was supposed to work with Kurt.

«Did he say Kurt's name?» asked Sally.

Laetitia frowned for a minute, then she said, Christelle translating. «No. He said I had to work with the mechanic.»

«He used the word «mechanic?» I asked.

When she nodded, I had to say «He's a very up-to-date saint. I don't think they had mechanics in the middle ages.»

«He didn't mean bikes either, I bet.» said Kurt.

Sally looked at Kurt and he nodded. He knew what she was asking.

«The saint told Kurt you were coming.» she said.

When the girls looked shocked, Sally hastened to add that he didn't say who was coming but that he was sending someone to assist Kurt.

There was a potent silence as they took all this in. It was still the middle of the night but no-one seemed ready to go back to bed.

Sally made more tea and Christelle asked more about the saint. Who was he and what was his story? They had never heard of a saint like that from Alsace. We did our best to channel Agathe, telling the old story of the magical cure of the child and then Kurt retold his part of it, the visions and his visit to the cave. As they listened, you could see that the girls were beginning to believe in it. Laetitia still scowled darkly and you could tell that she felt she had been thrown into something without her permission and she was not happy about it. She made an endless supply of roll-your-owns and the salon filled with smoke.

«Why do I have to help Kurt? And anyway,» she sneered, «I fix bikes, so why does a saint want me? I am as big a sinner as you can imagine.»

«Are you Catholic?» I asked.

«Shit no.» This was a bit rough for Christelle to translate «Well I grew up in a Catholic family and I was beaten up by the school nuns as a kid, but I am certainly not now any kind of Catholic.»

We had no answer to why she was chosen.

Then Kurt chortled: «Hey maybe this saint has a sense of humour and he chose the most unlikely candidates to be his, what you might call, disciples. You and me both.»

It seemed like no-one wanted to go back to bed, so as the first rays of the morning began to appear we got dressed and went round to the church. We pulled out the big key from its hiding place and opened the heavy oak doors.

Both Yvette and Christelle paused at the door, dipped their fingers into the bowl which would have held holy water if it wasn't bone dry and then they genuflected. Laetitia did no such thing, but she stubbed out her cigarette before she went in.

As we walked towards the altar, the sun was just coming up and the rays began to bring the stained glass window to life very nicely.

Laetitia gazed up at it.

«C'est lui. That's him.»

As we went back, I quietly said to Sally: «How much of this do we tell Patrick and Gwyn?»

«Good question.» she said, but she obviously had no answer.

Kurt heard me and he muttered «Let's wait and see what happens.»

It seemed like the only solution.

Sally and I made breakfast while the girls began to pack their things for the return journey.

Kurt came up as the kettle boiled.

«Gonna miss those chicks.» he said. «Haven't had that much fun in years.»

«You don't think Laetitia is going stay behind and be your assistant?» asked Sally.

«Nah.» he said, «I can't see that happening, though I wouldn't mind. Never found a girl who could mend bikes like her, I mean a real girl mechanic.»

«If she stayed you'd have to learn better French or teach her some English.» I said.

«Yeah.»

We could see the whole idea had intrigued him.

«Anyway,» he said at last, «I don't think she's into it. Freaked her out too much.»

The girls came up and we had a quick breakfast up on the roof in the morning sun. Laetitia rolled herself several cigarettes, one after the other. She was still not entirely recovered from her night visitor. Nobody else said anything more about saintly midnight incursions, as if the whole thing had been just a bad night, but you could see she couldn't shake it off.

She certainly showed no sign of thinking she should stay behind.

They planned to get back to Alsace in one very long day, so straight after breakfast they announced it was time to hit the road.

We went back to the grange as they loaded up their saddlebags and put on their leathers. Kurt pulled back the big doors which had been re-hung and well hinged, and the morning sun poured in.

They kissed us all on both cheeks before they put on their helmets, reserving the most lasting and sexy kisses for their host, who actually ended up blushing. Then they roared their bikes into action, filling the grange with the heavy whiff of motorcycle exhaust, kicked off their stands, and with last waves took off up the street.

We watched them go.

«Well,» said Kurt when the sound of the bikes had faded away, «I hope the saint isn't too upset that his plan didn't work.»

Sally patted him on the shoulder. «You never know what's still going to happen.»

He narrowed his eyes as he looked down at her.

«What do you mean?»

She shrugged. «I don't know. I just have a hunch this is not the end of it.»

«Yeah, well...» Kurt turned his back on the empty street and heaved the big doors closed.

The morning started in earnest as workmen arrived to lay a new layer of cement on the ground floor. Because it had been various different rooms during the hotel's existence there were all sorts of different floor levels and coverings, rotten lino in one place, old cracked tiles in others. The workmen had scraped it all clean and filled in the different holes but it was still uneven. So now the plan was to cover it all with self-levelling cement. Once that was done then Kurt could decide what to do with the space.

In reality Kurt still had no idea what this ground floor could be. He'd had the old kitchen completely removed, the huge old stoves and the walk-in pantry had all gone, but still he had insisted that the plumber ensure hot water access from front to back, and the electrician installed power points all over the place. Just in case.

A massive multicoloured cement mixer truck blocked the street for half the morning while the men ran back and forth with wheelbarrows. The Mayor turned up and yelled at Kurt that he should have applied for a road closure permit and he threatened to stop the whole operation. Kurt had learned the French word for «sorry», and he said «Désolé, mate» half a dozen times when he worked out roughly what the Mayor was yelling about. Then he went upstairs and came back with a bottle of Bordeaux Grand Cru as a peace offering, which the Mayor accepted, and that was that.

Once the cement was down, it had to dry for two days before anyone could walk on it. This meant there was no access to the grange except to walk round the block and in through the big double doors.

After watching the cementing for a while, Sally and I went off to visit Jean-Pierre for new books and French language practice. He still hadn't accepted any money from us so he was more like the local librarian than the local book shop.

Actually the word for bookshop in French is «librairie», while a library is called a «bibliothèque.»

He looked up from whatever book he had his nose in as we approached. «Bonjour mes amis.»

We had begun to think of our visits to see him together as our almost daily exercise in speaking French. He was a patient teacher and we really enjoyed extending our vocabulary. He obviousy enjoyed having someone to talk to.

That morning he asked us about our visitors. Nothing happens in this village without everyone knowing at least the basics. He asked simple French questions and we did our best to describe the girls in French, where they came from, what work they did and where we took them for sightseeing. We did not mention their penchant for taking their clothes off. He complimented us on our linguistic progress and we spent a happy morning and came away with some new books. Sadly neither of us was willing as yet to read anything in French.

We made salads and took them up on the roof in the warm sun. Kurt came up with splotches of cement on his jeans.

«We're all set down there.» he said triumphantly as he came out onto the terrace.

«Except the cement you mean.» I said, very pleased with myself.

He made the face of someone who has no tolerance for puns and helped himself to the bottle of cold cider we had just opened.

As we ate lunch, we tried to imagine what the ground floor was going to be used for. We got a bit extravagant in our ideas and we ended up laughing at the idea of Kurt in charge of a formal ballroom, or wearing a glitter jacket as the DJ in a wild nightclub with a disco ball.

In the middle of all this we heard a horn tooting insistently in the back street.

We looked over the back balistrade and there was a flatbed truck with a Harley Davidson on the back. Laetitia was banging on the big doors of the grange.

«Hang on!» yelled Kurt. Then he turned to go downstairs, but just as he was about to disappear he sneered. «Typical Harley. Shit bikes.» and was gone.

Sally looked at me and smiled her sweet «I knew it» smile. Then she said «Our Saint has a wonderful sense of humour.»

Then we hurried off downstairs and round the block to find out what the story was.

«Joint de culasse soufflé.» was the snarled verdict from Laetitia.

The bike, held by thick straps, sat upright on the tray of the truck in a pool of oil. The driver unchained it and pulled out a ramp from under the tray and Laetitia expertly ran the heavy bike backwards onto the road. She then paid the driver what looked like a lot of euros, he nodded to us all, and the truck took off.

The dead Harley was wheeled into the grange.

Kurt had no idea what she had just said but when she pointed and showed him he said: «I'm not surprised. She's blown a head gasket.»

«Get new.» she said. «C'est foutu.»

«Sure is.» said Kurt. He knew that word. «Trouble is there's no Harley dealerships round here, not that I know of.»

She didn't get it and I tried to find the best way to say it. Then she nodded «Bordeaux.»

«Yeah, probably.» nodded Kurt, then he tapped her saddlebags and gestured vaguely in the direction of upstairs. She opened them up and we helped to carry everything round the block because of the wet cement. As we walked I tried to find the right words for wet cement but she didn't get it, so as we passed the front door Kurt opened it and showed her.

She nodded and we went upstairs.

«Nous avons un bon salade.» I said, as we put her things in the guest room. She nodded again and we adjourned upstairs.

While we polished off the salad and a bottle of brut cider, we tried to work out what happened. Sally ran off and found a tatty old map of France so Laetitia could show us where the bike broke down. They were up near Limoges so they had been travelling fast.

«Ha!» said Kurt. «No wonder she blew a gasket, the Harley couldn't keep up!»

The other two girls had decided to keep going on their Kawasakis, once they had found the transporter for the dead Harley. We didn't have the language skills to ask her why she decided to come back here rather than go home.

Nobody dared to say anything about Saints.

After lunch Kurt and Laetitia went round the back to the grange and pulled the Harley apart to remove the offending gasket. We dropped in part through the operation and it was obvious she really knew what she was doing. Kurt mostly watched, passed tools and nodded in approval.

«She knows one end of a spanner from the other.» he said as we came in.

It was fun to watch. He would say the name of a tool or a bike part in English and she would say it in French. They were teaching each other linguistic mechanics.

Later in the afternoon they went on-line to see if they could order it. Evidently you can, but it would be a while before it was shipped. Somehow, mostly because of the pandemic, anything to do with shipping was now deeply backlogged. There was no getting round the fact that Laetitia would be with us for a good long stretch. They ordered the gasket using her credit card and gave Kurt's address.

And finally, at the end of the afternoon, we all went up onto the roof for a few cold beers in the warm sun, Laetitia rolled herself a smoke, and then she said: «On pense que c'est cet homme, le saint?»

Sally nodded and in her best French said: «Sans doute.»

I told Kurt what was said.

«You reckon?» he said, but you could see he had already thought about it.

Then he took a long haul on his beer and said: «So now what?»

None of us had any idea.

9.

Just as Jean-Pierre knew all about the three biker ladies, so did Agathe. She stopped by the following morning and, finding the door open, came upstairs. It seems in this village it is quite OK to just wander into someone's house if the door is open and yell: «il y a qu'un?», kind of like «Is anyone home?». We called back and she came up.

We were finishing off a late and leisurely breakfast, thankfully after a night with no interruptions of any kind, saintly or otherwise. Sally and I had lain in bed wondering if anything would happen, but all was quiet. As far as we could tell both Kurt and Laetitia got a good night's sleep.

«Good Morning.» Agathe said, as her head appeared at the top of the stairs of the second floor.

We invited her to join us and then she saw that Kurt no longer had his cast.

«Ooh-la-la. You are all fixed?»

«Yep. Good as new.»

«Was very quick, yes?»

«Yeah. Bit of a miracle really.» He shot us a warning look.

She seemed to accept this. Then as she looked around and admired the newly acquired furniture, she noticed Laetitia. «Bonjour,» she said, then added: «You are Australian?» She spoke in English but probably guessing Laetitia was not.

Laetitia sipped the last of her coffee and shook her head.

«Française?»

When Laetitia nodded, Agathe launched into a very direct French interrogation, which as far as I could tell was asking her who she was, where she came from, and was she part of the biker women that someone had told her about. Laetitia answered in monosyllables, including the fact that two of them had gone home. When asked if she spoke any English, Laetitia smirked and said: «pas de tout,» not at all.

Sally asked Agathe if she would like a coffee and Agathe took this as an invitation to sit. Sally had kept up her coffee skills and Agathe was impressed. She also helped herself to a plate of little sweet croquettes that Sally had made.

«So, Monsieur Kurt,» she said, «what is this hotel going to be?»

«How about a bat museum?» he grinned.

«You are not serious?»

«Nah. Truth is I don't know yet.»

Then she turned to me. «Did you go back to the caves?»

«Yes we did.»

«You find more things?»

«Um,» I had to think about that, «no not really.» I knew Kurt was keen not to mention his visit down there.

«So maybe I go with you next time and we look. Maybe we find more things.»

I suppose our penetration into the caves had re-ignited her interest as an historian.

«Yeah, sure,» I said, trying not to sound too enthusiastic.

Then Patrick yelled: «You hoo» from downstairs and came up.

«Hello,» he said when he saw we had a new guest.

«Bonjour,» she replied.

Then we had to explain who she was, how the three girls had appeared, and that on their way home her bike had broken down. Kurt enjoyed describing that bit. Evidently Patrick knew what a head gasket was.

Laetitia followed all this, asking Agathe every now and then to make sure she was not being slandered.

«You're a mechanic?» asked Patrick smiling at her.

She knew what he said and she smiled back: «oui.»

«So she'll fix it herself?» He looked impressed.

«When it gets here. Bit of a delay in the ordering pipeline. Anyway I don't enjoy tinkering with Harleys. Waste of time. She seems to know what she's doing,» said Kurt.

«Hey maybe she'll get all your old clunkers up and running while she's waiting.»

«She only does bikes, far as I can tell.»

Agathe turned to Laetitia and obviously wanted to know if she was in fact a certified mechanic. The response was long and I lost much of it, because the French talk fast with each other, but I gathered Laetitia told her the end of the story because I recognised the «joint de culasse soufflé».

Now that Agathe was with us and could translate, I took the opportunity to ask Laetitia if she had heard from Yvette and Christelle.

They had made it home safely, she said. She had a text message from them on her phone. She had also called her brother to tell him he would have to manage the workshop on his own for a while.

We asked Patrick about his trip up the Tarn and he said it was fine. He said they'd both got a bit bored just sitting on a slow-moving barge watching endless avenues of plane trees float by, but the dogs had fun. He was sorry he had missed the laying of the self-levelling cement. Agathe wanted to know where he and Gwyn had been and who his friends were, and I got the impression she was a kind of collector of stories of all sorts.

Eventually Agathe took herself off with vague promises to make a date for more cave exploration. Laetitia thanked her for translation. Agathe smiled at her, although Laetitia had not been all that friendly towards her, and told her she should learn from these Australians how to speak with an Australian accent.

Once she had gone Kurt grinned at Patrick, «Well mate, you missed a few pretty interesting things.» So then we filled him in on the recent saintly interventions, the three of us chipping in with the details if one of us missed something crucial. I think between us we painted a pretty thorough picture. Of course we would have to do it all again for Gwyn's benefit. Laetitia watched all this and, with what French I had, I told her what we were talking about.

«Il connait ce saint?» she asked.

As best I could, I told her that he had been with Kurt in the cave.

«On croit qu'il est un vrai saint?» she asked him.

«Yeah,» he said, «he's real enough.»

«Vous l'avait vu?»

«Not yet,» then Patrick grinned. «Looks like he only appears to mechanics.»

We went on like this for a while with our fraught «Franglais», but we managed.

Patrick went home to report to Gwyn so hopefully we would not have to repeat ourselves. No doubt Gwyn would be up soon enough to check out Laetitia for herself.

It took her ten minutes and she came, ostensibly to invite us all for lunch, but we knew the real reason. She eyed Laetitia up and down and you could see Gwyn was a bit suspicious.

As we walked round there Laetitia smoked, and I began another of our mixed and messy conversations but we were getting better at understanding each other. She hadn't quite understood how we related to Kurt, so I did my best.

Gwyn put on an impressive spread, seeing that they had just got home and we shared all that had happened over the last few days. They shared their barge trip with dogs, while we shared our bike girls and saints narrative. Gwyn has some French, more than Patrick, so she could help me filling in what was being said for Laetitia who seemed to relax a little more as the meal went on, and even came out with the occasional English expression.

It was Gwyn who brought up the question that was really begging to be discussed.

«So why, in heavens name, if you will excuse the expression, does the village saint, if he really is a saint, want two mechanics to work for him? «

«Good bloody question,» agreed Kurt.

«Well,» I said, «the first time it might have just been a side issue, kind of irrelevant - Kurt being a mechanic», I said. «Our saint obviously wanted Kurt, for some reason. But you are right, now there are two mechanics, it's not looking like a coincidence any more. It has to mean something.»

But what it meant, none of us had any idea, except for Kurt's muttered: «If you believe the bible, you could say God was the original mechanic.»

When we all looked puzzled, he said: «He put the world together didn't he, gave it wheels, oiled it, greased it and got it rolling.»

It was an original interpretation of the creation of the world, but kind of made sense.

10.

The next couple of days were uneventful, at least from the perspective of saintly intrusions. The life of the Bat Hotel found a sense of equilibrium where Sally and I took care of the «menage», the cleaning, the cooking and tidying up, while Kurt spent most of his time in the grange with Laetitia.

He had been wrong about her. She knew her way round cars just as well as bikes. While he continued to get the Simca into roadworthy shape, she had taken a fancy to the little red Deux Chevaux. When we wandered in, she had her head under the bonnet.

She told me, with a few misunderstandings along the way, that her father had owned one of these and that she had learned at a very early age how to work on it. I asked if her father was a mechanic too and she said no, he ran the post office but he loved cars. That was why both she and her brother had gone to mechanic school. I asked her if she was the only girl in the class and grinned. «Beaucoups de copins.» Lots of boyfriends.

By the second day she had not only cleaned out all the cobwebs, but more impressively she had the engine running, by no means sweetly and with an awful cloud of pungent smoke, but it was going.

We heard it from upstairs and came back to the grange to see what was happening.

When she saw us, she revved it and the grange filled with the acrid smell of its exhaust.

«She's a hot-shot mechanic this chick,» yelled Kurt over the noise.

Once she had turned it off, Kurt told Sally. «Now you'll have to learn to drive the French way, cause this baby is yours.»

Sally had to admit it was a very cute little vehicle.

We were almost at the point of thinking that the episode of saintly visitations might have, if not totally finished, at least taken a pause, but we were somewhat mistaken.

We discovered this in a most unexpected way.

Sally and I wandered into Jean-Pierre's «Livres Vracs» one morning to find him in his habitual armchair but without a book, as if he had been waiting for us.

«Alors,» he smiled. «I have something that you will find very interesting.»

He gestured at two of his other armchairs, none of which matched. We pushed the cats off and took a seat.

«As you know, this village is named after a saint.» he said, once we had settled back.

We nodded, wondering where this was leading.

«Many people are not sure if there was indeed a real saint or was it something fanciful, a myth.»

«We heard the story about the child,» said Sally.

«Yes, yes,» he nodded. «There was a time when our village enjoyed a little fame, and your hotel was quite busy.»

«But then it stopped,» said Sally.

Again he nodded. «It was not the right time for our saint to do his work, it was the war and everything that went with that.»

«So you definitely believe in this saint,» I said.

He looked at the two of us and then he smiled. «It is more than simply belief.»

«You have seen him,» said Sally. It was a statement, not a question.

«He makes himself known when he wishes.» Then he leaned forward, «As you are very aware.»

We both stared at him.

«He talks to you?» I asked.

He nodded.

«Does he talk to other people in the village?»

He moved his hand in the gesture of maybe, maybe not. Then he said: «Our saint is discreet.»

«What has he said to you?»

«Oh, every now and then he lets me know what he is up to.»

«But suddenly he wants to tell us that you know about us. I mean that we know about him.»

«He is a playful saint, you see. He likes to play. He likes to joke. He is a funny saint.»

Sally laughed gently. «We have seen that.»

«Do you know his real history?» asked Sally.

Jean-Pierre smiled. «Sometimes what is real and what is unreal is difficult to determine.»

«What about the story that Agathe told us about him, helping the poor people and having to run away?»

He shrugged «Who knows.»

«And the story about the child being cured? Is that true?»

«Of that there is no doubt. And there have been many others. I have seen this with my own eyes.»

«So you think he is a real saint?«

«You would have to answer the question what is a saint before I could answer you.»

«Well, in the sense that Catholics seem to have hundreds of saints. I mean every second village in France is called Saint something.»

Jean-Pierre nodded. «I would say this: if a saint is a man or a woman who performs a miracle, meaning something that is not normal for humans to do, then maybe that person could be called a saint. In that sense Saint Livraque, to my mind, is a saint.

«Did he do something for you?» Sally asked.

«Yes he did.»

«Was it miraculous?»

He smiled gently at her. «To me and to my wife it was.»

«Can you tell us?»

«I will make coffee.» he said. As we sat and waited while he went to the back of his shop and turned on an electric kettle, the cats whose chairs we had occupied decided to reclaim them even if we were still there. We ended up with a cat on each lap.

Jean-Pierre poured the hot water into his big glass «cafetière» to let it brew and came back to join us. The coffee smelled great and he brought three mismatched cups and a sugar bowl. There was no milk.

His coffee was strong and it seemed to dive deep into my veins and enliven them. Sally nodded. «This is great coffee.»

«It is,» he said. «My son is «un torrefacteur extraordinaire.»

It was not a word I knew.

«A torrefacteur is a maker of coffee, he imports, he selects, he grinds, he blends, he does magic.»

«Your own son?» I asked.

«He is. And he is the miracle granted to us by our saint.»

And then he went on to explain that he and his wife had known each other since childhood, both born just after the end of the war. He smiled as he described how they had told each other when they were still young children that they would marry and have lots of children. In those days the two schools were open in the village, girls at one end, boys at the other. After school each day they would meet in the middle and they would play together in the Halle in the middle of the village. After high school, she went off to Toulouse and trained to be a nurse, while he went to Bordeaux University to become a teacher.

«You never had any other girlfriend?» asked Sally.

He smiled. «Why would I want another girl friend? She was the one.»

I was beginning to guess what the miracle was.

«So you married her, of course,» I said.

«I did.»

«But you could not have children?»

«Sadly it is as you say. She became very sad. So sad that I began to feel that she might not want to continue to live.»

Sally put down her now empty cup and leaned forward, which tipped her cat onto the floor.

«But Saint Livraque did something, didn't he?»

Jean-Pierre smiled and stroked the ginger cat that had leaped up to occupy his lap.

«Our son.»

«Just one child?» I asked

«One is enough. He was an angel. He is still.»

«So what exactly did Saint Livraque do?»

«He came to her. She is a great believer in the power of prayer.»

«She was praying to have a baby?»

«She prayed every morning and every night for year after year. She prayed to the Virgin Marie.»

«But it didn't work?» I didn't want to be disrespectful, but I did want to know how our saint got into the picture.

«You are right,» he nodded. «Her faith was beginning to waver.»

«So how....? I let the question hang.

«There was a woman, a very old woman, who some people thought was a witch, and we children were frightened of her. She lived in a small house just outside the village, an old house, very neglected, where she lived alone with only chickens and goats for company.»

«She is still there?» I asked.

He shook his head. «She died many years ago. And no-one has lived in her house since.»

«What did she do?» Sally was impatient to get to the heart of the story.

«One day she came to our house. I was not there at the time, I was teaching at that time in the collège in Villeneuve. She told my wife that her prayers had gone to the wrong office.»

«She said «office»?» I asked.

«She did.»

«Did your wife know what she meant?» asked Sally.

«Not at first, but this woman was patient with her. At first all she said was that we should pray to Saint Livraque.»

«So this is how you come to know Saint Livraque?»

«We had heard of him of course but we had never thought that he was the kind of saint who could intercede. Quite honestly, up till then, I considered he was probably just a myth.»

«The old woman convinced you?»

«In a way,» he smiled. «That old woman was one of his. He sent her to us and she sent us to him.»

«Did he appear to you?»

«Not at first, but through this old woman he set us a test.»

«To see if you believed in him,» said Sally.

«You could say that.»

«What was the test?» I asked.

«We, my wife and I, should go into the cave, his cave. This is not something that anyone else in this village knows, but he wishes that I tell you. He told us that we should go at night on the next full moon. First we should drink the water that flows from the spring in the cave. Then we should, I hope you are not too shocked by this, we should take our clothes off and wash our bodies in that water. And then, in that cave, we should make a baby.»

«And then your son was born.»

«It was as you say. He is now forty years old.»

We sat there, trying to deeply understand what he had shared with us.

At last, perhaps to lighten the moment, I lifted up my empty coffee cup. «Thanks to Saint Livraque for this excellent coffee.»

It made him smile.

He promised that next time his son came to visit he would introduce us.

«Does he know about Saint Livraque?» Sally asked.

«He does. His name is Simon, and it was Saint Livraque who told us what his name would be.»

«But he doesn't live here?»

«No. He is in Toulouse and he has married and he has two children of his own.»

Somehow the sharing of his story was very moving and we sat with it, almost basking in its warmth. I was getting to feel rather fond of our saint.

However there were other things to think about.

«So why does he want Kurt to work for him and then Laetitia? What is all that about?»

«He didn't say.»

We both felt a bit deflated. It was amazing to discover that Jean-Pierre had a relationship with Saint Livraque, it was beautiful to hear his story, but it didn't answer our immediate questions.

He could see we were somewhat disappointed.

«I have discovered,» he said, «over the years, that one must be patient with our saint. He does what he does in his own way. He is special.»

Then he reached for a big Larousse dictionary and flicked through it, then he smiled. «The word «special» in French is not quite the same as in English.» He showed me the page. So our saint is a bit eccentric, maybe not quite trustworthy, unusual. It seemed to fit very well.

«Can we ask you who else knows about this?»

«Not so many. My wife and my son, one or two others.»

«Does Agathe know about this? « I asked.

He shook his head.

We sat there, the three of us and all his cats, letting it sink in. It was a welcome confirmation that we were not going crazy, it was not some kind of wild hallucination, so that was good, but it raised as many questions as it settled.

At last I broke the peaceful silence by asking: «So why do you think he has told you that we know about him?»

«He could see that you were a little doubtful. Even after he fixed the leg of your uncle. So I am here to help you to have more faith in him.»

«But what are we supposed to do? What is Kurt supposed to do? What is Laetitia supposed to do?»

«He did not say.»

«Can you ask him?»

«No.» Jean-Pierre reached, bent over, and fondled the ears of the sultry fluffy ginger who snuggled into his chest as he stroked it.

«It is not like that with our Saint Livraque,» he said at last. «He appears when he wants and he says what he wants. We, those who he considers to be trustworthy, we are told whatever he wishes us to know. That's how it is. C'est comme ça.»

«Can we tell Kurt and Laetitia what you have told us?»

He went on stroking the cat for a moment before he nodded. «You can. Perhaps it will be good for the girl from Alsace to visit me and I will tell her in a way she will better understand.»

We went back to the Bat Hotel and into the grange where Kurt was bent over the engine of the Simca. Laetitia stood back with the butt end of a cigarette in her mouth.

They had matching grease marks on their faces, like war paint. We told them where we had been and what we heard. Laetitia struggled to understand but Kurt just nodded. «Doesn't surprise me.».

Then we invited Laetitia to come with us to visit Jean-Pierre. She stubbed out her smoke, wiped her hands on a rag and Sally wiped away some of the more obvious grease marks on her face.

Then round we went.

He was sitting in the same armchair, and the cats had retaken theirs. He pointed to one of them for her to sit. She pushed the incumbent cat off and it growled. She looked around her at the shelves and stacks of books.

Jean-Pierre said:«I think it will suit best if you leave us. We can speak more easily I think.»

We left them to it, although we both wondered if Jean-Pierre had things to say to Laetitia that he did not want us to hear.

Kurt had decided to call it a day and we heard him singing in his bathroom when we went upstairs. He fancies that he can sing like Slim Dusty. It's a delusion.

After a while he joined us on the roof, bringing cold beers from the new fridge.

He wanted us to go over what we knew from Jean-Pierre. He nodded as we recounted the story of Jean-Pierre's son, and of course in the end he had the same question as we did.

«Here we are hanging out for the next instructions.» he said.

«Maybe Laetitia will hear more,» said Sally.

Almost on cue she came up, still in her mechanic's clothes.

Kurt poured her a beer and she sat.

«Ca va?» I asked, and she nodded. While she rolled herself a smoke, she added, which I translated as best I could: «It is good to talk to someone. I have not in my life ever had an experience that is religious. I am not a religious person at all. In Alsace some people believe in ghosts and spirits, many people pray to the saints, mostly it is the old people who believe in that.» Then she shrugged. «It is very strange.»

No-one could argue with that.

«But you believe what he has told you?»

She shrugged and took a long swig from her beer.

«It is hard to say, but I think yes I must. When the bike stopped, somehow I knew. Now this man is helping me to see it. I think he is telling the truth.»

«Did he say what work you are supposed to do?»

She shook her head.

Then there was the question of Gwyn and Patrick.

Should we tell them?

We hadn't asked Jean-Pierre about that but it seemed the obvious thing to do.

Laetitia went off to have a shower and I went round to invite Patrick and Gwyn to join us for dinner.

For the next hour Sally and I cooked. As we worked together we kept going over and over what Jean-Pierre had told us. And the tantalising question of what would happen next hung in the air.

The evening was warm and we took the meal upstairs and sat watching the sun dapple the far hills across the river. The sky turned crimson then paled into a delicate pink as the night set in. We demolished another bottle of red wine from Duras which was mellow and perfect for a warm evening.

Gwyn and Patrick nodded as we told them about Jean-Pierre and his son.

«I always thought there was something a bit mystical about Jean-Pierre.» said Gwyn.

«We have met his son. He is a very nice man.» said Patrick.

Then Gwyn chuckled «I love that our saint doesn't trust Agathe. I wonder why?»

«She talks too much.» muttered Kurt.

II.

And then our saint revealed a new way to communicate.

We had not met Jean-Pierre's wife and up until then I wasn't even sure where he lived. However, when we went back to see him the next day, she was there. She was a small woman, petite in every sense, with a tiny angular face, dark intense eyes, and grey hair cut short.

She was dressed in a housecoat and was standing on a wooden bench, dusting some of the higher bookshelves. She had tiny little feet.

When we came in she turned to see who had come and smiled at us. Jean-Pierre did the introductions, as she had no English.

Then he said «Elouise wishes that you come to our home for a dinner. She asks that you bring the two mechanics.»

Sally and I both smiled at her description of Kurt and Laetitia.

It turns out they lived right above and behind the bookshop. As we had only ever seen Jean-Pierre in the shop, it never occurred to us there was a residence behind it.

Jean-Pierre had said nothing about Patrick or Gwyn, so we kept the invitation to ourselves.

When we told Kurt and Laetitia, Laetitia insisted that we should bring something as a gift. Evidently that is considered the proper thing to do when you are invited for dinner.

They took the Ducati and I can only imagine the fun they had on the curves going down the hill. I am certain Laetitia is an expert at leaning.

They came back later in the afternoon with all sorts of local cheese. They had come across a farm that sold its own cheeses and they had stocked up. Laetitia explained how with cheese in France there is an etiquette. First you serve a light cheese, like a brie, then you offer a range, some cow, some goat, some sheep and some blue. The red wine that goes with the cheese should match the strongest cheese. When the cheese is cut from a wheel and a portion is served as a wedge, you mustn't take the thin end of the wedge for yourself. It's the sweetest part of the cheese. You should share by cutting diagonally.

We had a lot to learn about culture in France.

It was remarkable to see the effort Laetitia had made to smarten herself up. She wore a skirt. It was quite long and simple, pleated down the front, but it was the most feminine she had ever looked in our presence. Even Kurt had made an effort, putting on a clean shirt and pants. He had washed his hair and beard.

Jean-Pierre and Eloise live in a world of yester-year. The solid oak door that led to their house was next to the bookshop, and as soon as we walked in it felt like being in another age. There were old photos lining both the entrance hallway and the stairs going up to the main house which was above the bookshop. When we entered their salon it was crammed with objects and artworks all of which had age on them. It felt like we were in a milieu of sepia.

They had prepared an aperitif tray of small things to nibble, with various bottles of the alcoholic beverages that French people traditionally offer their guests before dinner: Ricard, Kir, Lillet and Cremeux. We were learning a lot as we went along.

Being a teacher by nature, Jean-Pierre delighted in telling us what everything was and how it should be enjoyed.

The talk during the aperitif was general, as Eloise wanted to know about life in Australia, and we in turn asked her about her early life as Saint Livraquaise. Jean-Pierre did a sterling job of translation both ways.

When we adjourned to their dining room, behind their salon, it was decorated in the same sense of period. A huge glass-fronted dresser had stacks of different kinds of plates and bowls, glasses of all shapes and sizes, many pitchers and carafes, serving dishes and tiny espresso cups. Much of what they owned they had diligently preserved from both of their families. Some pieces went back more than a century. Jean-Pierre assured us, as he proudly showed us the dresser shelves, that lots of the families in the village had this kind of heritage.

Their dinner table was classically set with linen serviettes and silver cutlery. In the middle of the table stood two tall candelabras with long red candles.

The meal itself was wonderful. Elouise was a classic French cook. I won't say chef, but it was homecooking of the very best. We began with tiny little canapes with all sort of pungent toppings, salmon, ham, herbal cheese, sundried tomatoes. Then her potimarron soup with a swirl of blue cheese swimming in it. When she served her «gigot d'agneau», lamb with vegetables, she said proudly that all the vegetables came from their potager. Almost every house in the village has a small plot of land outside the walls for growing vegetables, and most people still use them. She served us leeks, big purple tomatoes, red potatoes and topinambour. Jean-Pierre actually had to get up and flip his big Larousse, which he kept handily close by, for the translation of topinambour, Jerusalem Artichokes.

When the cheeses bought by Kurt and Laetitia were brought out with the baguette to go with them, there was a red wine from the Graves. Jean-Pierre told us the «chef de chai» of the château where it came from had been one of his students many years ago. The wine is termed »Grave» because it comes from gravel soil.

Finally, and I wondered how much more we could fit in, there was dessert. The crème brullé was perfect, the top crispy brown and the inside deliciously succulent. Jean-Pierre had done the «Brulling».

At the end of all this, as we sat back in the salon with the little espresso cups and delicate little cakes called «bienfaits», Eloise announced that she had a message.

Somehow there was a change in the atmosphere in the room as if someone had run an electric charge through it. Instinctively we all sat forward in our nineteenth century armchairs.

«He has asked us to talk to you.» she said.

«Saint Livraques?» asked Sally, just to be certain.

Eloise nodded.

«A saint does not die.» she said. «Saints continue with their work, but without the handicap of being trapped in a human body.»

She looked around the room to see how we responded to this. No-one could argue with that. What did we really know about saints?

«Sometimes» she continued «they withdraw from our world, waiting until it is the right time to resume their work.»

«Kind of like hibernating?» I asked.

She shook her head. «Not at all. They do not sleep like the bears in the Pyrenees. They retreat to a world that is full of saints and they commune together. It is a place of harmony. They send us their blessings and they hold us in their consciousness. They are full of love.»

«So,» said Kur, «for some reason our local saint is back on duty.»

«Exactly.»

Laetitia had listened to all this with a frown. «But why is he appearing to us, to Kurt and to me? What does it mean?»

«He has told you already. He has work for you.»

«But what work?»

Eloise smiled. «Ah» she said «that is not yet clear.»

«So what's the message? asked Kurt.

«First, you must prepare.» she said.

«How?»

«He will help you to become good conductors.»

«Conductors?»

That led to some discussion about the word «conductors» and, with the help of Larousse, we ended up with a sense of what was intended. For whatever reason, Kurt and Laetitia were chosen by the saint to be able to help certain people. They were to be conveyers of whatever the saint wished to be conveyed. Maybe it would be healing, like Kurt's leg, or maybe it would be messages, like Eloise was giving to us.

«But why us?» asked Kurt. «There's got to be better people than us, more, I dunno, saintly people. I mean we,» he glanced over at Laetitia, «we're not exactly the kind of people saints'd want to hang out with.»

Jean-Pierre laughed at the way Kurt said it, hunting for the right translation. Then he said: «You have too narrow an impression of saints.»

«It's something about mechanics, isn't it?» asked Sally.

«Perhaps. We must be patient.» said Eloise.

«So is that what he wanted to tell us? « I asked. «They should prepare?»

«It is not just that. He wants you to know that he will help.» said Eloise, then she leaned over and she took Laetitia's hand. «He knows about your burden.»

Laetita frowned but did not pull her hand back.

«You have heard of Oradour?» asked Eloise.

None of us had.

«It is a town not far from Limoges, where your bike stopped.» she said, looking at Laetitia with her intense eyes. «There is a reason your bike refused to go any further.»

«He did it?» asked Laetitia. «La culasse?»

Eloise nodded, still firmly attached to Laetitia's hand.

«Because of Oradour.»

«So what is it?» I asked.

Jean-Pierre leaned forward. «It is a town that suffered a terrible atrocity in the Second World War. There are different versions of why it happened, but almost all the residents of this small town were executed by the German Waffen.»

«Executed?»

«Something like 600 people, men, women and children were killed in one afternoon. Most people believe it was revenge for attacks by the Maquis.»

Kurt nodded. «I have found the anti-German sentiment in my travels. Sally and I have a German name. When I first got here they thought I was a Hun and weren't too happy about my bid.»

«You are right. Our memory of the Germans is bitter.» agreed Jean-Pierre. «Perhaps now it is changing a little with the younger generation.»

«So how does this relate to Laetitia's bike stopping in Limoges?» asked Sally.

Eloise looked at each of us, one after the other. There was pain in her look.

«Although it was the German Waffen who committed this act not all of the men in that company were German.»

«They were French?» asked Kurt.

Jean-Pierre nodded. «There were maybe two hundred soldiers in the group and some of them were from Alsace.»

A shock ran through Laetitia's body and Eloise felt it. She took both Laetitia's hands and held them tight.

«Is it because I am from Alsace?» whispered Laetitia.

Now Eloise's voice became very quiet as she leaned in and looked intensely into Laetitia's eyes.

«You carry a burden.» she said.

Laetitia gazed at the older woman and tears formed.

«We learned about the war when we were at school.» she said «Of course, but it was only a rumour that some people from our town had sided with the Germans. Most Alsacians prefer to remember those who resisted.»

«Can I ask,» I ventured gently «Why this is a burden for Laetitia? Is it a burden for all Alsacians?»

Eloise shook her head. «Not all.»

Then she turned back to look at Laetitia. «Both your grandfathers came from the same town, did they not?»

Laetitia frowned, but nodded. «My parents were encouraged to marry by their families. My two grandfathers had known each other all their lives. They went to school together. My family says they were like brothers.»

«But you did not know what rôle your grandfathers played in the war?» asked Jean-Pierre.

«It was never spoken of.» she said. «One of them died when I was very young, and I do not remember him, but my mother's father lived until he was ninety. At the end he had dementia and stopped talking.»

She saw both Jean-Pierre and his wife nodding.

At last, in a terrible whisper, she asked: «Are you telling me that they did that?»

In the long silence I realised that none of us seemed to be breathing. I looked at Sally and I saw she was almost crying. Kurt had an ashen look, and I felt like the excellent dinner we had just enjoyed was threatening to regurgitate.

Into this silence Jean Pierre said: «Those Alsacian men in the Waffen were conscripted. They called themselves «Malgré Nous» which means «against our will».

«But they participated in the deaths of all those people?» asked Kurt.

«In 1953,» continued Jean-Pierre «a military tribunal was held in Bordeaux and the few Waffen who had survived the war were charged. Fourteen others were French nationals whose home region had been annexed by Germany in 1940, and these Alsacians claimed to have been forced to join the Waffen-SS.»

«But still they did it? To other French people?» Sally asked.

«Yes. They were found guilty but at that time it was politically difficult and so they were were released.»

«No-one was punished?»

«Several of the Germans were, but none of the French.»

«Did they shoot them all?» asked Kurt. «I mean in that village?»

«No. The men were forced into barns and garages and were machine-gunned. The women and children were locked in the church and then they burned it.»

We sat in the horrified silence of that image for a long time.

At last Eloise said «We cannot and we must not get locked into the past. What is done is done.»

«What you are telling us is a terrible part of French history.» I said «But somehow, and I assume the saint has revealed this to you, you know that Laetitia is descended from two men who were involved.»

«It is what he has shown us.»

«But,» I couldn't see yet where this was leading, «you said that Laetitia carried a burden.»

Sally nodded. «Does it have to do with that terrible event?»

«It does. She carries the burden of guilt. She carries it for her family. She is the one who took on what the previous generation could not. It is the burden of history.»

That phrase, the burden of history, struck me. I had heard it before. Then I remembered. The village poet had said exactly that.

Jean-Pierre nodded when I reminded him. «All of us, in some way, carry the burden of history.»

«It is often the case,» continued Eloise, «that one member of the family carries the burden so the others do not.»

«But I wasn't there.» cried Laetitia «I wasn't even born.»

«For whatever reason, you were the one on whom this burden has been passed.»

«My brother doesn't have this?»

«No.»

«Why not? He is older than I am.»

Patting Laetitia's hand, Eloise said: «You can think of it this way: You are strong enough to carry it, perhaps he is not.»

«Wait,» said Kurt, suddenly sitting forward, «You said the saint was going to help. Didn't you say that?»

«I did.»

«So he tells you she has some kind of historical guilt or whatever it is. How does he help?»

«Will he take it away?» Laetitia had withdrawn back into herself and her voice was small.

«He has told us that he can if you are willing.»

«What should I do?»

«He tells you this: you can wash herself clean of this burden.»

It seemed to release something in Laetitia and she began to howl. She slowly bent forward and collapsed into the older woman's lap. It was painful to bear her anguish, but we knew we should sit there and be witness to it.

Jean-Pierre brought a box of tissues and we sat quietly till she quietened.

Finally Laetitia lifted her head and looked at us with her ravaged face.

«I always thought I was a bad person.» she said. «I never knew why. I just thought I was born like that. I always thought that nobody trusted me, or liked me. I was just bad.»

«Now,» said Eloise softly»you can let it go.»

«What do I have to do?»

«You know about the caves?»

She nodded. «They told me.» she said gesturing at us.

«There is a spring with water flowing down into a lower cave where there is a pool.»

We all nodded. We knew exactly what she was referring to.

«You will go there. You will stay there for a whole day, by yourself. You will wash yourself with this water, do it many times, and it will take away the burden that you carry. And then you will be ready to do the work that he has for you.»

«Can I go now?»

«Not yet. He tells you that the best day to do this ritual will be when there is no moon. The next new moon is in two days. You will go at sunset and you will stay there until the end of the following day.»

«What about the bats and the fleas?» I asked.

«You do not have to fear them.» she said. «They are his.»

«They didn't bother me.» said Kurt.

«You see?» said Eloise, smiling.

As we made our way back to the Bat Hotel, Laetitia rolled herself the first cigarette she had had since we entered Jean-Pierre's house. We walked in silence, each of us trying to make sense of what we had heard.

It was not just the horrific vision of what took place in one small French town more than seventy years ago, it was not just that Laetitia was carrying the burden of her family's deeds, it was not even that the saint had known all about this, but it was that somehow we, all of us, were plunging into a whole new kind of world, a world that none of us had any experience of and none of us really knew why we were in it.

In-drawn as we all were as we walked, when we got back to the hotel, Kurt suddenly enfolded Laetitia in his big arms and held her.

«Don't you worry.» he said. «We're gonna work it out.»

Then he gave Sally a hug and even me.

Then Sally hugged Laetitia and Laetitia hugged me.

12.

Sleep came unexpectedly easily.

I found myself going deep into a soft space of calm and protection. There were no dreams. When I finally woke and turned to Sally, in the early morning light, she had a gentle smile on her face.

«No saintly visions? I asked.

«I don't think we will have those,» she said, «I think we are assistants. Our rôle is to help.»

I had to agree. For whatever reason we were certainly part of this drama, but we were not the principal players in it.

Nonetheless, there seemed to be a certain kind of peacefulness as if we had arrived at some state of calm certainty that had no anxiety attached.

We got up, and as we passed Kurt's open door we saw that his big bed had a new occupant.

We smiled at each other and quietly went upstairs to start on breakfast.

When Kurt and Laetitia came up we said nothing about the new sleeping arrangements, but they did look very relaxed with each other.

Neither of them reported saintly dreams.

Breakfast felt like a gentle celebration. We found ourselves smiling at each other.

One thing that had not come up in all the drama of the previous night was again the question of what to do about Patrick and Gwyn. Should they be a part of this?

As we talked about it, me translating for Laetitia, it did seem obvious to include them. After all, they knew about the saint. The saint had even manifested in their house when he first appeared to Kurt.

Like us, they were part of the play of it.

We invited them up for morning tea.

When we told them what we had learned the previous evening they sat there open-mouthed, their tea untouched.

«This has got to be the strangest thing I ever heard,» said Gwyn.

«But you do believe it?» asked Sally.

«I suppose so. I mean that leg kind of tells the truth doesn't it,» and to make her point Gwyn leaned over and whacked Kurt on the leg that had previously been plastered. He flexed it for her to reinforce the point.

«The idea that the effects of something our parents or our grandparents did exists in us, well to me that is a bit frightening,» said Patrick. «It's kind of like psychic DNA or something. It makes you wonder what you inherited when you were born.»

I had no way of accurately translating that for Laetitia, but I did my best.

Gwyn looked at her and her face was compassionate. «You didn't know what your grandfathers did?»

She shook her head. «We all knew that they fought in the war. Everybody fought in that war. But no-one spoke of the details. Many Alsacians worked with the Germans, we knew that. My family never spoke about it.»

«Will you tell anyone about this?» I asked.

She thought about it. «I don't know,» she said. Then at last she added: «I am worried about the effect it would have. What would happen if I told my brother? I think maybe he would think I have gone crazy. I cannot imagine he would believe it. I would not tell my parents. What good would it do? They are old now and it would only hurt them. Maybe secretly they already know what their fathers did.»

«What about Christelle and Yvette?» asked Sally.

She shook her head. «Perhaps, after I do what I am asked to do. I don't know.»

Once Patrick and Gwyn had gone, to pass the time, the two mechanics retired to the grange, their place of familiarity.

We heard the Deux Chevaux revving, it has a unique voice, but it was beginning to sound more reliable. Once it had new tyres, specialty skinny ones, it would be ready to move out into the sunlight after its long hibernation. Its interior was certainly the next big job. Who knows who or what had sat there over all those years.

Sally and I cooked and cleaned up, leaving them alone in their automotive sanctuary.

As we worked together, Sally and I went over everything we had heard about our newly acquired saint. There were so many questions. I suppose for most, if not all, Australians, the whole idea of a saint intervening from the beyond would seem too far fetched. Neither of us had any frame of reference.

When we ran out of things to do in the kitchen, we decided to go round and put some of the questions to Jean-Pierre. At least he had a frame of reference.

We found him outside his shop sweeping the ruelle, the narrow alley that served as his forecourt.

He smiled when he saw us.

«I imagine you have many questions,» he said.

I was beginning to wonder if he was a bit psychic.

He invited us in and set up to brew his son's coffee. He was particularly fond of his son's Peruvian Arabica blend. Certainly the aroma as it brewed was intoxicating. He told us that the coffee from the mountains is very different from the coffee grown in the desert regions of Peru. He had brewed the mountain variety, promising the desert variety for another day.

Once we had settled with our cups in the armchairs and the cats had rearranged themselves to accommodate us, he said: «What would you like to know?»

Sally started. «If Saint Livraque is a real saint and he can do miraculous things, like you described to us, it seems strange to me that so many things have happened in this village, all those terrible things that Agathe loves to talk about. Why didn't the saint prevent them from happening? All those wars and battles, burning the village, people being killed.»

«Ah,» he said, «it is a worthy question. In truth we do not really know how the saints work, when they choose to intervene in the lives of men and when they refrain.»

«But,» I wanted to add, «surely when those young people were shot by the Germans at the end of the war, wouldn't that be something a saint should prevent?»

«You would be tempted to suggest that,» responded Jean-Pierre, «but in fact it is my belief that Saints do not prevent anything. They do not interfere in destiny.»

«He fixed Kurt's leg,» said Sally.

«He did, but only after he invited Kurt to go to the cave. You could say that he offered Kurt an opening and Kurt took it. For us it was the same. My wife and I both believe that the saint will only help those who are willing to help themselves.»

«So because the woman with the child who got cured believed in the saint and was willing to go into the cave, that's why her child was cured?»

He nodded. «That is the way we understand it. You could say it is matter of faith.»

Sally and I sat there with our excellent mountain coffee taking that in.

Finally I said: «Do you know of other times when the saint did something for someone in the village?»

«We know of several, although not so recently. For quite some years after the woman with the child being cured, there was a lot of interest in the caves and the bats with their fleas, and people came with all sorts of hopes. «

«And did the saint do things for them?»

«Certainly there were many stories of cures. Whether they were all real, who knows?»

«But then it all stopped. Do you know why?»

He shook his head. «The ways of the saints are hard for us to grasp. Maybe he didn't want the publicity.»

«Nothing during the war?»

«As far as I know, there was nothing. You can imagine that there was a very strong focus on other things than bats and caves and saints.»

Then I said: «When Patrick and I went into the cave, we found a Bic cigarette lighter. Do you know who would have left it there?»

«I cannot say for sure of course. There was a time, maybe some twenty years ago when there were a lot of drugs in this village. I think sometimes those people had to hide from gangs and people like that. Sometimes the police. It could have come from then.»

«Criminals used the caves?» I found that hard to align with all the saintly stories.

«You find it strange? Who knows what that means,» said Jean-Pierre.

«Are you saying that the drug dealers or whoever they were,» asked Sally, «they were aware of the saint?»

He shrugged. «It is possible that they did. And who knows, maybe they benefitted from being there.»

«Saw the errors of their ways, you mean?» I asked, feeling a bit sceptical.

He smiled his gentle smile. «It is not for me to say, or for any of us to say, what a saint does and why he or she does it. And even more, it is impossible to say what outcomes there might be. I do not think the saints ever guarantee a positive outcome. We must accept what we are allowed to know, what we are allowed to witness.»

That seemed to be the most sensible way to see it. What was happening to us was so out of our normal experience that we had no other way of thinking about it. But we had to accept that what was going on was something we were supposed to know about, because we did. We just had to go along with it as best we could.

We took ourselves off on a long walk in the balmy afternoon. There are some well- signposted walking trails leading away from the village, and we took one of them that weaved its way gently through spindly oak forests without dropping too drastically down off the hill tops. We had no intention of plunging down off the hill, only to have to labour back up again.

We found a grassy spot with a wide panorama of the valley, and we lay there in fresh grass among little yellow flowers. There was the mildest of breezes and bees busily worked their way round us.

As we lay there we saw two big birds, maybe eagles of some kind, wings outstretched and motionless, circling above us. The updraft from the river valley was lifting them higher and higher, effortlessly above us.

«I can hardly remember what Melbourne felt like.» said Sally dreamily.

I had to agree. We were living in a completely new and different world, although maybe that should have been several different worlds.

The one aspect of all this that puzzled us both was why we didn't seem to be able to be in contact with the saint ourselves. Sally had some intuitive sense of the saint which I suppose meant she had some contact, but I had nothing.

«It bothers you, doesn't it?» asked Sally as I mused on it.

«I have to admit I feel a bit left out.» I said.

«Well, maybe if he needs you for something he will let you know.»

And we left it at that.

At the end of the afternoon, when we got back to the Bat Hotel, we saw Kurt and Laetitia in the spa bath lying back with their eyes closed and the jets running. It obviously did not bother them that they had neglected to close the door.

Kurt opened one eye when he saw us and gave us a grin.

We left them to it.

The next day was the new moon. We double-checked that on the internet.

At breakfast we talked about how we should help Laetitia to be ready. I asked her if she would like to go down to the caves in the morning to see what they looked like and to think about how to prepare. At first she said she didn't need that. She preferred to work on the Deux Chevaux, but after a while she changed her mind.

Now that they knew the bats and fleas were not going to harm us, both Sally and Gwyn wanted to go and see them, too.

So mid-morning off we went.

We ended up being quite a party. Patrick of course brought equipment, just in case, with all his tools dangling from his belt as he walked along.

There was no sign that anyone else had been there, and in fact it almost seemed like the bushes had grown back to cover up the entrance to the cave with the spring in it.

Patrick hacked away at a few branches and we all helped to push them aside.

Then he turned on his big flashlight. Kurt had a torch too.

Inside it was deliciously cool and still. We stood there, once we had all inched our way in past the undergrowth. For the three girls, being their first visit, I could feel they were impressed. Patrick swung his flashlight round and we could see the bats, hundreds of them hanging on the crevices and ledges of the inner cave, but they showed no sign of moving.

Everyone seemed to be cowed by the silence and we spoke in whispers, as if we had entered a temple. I suppose in a way, knowing what we now knew, it was.

We walked to the far end of the cave where the spring came out of the rock face. The sound of it was subtle but constant. There was no other sound. The bats were silent witnesses.

Then Kurt led us over to the steep drop down to the lower cave.

«This is where our bloody saint threw me.» he said, but without any bitterness.

We scrambled down, holding on to each other for stability, dislodging a few pebbles and small rocks as we went.

Once we had all landed, we stood round the pool in silence and listened to the sound of the water running down from above. It whispered and sang gently in the background.

Laetitia knelt down and let the water run into the hollow of her palm. Then she scooped it up to taste.

«Belle.» she said. Beautiful.

Sally and Gwyn did the same.

«Next time we come,» said Sally, «we should bring bottles to fill.»

«So this is where I will come tonight.» said Laetitia.

«I will make you some food to bring.» said Gwyn and Sally added «and blankets.»

Laetitia nodded.

At last we ascended back to the main cave. The bats became a little restless and several flew around us. Sally clung onto me for protection and Gwyn used her arms to shoo them away.

Kurt chuckled. «The troops of the saint are getting edgy. Maybe they think someone needs to be bitten. Anybody need a cure for anything?»

Nobody did.

At last, when we walked out into the bright late morning sun, we needed to stop and breathe.

There was certainly an atmosphere in the caves that you could not ignore. It felt like we had been deep sea diving and had come up for air.

Nobody wanted to talk.

Then we had to, because Agathe saw us coming up.

«You have been to the caves?» she asked, looking a bit annoyed, and I knew why.

«Yeah.» said Kurt. «Laetitia wanted to see the bats.»

«Why did you not tell me? I would go with you and tell the stories.»

«That'd cost four euros each!» grinned Kurt.

«No, mais non, I would not charge for that.»

«Well,» said Patrick, «next time, we'll call you.»

«You didn't wear any protection?» Agathe had just recognised that we were not looking like apiarists.

«Nah.» said Kurt with a grin. «We Aussies aren't afraid of anything. Where we come from there are man-eating sharks and crocs and black widow spiders. Nothing scares us.»

«But you did wear something before, did you not?»

She was looking at Patrick and she knew he wasn't an Aussie.

«Yeah, we did,» he agreed, «but it turns out we didn't need it.»

«How do you know that?»

Kurt put his finger to the side of his nose. «Intuition.» he said. « We know what's dangerous and what's not.»

«And it's true,» added Sally. «We didn't get bitten at all. The bats just watched us.»

«Maybe the fleas only bite people who need it.» said Gwyn, trying not to sound too sarcastic.

Agathe shook her head.

«Me. I will wear protection.»

Then she turned on her heel and walked off.

As she watched Agathe, Laetitia said: «She is not happy with us.»

We had an early pre-sunset meal up on the terrace. Laetitia fortified herself with quite a few glasses of white wine from the Buzet.

Then as the sun found some western clouds to rouge, Laetitia gathered up her things and we escorted her to the cave, keeping an eye out to make sure we did not accidentally run into Agathe on the way.

«I go in by myself.» she said when we reached the entrance.

Patrick had given her his big flashlight with a new battery. She had a basket full of food that Gwyn had cooked, a bottle of armagnac, a couple of blankets, a towel and an empty bottle to fill with the spring water. Her backpack was quite full.

«Take it easy down that slope.» said Kurt.

«Do you want us to come for you at sunset tomorrow?» I asked.

She thought about it, then she shook her head.

«No thank you.» Then she gestured at her watch. I hadn't noticed it before but she had a big, man-sized wristwatch with multiple dials on it.

«I come.» she said.

«Good luck.» whispered Sally and gave her a hug.

Then we all did, including a long mutual hug with Kurt, before she turned and edged her way in past the bushes.

We stood there for a while, not wanting to leave, even as the shadows lengthened for the end of the day.

«Pretty weird.» said Kurt at last and turned to walk up the slope.

As we climbed Patrick said: «I am going to bring some tools down and clear the entrance. I have a feeling we are going to be visiting there pretty often.»

We knew he was right.

13.

Lying in bed that night, Sally and I wondered what it must be like for Laetitia deep underground by herself in the cave. What was happening? Would the saint appear to her? Although we tried to speculate what would come of it, in real terms we had no idea.

«She didn't seem frightened.» said Sally.

I agreed, although she did take the bottle of armagnac. It was hard to tell how she felt about it except that she was certain she had to do it. She was now convinced that she needed something to happen for her to be rid of the burden of history that she carried.

Once again we found ourselves marvelling at how easily and quickly we had arrived at an acceptance that this saint was real, could do things, and was aware of the world we lived in. What was it that made Laetitia accept it? What was it that made the saint choose Kurt, of all people, and then Laetitia? What were they destined to do?

The questions hung in the air as we dropped off to sleep.

Rising the next morning, half expecting, not really, that Laetitia had come back early, we made breakfast and sat up on the roof with Kurt as the sun began to warm the day.

After a while Kurt got up and disappeared into his «engine room». He and Patrick were going to organise a new coat of automotive paint for the old Citroen van. There was a «carrosserie» along the valley that specialised in repainting vintage vehicles.

Sally and I strolled around to visit Jean-Pierre.

As if he knew we were coming, the coffee was already brewing and the aroma reached to greet us as we turned into his «impasse». It was the Peruvian desert variety.

We carried chairs out into the sun and the cats deigned to join us. Eloise had baked little square brown cakes with cinnamon which were still warm.

As we sipped our coffee, Sally asked: «Has the saint said anything about what is happening to Laetitia?»

He shook his head.

«Our saint is what you might call taciturn. He does not make conversation. When he wishes something to be communicated he does it with precision. That is his way.»

«I suppose we will have to wait till she comes out.»

«And she may not wish to tell you.» he said. «It was like that for us.»

When we looked puzzled he added «There are very very few in this village who know.»

«Do you think there are other saints in other parts of France who are like this?» I asked.

He shrugged. «Who knows? Maybe. It is also possible there are, but they do not wish to be known.»

«Do you think it is only Christian saints, or do you think maybe in other traditions there might be the same thing?»

Jean-Pierre took a moment to respond as if he was checking inside himself. Then he smiled.

«I do not believe that Christianity has a monopoly on saints.»

«Maybe we have Australian ones that we don't know about.» I mused.

«It is possible.»

And then we just sat in the sun with the somnolent cats, the aromatic coffee and the sweet cakes, just enjoying being there.

We found things to do for the rest of the day, but the sense of anticipation was inescapable.

The sun sank at last on a cloudless evening, and we waited.

It was almost completely dark when she appeared.

The three of us were up on the roof, enjoying the last rays of the day with cold beers, but also with eyes on the street below. After a while Gwyn and Patrick joined us. They had seen her pass their house and they were not going to miss hearing what happened.

Kurt had procured half a dozen nearly new deck chairs going cheap in a village further along the valley, at a «vide grenier», French version of a garage sale, «grenier» being the attic. The deck chairs were a bit rickety, but they were going to get a lot of use.

Laetitia came slowly up the street carrying the things she had taken with her into the cave. We watched over the parapet but she never looked up.

When she came in we restrained ourselves from rushing downstairs and we let her take her time.

She disappeared into the room where she had first slept with the other girls, and we wondered if she was going to come up.

When she did appear her face was covered in red blotches.

Sally jumped up and gave her a hug, then put her hands up to Laetitia's face.

«Was it the fleas?»

«Les puces.» she nodded and then lifted her T shirt. She was bra-less and covered in red dots which gave her tattoos an interesting additional colour.

Then she turned round and dropped her track pants, and her buttocks were the same. The butterfly on each cheek had vivid red spots.

«Full coverage.» muttered Kurt.

She flopped down into a deck chair.

«Does it hurt?» asked Sally.

Laetitia shook her head.

«Can you tell us what happened?» asked Gwyn.

She shrugged and reached for a beer.

At last she said, with me translating: «I did as they told me. I took my clothes off, I washed in the water from the source. It was cool and sweet. I felt very good. Then it was like a fog came and covered me. Or like I had smoked really good dope. I was stoned and then I went K.O.»

«Unconscious?»

She nodded.

«How long for?» asked Kurt.

She took a long swig from her can, and then shrugged.

«Who knows? But when I opened my eyes I could see faces, people looking at me.»

«There were people in the cave?» asked Patrick

«No. I could see just faces, like a mirage.»

«Did you recognise them?»

«No, but I know where they came from. They were Oradour people, children, women, old men.»

«How did they seem to you?» asked Sally «Were they happy, sad, angry?»

She shook her head. «They just looked.»

That seemed to be the sum of it. She had nothing else to tell us. She said she stayed there till she knew it was the end of the day, then she came out.

Somehow we all felt there was nothing to say and we sat there silently as the darkness set in.

At last we went downstairs, Gwyn and Patrick went home, Sally found some cream to put on Laetitia's flea bites, and then we all went to bed.

14.

And then nothing happened.

Maybe we expected that something would come out of Laetitia's cave adventure, but her flea bites went away with the help of Sally's cream, and life went on. The two mechanics went back to work mostly in silence or at best with grunts and gestures. We cleaned house, cooked meals, went shopping and hung out with Jean-Pierre. He had nothing to add so it seemed like our saint had done whatever needed to be done, and then gone off to whatever plane of consciousness bodyless saints inhabit.

The three months were up and our visas were about to run out, both ours and Kurt's. We had to leave the Schengen European countries, supposedly for three months before we could come back in. However, we met several non-Europeans who told us that the frontiers were not strictly patrolled between Schengen and non-Schengen countries, and all that you had to do was to make sure you got a good entry stamp when you came back in. Rumour had it that Switzerland was the easiest and, being the closest, the most convenient.

By this time Kurt had three working vehicles. The old Citroen van, now splendidly grey in its new coat, was not going to serve as a long haul holiday transport, the Deux Chevaux was a bit short on luggage space, but the Simca was looking good. Kurt swore he had it in shape for a good thousand kilometer run, especially when he had found very comfortable seats to replace the tattered originals.

When we told Laetitia what we were planning, she shrugged. She didn't need a visa, so why bother going all the way to Switzerland? She still hadn't got her head gasket, and as far as she was concerned the Harley was the only way she wanted to travel.

So in the end we decided we would trundle off and leave her in charge.

Strangely enough this was confirmed, almost as soon as it was decided.

When we told Jean-Pierre of our need to leave the country, he said that it was fine with the saint, but that Laetitia should not go anywhere. He said she had to be still so that the work that was needed to be done inside her could be completed.

She snorted when she heard that, insisting that she would do whatever she wanted to do, but in reality we could see that she was quite pleased to stay put. I have to say I was a bit surprised that the saint even knew we were planning to go, but then who knows what saints know.

Kurt ran the Simca up and down the hill a few times and declared it was in perfect shape for a road trip. Laetitia patted the pale blue bonnet and said she thought it was ready. Always good to get a second opinion.

So we looked at maps of how to get to Switzerland and decided to avoid freeways most of the time. Kurt insisted that Sally and I both should become comfortable driving on the other side of the road.

We packed up small suitcases thinking we might be gone for about a week. Laetitia seemed very content to watch all this, and Gwyn invited her to come round for meals whenever she felt like it. Laetitia was impatient for her «culasse» to arrive so she could get her Harley back on the road. Kurt even offered to lend her the Ducati but she sneered and shook her head. That was one thing she and Kurt could not agree on at all. Their rides. She sneered even more when he tried to give her some money to live on while we were away.

«You think I am SDF?» she said poking him in the chest. Luckily I had just come across that expression. The French love to shorten things into acronyms and this was one everyone used. The words are «sans domicile fixe» meaning of no fixed address, homeless.

Kurt grinned and gave her a hug.

«Nah,» he grinned, «you're not a hobo.»

We set off on a crisp October morning when the valley below the walls was filled with a thick layer of cloud as if we were about to dive off into an unknown ocean.

Patrick and Gwyn waved us off, standing with Laetitia who had a scowl on her face. This was because at the last moment Kurt had tried again to give her a wad of euros by slipping them down the back of her trackpants.

The little Simca purred along very nicely as we dropped down into the fog with Kurt at the wheel. We spent the morning barreling along on roads that were mostly not much wider than the Simca, meaning that if we met a large combine harvester we had to take to the fields to get off the road. They are so big that an escort vehicle with flashing orange lights precedes them to warn oncoming traffic. It was always friendly, the drivers would give us a cheery wave and we would wave back.

We stopped mid-morning climbing to another bastide perched on top of what may have been an ancient volcano, so it had steep streets leading up to a small flat summit dominated by a big stone church with a square of shops around it. There was a cafe, which was also a tabac and bistro, a kind of one stop shop for coffee, lottery tickets, cigarettes and croque monsieurs. It had a few chairs and tables outside in the sun. As we sat there with our «grand crêmes» we saw an old man walk over to the Simca and lovingly run his hands along the bonnet. He caught our eye and we waved, so he came across.

«She is yours?» he asked.

When we nodded, he pulled up a chair.

«When I was young», he said, «I worked for a long time to be able to buy my first car. It was just like yours. You have taken good care of it.»

Then of course, like old people all over the world, he wanted to tell us his life story. I did my best to keep up and translate for Kurt and Sally. What struck me was how simple his life had been, how natural the trajectory had been. He grew up in this town where he could trace his ancestry back for generations. Half the males of his lineage had been killed in the First World War and his father had been interrrogated by the Nazis in the Second World War. He was born in the last years of the

War and worked for the local Mairie as a clerk. He married a local girl and had two sons both of whom had gone to work in Paris.

He made me think of Laetitia and her burden and I wondered if he had that. I couldn't tell. I guess you have to be a saint to know that.

When I asked him what he drove now, he smiled an almost apologetic smile. «Dacia.» It was an admission of poverty, Dacias being the low-grade version of Renaults built in Romania.

«C'est la vie.» he shrugged.

He waved us off when it was time to move on, wishing us «bonne route».

We found lunch in a spa town where there were natural springs. Every town in France that has a spring seems to be called something «les bains». Being a spa town, though, meant that the restaurants ought to be good and this one was. Being a work day, they had the «formule», the menu of the day, and it was extraordinarily cheap. We found ourselves in the company of the locals, many of whom were obviously workers, often wearing overalls with the name of who they worked for. They were on their lunch break, which is of course sacrosanct in rural France, and is long and leisurely. The «formule» included a carafe of red wine and complimentary coffee.

Life in rural France is good.

By the end of the day we were about half way to Switzerland. Sally had driven for an hour or so and managed to stay on the right side of the road, not the left, and then I did the same. I have to say it took some concentration, and by the end of the hour I was almost cross-eyed.

I used my phone to find a «chambre d'hôte» in the lower foothills of the Alps which were looming in the distance, then as the sun sank behind us we drove into a charming farmhouse complex, with wide-bodied yellowish cows in the fields around it. The big old farm house had aged cedar trees all round it with little statues of animals at their base.

We knocked on the front door but there was no answer, but as the door was unlocked we opened it and tentatively went in calling «Il y a quel'qu'un?».

We stood just inside the front door until finally we were welcomed by a small pooch of indistinct lineage who wagged his tail and then turned and ran back into the house, so we followed. He took us right through the big house and out the back door, through a well-used kitchen that smelled fabulous. Across the yard, littered with farm implements, was a big barn, and the dog stopped outside, waited for us, then barked.

This brought out what you would expect a farmer's wife to look like. She was a solid lady in a kind of housecoat, head-scarf and big boots. Behind her there was a lot of mooing.

«Bienvenu!» she called. «Nous sommes un peu pressé» meaning they were busy, then she turned back in and the dog followed, so we did too. The barn was impressive with a very high roof and several levels of what looked like hay storage above it.

At the far end was a modern automated dairy. We could immediately see why she and her husband were a bit pressed. They moved from the back of one cow to the next attaching pipes to the udders of the same kind of yellow cows we had seen in the fields.

We sat on some hay bales and the dog joined us while we watched. Every now and then the husband would stop, give us a wave and then turn back to milking.

Finally the woman came over to us with a jug and some cups so we could sample their product. It was still warm. I would have loved to have added it to a cappuccino.

At the end of it all, we went back to the house and she changed her boots for slippers and showed us to our rooms upstairs. It was a wonderfully homey house and must have had half a dozen bedrooms. Sally and mine overlooked the barn and we could see the cows milling around the back of it .

Although it was a bed and breakfast, the woman asked if we would like to have dinner with them. It turned out we were their only guests, and so she invited us to join her husband and herself. «You can have a walk.» she said, before dinner would be ready.

As the light faded we went for a wander around the farm yard which boasted exactly what you would expect: ducks and geese, pigs in muddy pens, a donkey in a little yard, outside of which sat a small cart which I supposed was what the donkey would pull, although it would carry not much more than a couple of children.

At the appointed hour we came down to her big kitchen and the cooking smells had become even stronger and wonderfully inviting.

«Sit, sit.» she said. There was a solid oak table in the middle with high backed wooden chairs. In the middle of the table sat a bottle of Ricard. As soon as we sat, her husband came in, and without asking, poured us each a big glass of it.

Then we held up our glasses and wished each other «bon santé !» Sally's face was a picture when the liquid hit the back of her throat.

Sally and I gently declined a second glass, but Kurt was game and he and the farmer polished off another two.

The first course was a crockpot of soupe à l'oignon, dark brown onion soup with chunks of what looked like toasted cheese floating on top. It was delicious and it was easy to accept seconds, although I was wary as to how many courses were to follow.

I was right, because then there was a plate of foie gras, which we were proudly told was homemade. Then we had little red fish with tiny potatoes. After that there was the plat principal, their own duck, which sat in a succulent red sauce with a mound of homegrown veggies. My weakness for duck was deeply rewarded.

While all this was taking place, we had to be grilled about who we were and where we came from. The usual French fascination with Australia was there, how far away it is, how dangerous all the creatures are. They thought of us as being pioneers in a wild and exotic land. Then when we told them about Kurt buying his hotel, they were astounded. «Why?» Kurt floundered around trying to find a decent justification, but failed.

To rescue him, I began to ask them about their lives and we learned a little about them, all their five children having left, some still studying, others working. None of them had expressed any interest in taking on the farm. The farmer was diffident about that. «Maybe,» he said, «when they are finished being children, and tired of the temptations of city life, they will see the wisdom of farming.»

«We pray for that.» said his wife, gesturing up to a large reproduction of a saint in an ornate gilded frame above the open fireplace.

«Well, she does.» grinned her husband.

At that point the phone rang and the husband left the room.

I asked her who the saint was.

«Saint Medard.» she said, and then when I asked what his story was she went off on to a long tale of what the saint had done and his miracles. He was local and the whole district regarded him as their saint.

I had trouble keeping up with the translation of all this for Sally and Kurt, but I was managing.

Sally asked whether the farmer's wife believed in the miracles and the woman gazed at her incredulously. «But of course.»

«Did he do any miracles for you?» asked Kurt.

She looked at him steadily for a long moment and then she asked «Do you have saints in Australia?»

«Not that we know of.» I said.

She nodded, and I could tell she was not sure about what she ought to say. Then Sally said «In Saint Livraque we do and we know what he does.»

Then we had to explain and Kurt had to talk about his leg, by which time the woman was smiling broadly.

«My husband does not believe in any of that kind of thing, but I am glad that you do. Saints are real and they exist everywhere, but only certain people have the good fortune to know them and to see what they do. You are lucky.»

Then her husband came back and we changed the subject.

We slept well and woke to the sound of cows and the donkey. Looking out the window we could see that morning milking was well on the way.

We got dressed and went out the back to watch.

When it was time for breakfast, we sat at the same kitchen table to be greeted by a small mountain of freshly baked crepes served with their own cream, home-churned butter, her homemade jams and cheeses from a local fromagerie.

The farmer was soon gone but his wife stayed.

Having put away the dishes, she came back to the table with her coffee and leaned in with a conspiratorial look.

«So, your saint came to visit.» she said.

She smiled as our collective eyes widened.

«He is looking after you.» she said. «You will have a safe journey. And the girl with the motorbike is doing good work.»

This caused Kurt to start laughing. «That's our saint!»

Then we had to explain about Laetitia.

The woman nodded.

«Thank God for our saints.» she said, and crossed herself.

And that was that.

We had a leisurely start to the next leg, perhaps buoyed by the knowledge that we had saintly protection.

The farmer's wife decided she knew us well enough to kiss us all on both cheeks and to remind us of our blessings. She gave us a box of homemade biscuits for the road.

Sally said to her «I am certain your saint will bring one of your children back to the farm. You will see.»

The woman stroked her cheek and said «Maybe your saint will help.»

The day grew quite grey as we wandered along the narrow country roads, now quite hilly. We missed seeing the Alps as we approached, hidden under layers of cloud, but at the end of the day as we neared the Swiss border the sky cleared and there they were, radiantly pink in the last light of the day. We worked out which one was Mont Blanc, using the GPS on the phone. Evidently it is called Monta Rosa from the Italian side, and it was certainly rosy pink when we saw it.

We spent the night in a little inn that smelled of mould, but was located in a picturesque village clinging to the slopes of a foothill. Outside was a lot more attractive than inside. There was no talk of saints and we discovered that not everyone in France cooks well. It was very cheap in every sense.

Early the next morning, after dishwater coffee and a stale baguette, we went the last short distance up a long hill to cross the border. At the customs check point, a small hut on a narrow road, it was deserted. The whole reason for our coming to Switzerland was to get a stamp that showed we had left France.

We parked the Simca and looked around. There were a few houses clustered a short distance away and we decided to take a walk to see if we could find a customs person.

It was a crisp morning and the air was wonderfully fresh. We must have been several thousand meters above sea level at that point.

In the centre of what turned out to be a tiny village, in France they call them Lieux dit .... , which means «a place called....» and then you add a name, there was a sort of little café and sitting on rickety chairs outside were two men in uniforms.

«Duanes?» I asked.

They nodded and when I told them what we wanted, they said they couldn't help us till nine o'clock. «That's the law.» they said, and invited us to join them for breakfast.

There was an air of alpine relaxation and no-one seemed in a hurry to do anything.

They wanted to know who we were and why we were travelling in the back roads of eastern France in a 1960s Simca. Obviously life was pretty boring in a two-man shed on a mountainside marking an otherwise invisible national border.

When we told them why we were crossing the border they lowered their voices, although who they were trying to avoid was not obvious.

«You need a stamp that shows you left for three months, then you come back.» one of them said.

We nodded.

«Maybe if you give us a little present we can fix it for you.»

So we never went to Switzerland.

I am sure our stay there would have cost a lot more than a fifty euro note to each customs man, plus the price of their baguette and coffee, both of which were superior to what we'd had for breakfast.

We shook hands and the Simca headed west again, with our passports purporting to show we had left for three months and then came back. It was a little risky in that our re-entry dates were three months in the future, but they assured us that we would be fine. «Unless you commit a crime.» grinned one of them.

We promised to be very law abiding citizens, but I doubt my French version of that promise was as erudite as that.

As we drove off away from the Alps we all felt the desire to get back to Saint Livraque as soon as possible. We got what we came for and somehow we felt the itch to get back, ready for whatever action our local saint had in mind.

15.

The return journey took two days and one night, staying in another picturesque town on the Rhône River, famous for making nougat. The town wasn't all that big but had four nougat shops. We bought several chunks, each filled with a different extra ingredient: nuts, fruit, Nutella. I have a low tolerance for nougat which seems to tenaciously lodge in your teeth and stay there for days. Nonetheless, we felt we should support the local artisans. The hotel was part of a national chain and had standard everything. In French the word «standard» means the basics. We didn't complain.

We all took turns in driving, resorting to freeways to speed up the journey towards the end. It's much easier to remember which side of the road to drive on when you are on a freeway. The dear old Simca wasn't quite up to the 130 kilometers an hour permissible on French freeways, at which speed she began to shudder, but she seemed comfortabe enough at 110. That's the speed you are supposed to observe if it's raining. It did rain for a while on the second day, but still everyone else on the freeway powered past us at or more than the 130 limit. Definitions of when it is raining seemed to be variant.

Coming up the last twisting incline felt like coming home.
We had missed it.

There was no-one home.
When we pulled back the big door of the grange to park the Simca we saw that the Harley was gone. The «culasse» must have been delivered.
«Ha, I can imagine,» grinned Kurt. «the minute it turned up, she had it back in and couldn't wait to try it out.»

We unpacked and wandered round to say «Bonjour» to Patrick and Gwyn.

«Anything interesting happen?» asked Kurt as we came in.

«It all depends on what you might call interesting.» replied Patrick, who was up a ladder, dutifully cutting the branches off his platane tree. Evidently this is a French tradition where you cut off all the new growth at the end of the summer so the tree is left with only the solid trunk and major branches with fist-like ends that then sprout fresh growth in the spring. It's called pollarding in English, I believe.

He came down off his ladder and we sat down for a cup of tea in Gwyn's kitchen.

They hadn't seen Laetitia for a day or two, but they did know her package had arrived.

«Maybe she'll turn up at the end of the day.» said Patrick.

«Maybe she's gone home.» said Gwyn with just the subtlest of smirks, knowing that Kurt and she had begun something of a relationship.

«Nah,» he muttered. «her stuff's still there.»

«And anyway,» I added, «she's got work to do for our saint.»

«Maybe,» said Sally «Saint Livraque has sent her out on a mission.»

That was an interesting thought so, after tea, Sally and I went round to see Jean-Pierre.

He had the coffee brewing as if he knew we would turn up.

«Did you have a good trip?»

Sally told him about the lady who had her own saint, and he smiled when he heard that she had a sense of our saint.

«There are people like her everywhere, but you won't know who they are unless they sense that you are one of them.» he said.

However he had nothing to tell us about Laetitia. He hadn't seen her since we left, and our dear Saint Livraque had been equally non-communicative.

«So it is quiet.» he smiled.

It was all something of a letdown. I think secretly we had hoped that there would be a hint of what was going to happen next.

Back at the Bat Hotel, we cleaned up, it being somewhat obvious that Laetitia was not into housekeeping. We cleared the kitchen sink of what she had not taken care of and put on a load of washing in the new machine. We had decided to be environmentally responsible and instead of a drier we ran a clothesline up on the roof.

After that we went shopping in the Simca, with Sally at the wheel. She had rapidly grown confident driving on the other side of the road. Kurt had decided it was time for us to be independent so he stayed at home.

We were coming back up the hill which the Simca always found a bit of a challenge, when two big bikes came up behind us and one of them kept flashing its high beams. Sally thought it was the police so she pulled over just below the village walls.

It was Laetitia.

Of course she recognised the Simca.

As soon as she took her helmet off Sally jumped out of the car to give her a hug and I followed.

«Where is Kurt?» she asked.

«D'accord.» she grunted when I told her we had just come home earlier in the day. «You see my culasse is fixed, so I go out for a test.»

Then she turned and beckoned to the rider of the other bike.

As he walked towards us he took off his helmet. He was a very tall man with a thick head of pure white hair and a trimmed white beard. His leathers were very impressive, with thick padding over very fancy boots.

«I wish to present Erik.» said Laetitia.

He pulled off his bike gloves to shake hands and then, with not too much of an accent, he said: «I am pleased to meet you» in very english English. He was riding a top of the range Honda Gold Wing.

They remounted, powered around the Simca, and preceded us up into the village like a police escort.

We pulled back the big door and there was Kurt with his nose under the bonnet of the Citroen.

He had the biggest grin on his face when he saw the Harley.

«Ca marche?» he said with his horrible accent.

«Parfaitement.» and she gave him a juicy two cheek kiss.

«And you picked up a sidekick?»

I had no way to translate that, but Erik said: «Un acolyte.» I was impressed. I was hoping he was going to stick around.

Kurt shook hands and looked at the Gold Wing. «That's the Rolls Royce of bikes that is.» he said. Then he grinned. «But I am a bit surprised that Laetitia was prepared to be seen in the company of the enemy.» Then he had to explain that evidently Honda owners and Harley owners do not see eye to eye.

You could see that Erik was rather impressed with Kurt and even more so when Laetitia pointed out the Ducati. As they talked about bikes, Erik took off his leathers. He was surprisingly thin. He had long limbs that seemed to hang from the central axis of his body like limp branches on a tree. As I watched him talking, although animatedly with Kurt, I had the distinct sense of deep sadness in him. Even his face seemed to have the same downward inclination as his limbs, his eyebrows slanted downwards, and the corners of his eyes and the edges of his mouth were turned down.

It was that time of the afternoon when the French enjoy « un aperitif». It was still warm enough to take our drinks and nibbles up to the roof.

And then of course we had to catch up. Laetitia wanted to know how our trip went, and chuckled when we said that we never set foot in Switzerland. «C'est comme ça, n'importe ou.» she said. «That's the way it is, no matter where.»

Of course we were keen to know Erik's story. Sally had already quietly said to me that she thought he was no accidental pick up.

Now we had a fluent English-speaking French person, Laetitia felt she could rattle away as fast as she liked and he would translate. He was very good at it. So she talked about getting the gasket delivered the day after we left and how once it was installed, she took off.

She had pulled into a service station up the valley and there was the Gold Wing. So they got talking. He was retired and had hit the road on his own. Then he picked up his own story in his impeccable Anglais. He had been the CEO of a mutual health fund, of which France has a lot. However, he had handed over its management to a new CEO, a young man he had been mentoring.

«I decided to retire early.» he said. «I left the company two years ago because my wife was quite sick. I decided I should take care of her.»

We nodded sympathetically, aware that the wife was not there.

«I bought the Gold Wing for our fortieth wedding anniversary five years ago and she loved to ride with me. We had matching leathers, bike intercoms, and we could listen to music in our helmet headsets. She was very fond of Brahms. We toured all over the South West. But last year she became too sick to ride any more.»

He sipped his Ricard.

«She passsed away this year.» he said.

I caught Sally's eye. She was nodding and then she leant forward and patted his knee.

«You must miss her.» she said softly.

«Very much.» He finished off his Ricard, then he said: «I have been revisiting some of her favourite places.»

«Did you ever visit Saint Livraque with her?»

«Sadly we did not.»

I could see how the experience of losing the woman he obviously loved had transformed his whole being, body and face. If anything, as he was speaking, it was even more down-turned.

As the sun set we went downstairs to make dinner, and Erik took his gear out of his big saddle bags. We hadn't got round to buying a bed for the guest room yet, but Laetitia offered to lend him her blow-up mattress and he had a sleeping bag.

There was a warm sense of camaraderie, and we chopped and cooked and everyone seemed happy to join in the preparation. Kurt and Laetitia dived into peeling and cutting vegetables and they kept throwing veggie scraps at each other like two wild kids. It was touching in a way.

It turned out that Erik loved to cook, and while his wife was alive he had been the principal cook in their house. He created a spicy rich sauce for the duck Sally and I had just bought. Duck was becoming a regular menu item.

Somehow we were creating quite a feast, so Kurt went off to invite Patrick and Gwyn to join us.

For most of the meal we made happy catching-up small talk, but somehow at a certain point Saint Livraque edged into the conversation. We were talking about our experience of arriving in a small village and learning to adjust to the local culture. Maybe it was Sally who first gently alluded to our saint. There was a moment when we looked at each other, wondering what Erik might make of it. After all he was a businessman, obviously successful in life.

However, he leaned forward when she mentioned the village namesake.

«Are you saying that the presence of the saint is felt, even today?»

It was Laetitia who decided to assure him it was so. This was interesting because she was talking about her own experience in French and he was not translating. He studied her carefully as she spoke and I tried to keep up as best I could for the others. She talked about Oradour.

He had listened to her with a gentle frown as if not sure about what he was being told.

«Ordour.» Then he said, in English «My wife and I have been there. It is perhaps the saddest place we have ever been.»

Then Laetitia told him how she had learned about her burden. This meant introducing Jean-Pierre and Eloise and their relationship to Saint Livraque.

«This is something I have never thought about. We French have a lot of burdens to carry and we have a long and dark history. But that we might carry the burden of our forebears, this is a new idea.»

Then Laetitia went on to describe going down into the cave and sitting naked by the pool. She lifted her shirt but the bites had subsided.

«Do you feel something changed?»

She shrugged. «Qui sait.« she said, who knows.

«But you believed what this couple told you enough to spend a whole day being attacked by fleas?»

She nodded.

Then she said: «I feel better, I really do.»

«What do you mean?»

«It is hard to describe,» she said, «but something has gone. I cannot say what it is, but it feels better.»

Then she laughed. «But one thing has gone which I am not happy about.» Then she leaned forward and pointed at the coffee table. On it sat her tobacco and papers for smoking.

«He does not let me smoke.»

Sally was impressed. «Did he say that?»

Laetitia shook her head. «No. But every time I try to have a smoke I feel sick. He made me allergic.»

Erik looked at us, one after the other, as if perhaps wondering how serious we were.

«For you all, this saint is very real and in a sense very alive?»

We nodded.

To reinforce the point, Kurt told him about his leg.

Erik sat back in his chair watching us. It was as if he was gauging our sanity, or at least our belief system.

Then something very unexpected happened. Erik closed his eyes. Then a tear began to run down his cheeks.

We sat quietly and waited.

At last he breathed in deeply, blew his nose and opened his eyes.

«She believed in this.» he said. «I never did. I am what you would have to call an atheist, or at least a non-believer in anything mystical.»

«Your wife?» Gwyn asked gently.

«Gaelle.» he said.

We cleaned up the dishes and said goodnight to Patrick and Gwyn and headed off to bed. There was no sound from Erik's room but we did hear some wild laughing from Kurt's spa bath, suggesting a joyful reunion.

As we lay there, smiling at what we were hearing, Sally whispered: «I wonder if our saint is about to convince Erik that he is real.»

Our saint chose not to, or if he did, it was not obvious.

When Erik joined us for breakfast, he looked refreshed and at ease. He slept well, he told us.

He had no real plans to move on and Kurt assured him he was welcome to stay as long as he liked. Given his level of English I was hoping he would.

While we were heading to Switzerland Laetitia had been working on the Deux Chevaux, at least until her culasse turned up. Although the little car needed a lot more cosmetic touches, especially the interior, it was now ready to be registered.

We waved it off as Laetitia and Kurt headed down the hill to get it done. Laetitia had not quite managed to get the engine totally clean so there was a faint pale blue trail as it took off.

We offered to take Erik on a guided tour of our little village, deciding that we now knew enough not to need Agathe, thereby saving Erik four euros.

The sun was a lot lower in the skies these days as winter was approaching, but even when the river valley was lost in thick fog, our little hilltop refuge was very often bathed in sun. We started out at the lookout and talked about the caves underneath. The lookout was a bit useless otherwise, as below it, as far as the eye could see, the outlook was thick cloud.

We did the circuit of the village and ended up in the little alleyway that concealed «Livres Vracs.» The coffee was brewing and the delightful scent welcomed us.

I have to say that, as we approached, I was curious to see what Jean-Pierre had to say about, or to, Erik.

He was sitting at a small table mending some damaged books and he lifted his glasses up to his forehead to greet us.

We introduced Erik who was delighted to see shelves and shelves of old books.

Jean-Pierre poured the coffee and we dislodged enough cats for everyone to have a seat.

Erik complimented Jean-Pierre on the coffee and then heard the story of where it came from.

And then our saint chose to put in an appearance.

This was in the form of Eloise. She appeared at the doorway from upstairs with a plate of fresh madeleines.

Jean-Pierre poured her a coffee and she gently dislodged another cat so she could settle. She very rarely came downstairs so Sally and I exchanged a look.

Eloise caught it and nodded.

Then as she proffered the plate of the little shell-shaped cakes to Erik, she said: «She wishes to talk to you.» She used the intimate «tu» as if she and Erik knew each other well.

He stared at her, clearly unsettled and maybe already sensing who the «she» was.

The air was potent and it seemed like none of us could breathe.

«The sadness that you carry,» continued Eloise softly, «it holds her back. She cannot move on.»

He nodded but could not speak.

At last he said, almost in a whisper. «I do not know how to be less sad.»

«She will help you.»

«How?»

Eloise smiled and leaned forward. «You have heard of our saint of course.»

He nodded.

«Our saint is very mysterious. He chooses when to be with us and when to be absent. He has decided to help you to move on.»

He studied her face, her quiet serious look.

«You said she wanted to talk to me.» He was using the intimate «tu» as well.

«Our saint has enabled this.»

We waited till Kurt and Laetitia returned with the Deux Chevaux, newly registered, and then we went down to the cave. By the time Gwyn and Patrick had joined us we were quite a party. It was late afternoon when we went down.

The entrance had been completely changed. Patrick had been working on cleaning up the steps that led down, removing the moss and sludge and reinforcing the loose stones, and then he had hacked away at the sumac and brambles around the entrance to the caves.

«I knew we 'd be having a lot more traffic.» he said. «We might have to put in a lighting system soon.»

We had torches.

There was no real idea as to why we were all going, why all of us felt we needed to be there, but no-one wanted to miss how Erik's wife would communicate. Eloise had simply told us he should go there.

He didn't seem to mind us all coming along.

The bats began to fly about as we entered the first chamber. The sound of bats flying is very subtle, a gentle rustling and occasionally a small high pitched squeal. We stood still until they settled. None of us wore protection any more. There was a profound silence as we stood there, waiting to see what would happen.

Nothing did.

We helped each other to descend to the lower chamber where Laetitia had spent her twenty-four hours and where Kurt's leg had been fixed. We talked quietly as if we were in a place that commanded our respect, which of course it did. In the lower cave, there were no bats and the gentle rippling of the water from above was the only sound.

As we stood looking down at the pool Erik began to murmur, a sort of humming sound.

We watched him as he stood still with his eyes closed. It was incredibly peaceful and we all seemed to melt into it. We turned off the torches and sat down round the pool. Everything became still, no sound and no light, and very soon we all had our eyes closed.

How long we sat there is hard to say but it was a delicious feeling.

At last it was broken when Erik began to speak softly in French.

«Bien sûr.» he was saying, «Of course».

As we opened our eyes and turned our torches back on, their light seemed so harsh. However, looking at Erik we could see that he was smiling and his eyes were shining.

«As she said,» he murmured, «she wanted to talk to me.»

«What did she say?» asked Kurt.

«You don't have to say anything.» said Sally putting her hand on Erik's shoulder.

«No, no. It is OK». He turned to face her. «She knows you are all aware, so it is OK to say. She says that I am lucky to have found you. You will help me, she says.»

There was another silence, then he laughed gently. «She says the saint believes in the goodwill of mechanics.»

«Course he does.» grinned Kurt.

«So now what? asked Gwyn.

He looked at us, standing round him in the glow of the torches. «She has asked me to allow her to move forward. It is exactly as Eloise said. Gaelle told me that my sadness was holding her back. She said it was as if she was like a prisoner stuck on the back of the Gold Wing still riding with me, but she wishes to move on. I must let her go.»

«Where is she going?» asked Gwyn.

He shrugged. «I don't know, but she said there are people waiting to take care of her. She knows them and she wants to go with them, but she can only do that if I let her go.»

Then he repeated what he had said for Laetitia in French, and she nodded.

«Un autre fardeau.» she said. «Another burden.»

He nodded.

We climbed back up to the main gallery above and the bats were undisturbed. They hung there like so many dark drapes in a shuttered mansion. And yet, although bats have a certain negative reputation, there was a peacefulness in the cave.

Coming out into the last of the daylight, the glow of the sunset was glorious. We stood and watched it, radiant crimson where the sun had just dropped below the horizon with an orange aura, while across the sky above us there were undulations of gentle pinky grey clouds.

Nothing needed to be said, and as the last light faded we turned and mounted the newly refreshed steps.

16.

Then once again things went quiet for a while.

Erik seemed in no hurry to go home and we were enjoying his quiet company. We could see that he needed time to get used to what he had experienced in the cave. He spent hours sitting up on the terrace roof just being quiet.

We left him to it.

Meanwhile, we kept house and the mechanics retired to the grange.

After a couple of days Kurt suggested we go on an outing and we returned to the château that had the restaurant. To get there we took three bikes. I got to ride behind Erik on the Gold Wing, which was like sitting in an armchair and I felt incredibly safe. Leaning out was almost a pleasure. We chatted over the intercom as he drove. Sally rode behind Laetitia and they leaned with ease. Kurt swerved dangerously out in front just to show me how leaning should be done, at least that's what I thought he was doing.

The restaurant owner was delighted to see us back and asked where the other girls were. This time he actually had other patrons, which was a good sign. At the end of another excellent «formule» Erik insisted on footing the bill.

Then after lunch Kurt decided it was time Sally and I got our own leathers and helmets so we could become properly outfitted bike people. This was an education, as there are so many bike outfits to choose from in the local bike emporium. Each item seemed to have its own implicit cultural message, especially according to the bike of the rider concerned. As we were non-aligned, bikewise, we basically went with what was comfortable. It was a little embarrassing to have Kurt pay for everything, but he loved it.

Our other shopping venture before charging back up the hill was to furnish the guest room properly for Erik. The girl in the big box store was very pleased to welcome us back. The double bed with matching dressing table and chest of drawers would be delivered the next day, free of charge.

When we got back, Patrick and Gwyn came to see us with some interesting news. Patrick had been down to the cave again to work on opening up the entrance. Agathe had seen him going down there with his tools and wanted to know what he was up to. He had tried to obfuscate as best he could but she was suspicious. She told him that technically the caves were on private land and he was, in theory, trespassing. When he asked her who the owner of the caves was she didn't want to say.

After she left he had done what he wanted to do anyway, whoever the owner was, but after he told Gwyn she decided to go up to the Mairie and look at the cadastre. This is the plan of the town with all the plots of land on it and you can check out who owns what.

It was true. All the plots of land under the walls of the town were broken up into small lots owned by many different people. At one time the village was known for dried figs and so most of the lots had old fig trees on them, now significantly old and gnarled. As far as she could see, the four caves were in four different lots and it was not clear who owned which cave. Obviously it would be a job for a surveyor.

I asked her if Agathe or her family owned any of the plots and she didn't think so. She didn't recognise any of the names.

We decided Agathe was just miffed to be left out of whatever we were doing and thought no more about it.

The next day the furniture arrived for the guest room and Erik no longer had to use camping equipment.

Sleeping on a proper mattress seemed to have an immediate effect. The next morning when he joined us for breakfast he looked downright joyful. Sally gave him a good morning double-cheek French-style kiss and said he had obviously slept very well.

He nodded. «Oh yes. Perhaps the best in more than a year.»

Kurt grinned. «We must have hit on just the right mattress.»

«I am sure you did,» he replied, «but that is not why I had such a good night.»

Sally poured the tea, and as she handed him a cup she said: «So what was it?»

«Gaelle.»

«You had a dream?» I asked.

He shook his head. «It was more than that. She was there. She lay beside me like she used to. We talked and she told me what I must do.»

We waited, knowing he would say more, after he had translated for Laetitia.

«I must buy a house.»

«You don't have one already?»

«In Bordeaux I have a big house and we have a chalet in the Pyrenees, but she said I have to live here in this village and I have to buy a house.»

Kurt grunted. «Plenty to choose from, especially if you're into reno.»

So after breakfast we went for a walk. There were quite a few houses on offer, in varying states of repair and with signs indicating that some had been «a vendre» for quite a while. We stood in front of each one and Erik seemed to pause, wait, and then shake his head. «No, that's not it.»

«She is helping you choose?» asked Sally.

He smiled. «Something like that.»

At the far end of the village, overlooking where the end of the moat would have been, was one small totally detached house made of stone. It had no «a vendre» for sale sign, but the windows were boarded up and it looked utterly desolate. In the rear there was a wooden door that was not properly closed, so we pushed our way into what had been the kitchen, now with rubble on the floor where some of the ceiling had collapsed and a dead pigeon in the sink.

Erik stood in the middle of it all and nodded.

«I think this is where I am to live.» he said.

We went up to the mairie to look at the cadastre to see who owned it. The owner was listed as a woman who lived in Lyon. After some more digging, we found a phone number and Erik tried it. The woman was astounded to be called about the house. She said she had inherited it from her elderly aunt who had died several years earlier. She had been meaning to get rid of it but her husband had been very sick and was now in a hospice. She was more than happy to sell it and asked what he was willing to pay for it. He could have probably asked for a very small amount after what she had said, but he gallantly offered to engage a real estate agent to value it. She was almost in tears in her gratitude and thanked him profusely for calling. He promised to call her back as soon as he could.

As we walked back to the Bat Hotel, Erik took down the numbers of two agents who had posted rather battered signs up on houses for sale.

One of the numbers proved to be a dead end, as the agent had retired but neglected to take down his old signs. The other call, however, was answered by a young woman who said she was just training and that the owner of the agency was on vacation. She would be delighted to do a valuation, she said, because she had just finished a course in doing exactly that.

It sounded a bit dubious to us, but Erik took it all in good spirits and invited her to come up to Saint Livraque as soon as she could. He would of course be happy to pay for her time.

«Well that was quick.» said Kurt when he heard the story.

He and Laetitia had started the task of bringing the Panhard back to life. He had shown us some of the history of Panhards (including how to pronounce the name in French: «pan ha.») I had never heard of them but in France they were one of the earliest auto makers. This one was called a Dyna and dated, as far as Kurt could tell, from 1963. They died out when Citroen bought the company. Kurt was sure it would be a hit at local motor shows, once he got it back to working order.

So he and Laetitia were more than happy to leave house-hunting with Erik to me and Sally.

That afternoon, the girl turned up in a pale pink Fiat Punto that had obviously done a lot of mileage. It smelled vaguely as if it was about to catch fire, having laboriously ascended our long uphill approach.

While we waited for her, we had brought torches to penetrate deeper into the cottage. What eerily appeared in the torchlight was not encouraging.

She must have been no more than twenty, and was a bit giggly as she talked about how excited she was to be a real estate agent. The expression for that in French is «agent immobilier», meaning someone who sells things that don't move. It makes more sense in a way than real estate.

We pushed open the back door, turned on our torches again and toured the premises. I had half expected to find bats but there weren't any. The house layout was quite simple. It had a corridor in the middle that ran from the front door, past two front rooms, both with ratty old single beds in them, past an ancient bathroom and a third very small room full of empty milk churns, before opening out into the kitchen at the back.

The girl had a laser device for measuring and she dutifully recorded the dimensions of everything so she could calculate the total square meterage, which in France is always the most important starting point for evaluation. She had a small electric tablet to record everything.

«This could be a very cosy little home.» she said, sounding like a true trainee real estate agent.

«I believe it will be.» said Erik.

«Probably you should get someone to inspect the roof.» she said, having pointed out a number of spots where water had come in.

«I am sure it will have to be replaced.» he said, sounding not at all worried. In real terms it was as if he had already bought the house. All he needed was the price.

The floors were covered in cracked tiles which would have to be replaced but the walls, as far as could be ascertained, were solid. Some of the interior walls had been plastered and had lots of cracks but the outside stone walls were almost a metre thick and apart from a few signs of slippage looked totally solid. The windows were old, single glazed and most had cracks. The plumbing and the electrics would all have to start from scratch. Not only did Erik seem unfazed by any of this, he actually seemed to be energised by it.

Having heard from Kurt how easy it was to get artisans and work teams in the village, he couldn't wait to get started.

Before she hopped back into her Punto, she shook hands with us and thanked us for inviting her. She would call Erik by the end of the afternoon she said, after she had looked up different kinds of information, comparisons of like properties, and checked in with her boss. She didn't think it would be a very expensive purchase.

Clearly she had nothing else to do, because she was back on the phone by the end of the afternoon.

As he listened to her outline what she had discovered and what she thought the price should be, Erik was nodding. Her boss had been contacted and had agreed with her assessment. The enthusiasm in her voice was obvious. Erik told her that he would pass on the price to the owner, and that as far as he was concerned she had just made a sale. We could hear her excitement as she admitted that in fact it would be her first sale. As a trainee she had only helped out, never had a sale in her own right. Erik asked her to find out from her boss how much she would be owed for her good work.

The owner in Lyon was just as excited as the agent immobilier trainee. «Mais oui, mais oui.» we could hear her say.

Then there followed a conversation about notaires, the lawyers who handle all the paperwork. Erik had his own who had taken care of all his business for years, so she accepted to use the same one. Everything was moving fast. The last thing the lady said was, that as far as she was concerned, if Erik wanted to start doing anything to the house, she gave her permission. He promised to send her photos so she could see what was happening. She was absolutely over the moon by the end of the call. She was not going to be all that much richer after the sale, given that the price was less than you would pay for a midsized Peugeot, but at least it was no longer something she had to take care of.

After the call, Erik sat back with the biggest smile on his face.

«I will go and buy champagne.» he announced.

We had a celebration dinner not only with the champagne but several bottles of very good Bordeaux Grand Cru from Pomerol, which by then I knew was not cheap. Not only had Erik splashed out on good things to drink, he had come back with all sorts of cheeses, a ham, and organic veggies.

Sally dutifully performed the rôle of sous chef, but Erik did the whole thing himself.

Patrick and Gwyn joined us and there was a certain euphoria in the air that was undeniable.

The next couple of days saw Erik visiting the house every day. When he took Laetitia and Kurt, he was already describing what he planned to do with it.

With Kurt and Patrick's help he was off lining up his workers. He had a long conversation with the Mayor about getting permits but as he didn't plan to demolish anything external, extend the property in any way or majorly alter the look of it, except to replace the roof, the Mayor tended to suggest that he could just get it done, as long as he didn't make too much noise about it. Nonetheless, the Mayor was also very happy to give a quote for the work that his teams could do. If the Mayor did the roof then there certainly would be no need for formal permits.

The first step involved all of us, even Kurt and Laetitia, taking time away from their «babies», as we began clearing out the junk. Patrick contacted the same local farmer who was more than willing to hire out his trailer, a few euros into his back pocket, and we loaded it up with old furniture, ruined tiles, dead antiquated appliances and accumulated rubbish. The farmer got to keep the milk churns. By the end of the first day, after several trips to the «dechetterie» where everything was dutifully triaged, the house was effectively empty. It echoed with our voices, and when the boarded-up windows had been liberated, a pale light poured in, filtered by the lacework of many years of spiderweb.

Erik was very pleased.

Once the neighbors got wind of what was happening, they felt called upon to drop in, lend a bit of a hand, and tell stories about who lived there previously. Agathe of course was the best at that, although most of the house's history was mundane. Generation after generation of Livraquais had lived, worked, married, propogated and died in these little rooms. She sounded almost apologetic.

The next phase, while the notaires did the paperwork, was deciding the layout of electrics and plumbing, but once Erik had decided where it should all go, there was nothing much to be done so he decided to head back to Bordeaux for a day or two.

He left the big Honda in the grange and Kurt took him to the nearest railway station on the back of the Ducati. He would return with his car and some of his things. He had a lot of decisions to make.

Things went quiet again as the first blasts of winter began to be felt. It wasn't cold exactly, but we had to wear more layers. There were no longer so many opportunities to go up onto the roof for tea or aperitifs.

As winter was in the air, Kurt had commissioned the Mayor and his team to redo the terrace on the roof so there was no further need for buckets to collect the leaks below. Since then a couple of decent downpours had demonstrated the Mayor's expertise. The terrace now had a gentle two-way slope from the middle out to the front and the back walls so that rain easily ran off, out through small holes at the base of the balustrade and left the lounge and kitchen underneath perfectly dry.

When it was all done we had a celebration aperitif, rugged up against the increasing cold but very happy. The slopes were so gentle we hardly noticed and the deck chairs didn't budge. The Mayor dutifully accepted our compliments when he joined us.

Every now and then Kurt would insist that we go off on the bikes, now that Sally and I were decked out in our new outfits. I was getting a little better at leaning into the corners.

One of those outings was prompted by a dream.

Laetitia told us that Saint Livraque had told her to go to visit his brother in Rocamadour. We had never heard of it, so we surfed the internet. According to Wikipedia, it is an ancient religious site, clinging to the side of a cliff over a small river in the Lot, the department named after the biggest river that runs through it. Rocamadour is named after Saint Amadour, whose supposed relics were uncovered there in the 16th century. His relics, real or not, had a bit of a hard time, rather like our village, ransacked and burned by the Protestants during the religious wars and then desecrated again during the Revolution. Just a few charred bones are left.

I read that the whole notion of a saint having lived there was highly debatable, but I decided it was best not to say anything.

A legend is a legend.

Who knows what the truth is?

So off we went on the two bikes.
The road winds for a couple of hours over rugged terrain mostly following the river and I had lots of practice at leaning.
We got there in the late morning on a day that was nicely sunny.
At first it just looked like a small relatively flat modern town with a pharmacy and a bank, a few restaurants scattered around a medieval château, and an expansive carpark. Being the off-season, there weren't many cars.
This all seemed rather disappointing until we walked over to the château and looked over the parapet. The town below was entirely different. It came into being in the 12th century and was almost vertical, all the buildings one on top of the other, attached to the side of the cliff below the château, overlooking the small river at the bottom. Steep stone stairs ran down zig-zagging back and forth from top to bottom.
As we descended it became clear that there are distinct layers to the town. The château on the top is obviously intended for security, guarding all below it. The middle level is the religious heart, the church with its black Madonna, the chapel with the relics, and the monks' housing. Then towards the bottom there is the area of commerce, rows on either sides of the steps of souvenir shops, cafés and little stone houses backed into the cliff face, the single descending walkway of cobble stones eventually arriving at an arched gateway leading to an open parking area beside the little river. This was mostly occupied by big tour buses and all sorts of caravans with different European number plates.

Going down was easy and we found ourselves a sunny spot outside a coffee place almost at the bottom. Tourists came and went and there were smatterings of quite a few different languages.
After a decent coffee and croissants, we started the steep climb back up.
Laetitia suddenly stopped in the middle of the stairs at a place which opened out into a wider plaza. I thought maybe she had run out of breath and needed a pause but she shook her head.
«His brother is in there.» she said, pointing to the chapel.

We trooped into the crypt where the relics are held in an ornate urn at the far end, and looked around. The low curved ceiling kept the sound to a minimum and it had an atmosphere not unlike our own caves.

There were wooden benches and we sat, still wearing our leathers. Sally's and mine, being new, still creaked a bit if we moved. Other than that it was very quiet in there.

Suddenly Kurt started laughing and then Laetitia joined him.

«Oh yeah!» shouted Kurt. «Look at 'em!»

Sally and I couldn't see anything.

«What is it?» I demanded.

«The pair of 'em.» he said, pointing at the front of the room where the relics were. «You can't see 'em?»

Laeitita looked at us as we shook our heads.

«Ils dancent.» she said. They are dancing.

I tried squinting to see if that might help but nothing changed, until suddenly Kurt jumped to his feet.

«Oh no!» he yelled «Hey! Come back!»

«They are going for lunch.» said Laetitia.

Sally said: «You could really see them? I mean two of them?»

«Clear as I see you right now.» said Kurt.

«What did they, I mean, was it our guy?»

«Yep. Our guy.»

«But there were two of them?».

«Yep.»

«What did the other one look like?»

«Bearded. Yellow robe.»

«C'est lui.» said Laetitia, pointing to an icon that I had not noticed hanging on the wall of the crypt.

«Yeah,» said Kurt, «that's him.»

We sat there for a while longer and then I suddenly recognised that, although, outside, people had been coming and going up and down the stairs and into the different parts of the church toting cameras and phones, while we sat in this crypt, no-one came in.

«Private audience.» I said.

«He wanted us to meet his brother but something else as well.» said Laetitia.

I translated for Kurt and Sally.

«We've got work to do.» Kurt nodded.

When we asked the obvious, neither of them knew what kind of work it was supposed to be.

Finally other people began to filter in, so we walked out, feeling as if the doors had just been re-opened to the public.

We climbed the long steep stone steps back up to the top by the château. The stones were quite worn in the middle of each step and I imagined just how many people must have climbed them over so many centuries. Pilgrims, ransackers, penitents and tourists.

At the top we found a restaurant with tables out in the open under a Linden tree.

Looking around, it all seemed a bit unreal. Two saints had been dancing in the crypt but up here cars and trucks went back and forth and there were jet trails overhead.

What was real?

Coming back to more mundane matters we looked at the menu.

It featured Rocamadour cheese. When in Rocamadour....anyway, we made sure to include some in place of desserts. Restaurants in France often offer a cheese plate instead of dessert. It turned out to be a round creamy sort of goats cheese, and it was pretty good. Before that, the cuisse de canard was pretty good, too. I like a good duck.

We were at the cheese stage of the lunch when we heard bikes. Immediately Kurt and Laetitia looked round to see what they were. It was a group of five who all pulled into the parking lot next to the Ducati and the Harley.

As the riders stood their bikes up and took off their helmets, we saw they were all young and male. The bikes were a mix but none of them were big fancy bikes. Several were not much more than dirt bikes.

They stood round our two bikes with undisguised admiration.

Kurt stood up and yelled in his appalling accent.

«Bonjours les mecs.»

Seeing him still in his leathers, they all came over.

There was a bit of conversive confusion as several of them started talking at once. They had an accent which was really hard to follow. Laetitia took charge. She invited them all to pull up chairs round our table then she did an introduction. I did a bit of translation on the side but it wasn't all that necessary.

It turned out they were locals, more or less, coming from the nearest bigger town called Gordon.

After the exchanging of names which led to their fascination that three of us were Australians, Kurt asked if they'd had lunch. They had not and he told them he would buy them all a lunch. They were amazed and at first said they couldn't possibly accept, but when he insisted, Kurt had friends for life.

It was interesting to watch the waiter, who had been deferential enough to us, looking with narrowed eyes at these young men who, I suspect under other circumstances, would not have been quite so welcome.

They were a bit shy about ordering and chose the simplest thing on the menu. Five burgers. It still amazes me that the French even like burgers, but there are burger places everywhere doing fine. They even give an annual award for the best «french» burger. There is another one for «frites», chips or as the Americans say «french fries».

The boys asked about us as we waited for their burgers, and we asked about them. They had all grown up together in the same part of Gordon. They were in their early twenties and all were training to be apprentices, a couple of mechanics, a plumber, a pastry cook, and a roofer. Two of them were brothers, where the older brother did all the talking and the younger brother never said a word. The younger brother was one of the trainee mechanics.

When they heard that Laetitia was a bike mechanic they were very impressed, especially when they realised that the Harley was hers. They had thought that Kurt and I were the owners of the bikes and that Sally and Laetitia were our pillion companions. Laetitia had great pleasure in scolding them for their chauvinism and they looked suitably abashed.

Later in the conversation after the burgers had been served that I tried to engage the younger of the two brothers. His name was Guillaume.

With my accented French I thought maybe he wasn't following what I was saying, although he would nod with a shy smile. His brother leaned over and said: «Il ne parle pas.» He doesn't talk.

«Why?»

«Il bégaie.»

I did not know the word and one of the other boys did an imitation of stuttering.

Guillaume looked down at his burger as this happened and I felt very sorry for him. But Laetitia's eyes widened.

She put her hand on Guillaume's arm and she said: «Vous voulez parler?

He lifted his eyes looking puzzled.

«If you want to talk then there is something you can do.»

Kurt and Sally and I instantly knew where she was going.

Guillaume studied Laetitia's face for a long moment, then he nodded.

Guillaume did not come to Saint Livraque right away because he had classes he had to attend, but after a couple of weeks, at the end of the semester, he and his brother Raphael came together, their two small Yamahas standing in the grange, hot and smokey, in stark contrast to the Ducati and the Harley.

They brought their tattered backpacks upstairs and we installed them in a room that we hadn't got around to doing anything much with so they had sleeping bags on the floor.

Naturally Sally and I were certain about what would happen: Guillaume would get cured by our saint and go on to be a chatty young teenage mechanic.

How wrong can you be.

Our saint has some tricks up his ecclesiastic sleeve.

Laeititia took charge the next day and decided that she would take Guillaume by himself. Raphael seemed more amused about all this than anything else. He came along for the ride, and his parents would not have let Guillaume come on his own anyway. He listened to what we told Guillaume about the caves and the saint and cures with a slightly puzzled look. Kurt told his broken leg story quite well in French. He was getting used to telling it. Guillaume nodded and smiled and seemed to be quite open to everything, while his brother laughed now and then. He shrugged when I asked him what he thought about it all. «Je ne sais pas.» I don't know.

So the next morning Laetitia took Guillaume, quite willingly, down to the cave and we did not see them for several hours. Raphael hung out with Kurt in the grange.

When they came back Guillaume was radiant. He really looked totally different.

«You can speak now?» I asked.

He shook his head.

Laetitia told us what had happened.

They had sat together by the pool in the deepest cave. She said nothing happened for quite some time until very gradually the air changed. She said it was like that when she had been there by herself. Very gently, she said, the air began to be filled with voices singing. She said the voices were like angels and Guillaume began to cry when he heard them.

Then one of the voices rose above the others and sang to Guillaume telling him that he was one of them. He had no need to speak. His life's work would be in silence.

Raphael shrugged when he heard this and refused to comment on it.

The boys stayed with us for another couple of days and most of the time they were down in the grange messing about with bikes. Their two Yamahas were retuned to perfection so that when they left again they purred off without any smoke.

That seemed to be the end of it, until some months later we received a postcard from the Jura mountains, not far from where Laetitia had lived.

Guillaume had been accepted as a novice in a silent monastery.

17.

After the boys left, Kurt decided he needed to set up more guest rooms. Who knew when the next candidates for saintly interaction might turn up.

Back we went to the same big box shop where we had become their best customers. They had insisted that we get a «carte de fidelité», a loyalty card where you get points. We got two double beds for the price of one.

We set up two more rooms just in time, because the next guest came the next day.

When Erik came back in his big Range Rover, it was packed with stuff, and his brother-in-law.

Didier, who was about the same age as Erik, had just retired himself and obviously had time on his hands. He had started and run one of the fanciest Bordeaux riverfront restaurants, complete with a Michelin Star. Now he had sold it to a world famous English television chef who was establishing his brand in big cities all over the world.

Erik told us that he had known Didier longer than he had known his own wife, they had gone to high school together, and that it was Didier who had got them together.

The work on Erik's little house had begun in his absence but not nearly enough for him to move in. We helped him carry all sorts of things up to his room, his computers and electronic gadgets, a couple of suitcases of clothes, and some of his prized cooking utensils. He was promising to make us some of his favourite recipes.

Didier just had a small suitcase.

While he was away, Erik had finalised the purchase of the little house, and the lady in Lyons had sent him some fine Burgundian wine in gratitude.

He brought the case with him.

He was now officially Saint Livraquais.

That night we sat up in Kurt's lounge with the woodburning stove glowing in the corner, as it was starting to get cold at night.

Erik had told Didier all about what had happened to him, and Didier seemed remarkably open about it. He and his sister had been close he said, and when she died he grieved for a long time. It was clear that what Erik had told him had the effect of alleviating some of his grief.

He was very keen to see the caves where it all happened.

Didier's English was as good as Erik's, although he didn't quite have the polished accent. Nonetheless, it was good having another bilingual guest.

Next morning Erik took Didier off to the caves and they spent all morning in there. Sally and I had wondered if our saint had any plans for Didier, but when they came back all he said was that it was wonderfully peaceful in there.

Perhaps in a way he too was letting his sister move on.

For the next couple of days they would take a morning walk round the village and then go together down to the caves. There was no hint of saintly intervention, and Jean-Pierre showed no sign of receiving any messages.

However, Jean-Pierre's coffee was very impressive to Didier. He wanted to know all about the torrefaction and what blends were used. He obviously had a deep and passionate interest in the subject. He sipped his coffee with the air of a connoisseur.

This led to a very interesting conversation about why our village did not have a coffee shop. With that kind of coffee available it was a terrible omission. We had to agree, given what we used to do in Melbourne. And that's where the germ that had lurked subtly in the background all along began to sprout.

The next time Didier walked into Kurt's ground floor he was eyeing it with a restaurateur's persepective. He could see a bar on one side, resurrect the big old fire place, bring the kitchen back to life, after totally replacing the previous version.

Kurt followed all this with narrowed eyes but did not knock it on the head.

«You want to start a business?» he muttered.

«Do you want a coffee shop? said Didier.

«Doesn't bother me one way or the other but I am not running a coffee shop.»

«But we could!» remarked Sally. «That's what we do. At least that's what we did before we went bust.»

So then we had to describe to Didier about the Crooked Nook.

Of course there was the initial excitement of creating visions of how it might look but the reality of bringing it into being was something else. For a start, we had visas that prevented us from working. Didier didn't see that as an impediment. We could just be what he called consultants, unpaid of course.

Sally and I spent a few late nights wondering about whether we would be coffee shop folk once more.

Just like Erik, of course Didier was a wonderful cook, and Sally and I happily allowed ourselves to be demoted to onlookers, the occasional sous chefs and dishwashers.

Then, the following weekend, we were witness to some of their cooking on a grand scale.

They gave a banquet.

Erik had told his Gold Wing buddies, a kind of informal top-end biker's club, about Saint Livraque and buying his house. He invited them all to come and have a look.

He booked all three of the town gites for them and they came en masse, well seven of them on five bikes. A small fortune in top of the range motor cycle hardware was parked in the square by the church.

On the Friday, Sally and I got recruited as serious sous chefs after an extensive shopping run to the Friday market up the valley, and Kurt's kitchen turned into a hive of culinary chaos. Much of the cooking got done that afternoon, so when the bikers arrived Erik would be free to host them.

I don't think our village has ever seen so much upmarket leather. They were all of a certain age, and most of them seemed to have been in big business of one kind or another. Two brought their wives.

We started with coffee up on the terrace now that we had acquired our own supply of Jean-Pierre's son's excellent brew, but it was a chilly morning, threatening to rain so we didn't stay long. There was no sighting of the Pyrenees.

Then we walked with Erik to do the tour of Saint Livraque where Erik had imbibed quite a bit of the history already. It was interesting to see that he made no mention of the caves, and Sally and I wondered about that.

We paused at «Livres Vracs» where Jean-Pierre was very gracious. He had probably never had so many browsers at one time. He did get a couple of sales for old books that one of the guys, who was a lifelong bibliophile, took a fancy to.

It crossed my mind and I did say something quietly to Sally that maybe Jean-Pierre might pick up something about some of the bikers, but he showed no sign of it.

Luckily Agnes did not get wind of the fact that her territory was being invaded without her getting her four euros per person.

It started to rain so our tour was a bit short, and we retired to Kurt's to finish getting lunch ready while Laetitia and Kurt led their own tour to the grange and the collection of wheels. The five Gold Wings got to shelter with the Ducati.

The lunch was sumptuous and washed down by several bottles of what I guessed to be rather expensive Bordeaux Grand Cru Superieur from the Medoc, which had come in someone's saddle bags. I had certainly heard of the saintly chateaux they came from.

Well nurtured and relaxing in Kurt's new lounge chairs and couch we talked about the village and how we got there. Inevitably we got round to the caves and the bats and their fleas. Several of Erik's friends were fascinated and wanted to hear all the stories. It seems the French have a certain tolerance for the mystical, and after all there is no shortage of saint-based miraculous tales in French history.

What intrigued them was that our tales were contemporary and some of us had had mystical experiences. Laetitia's story had them really thinking about their own past. However, several of them were totally sceptical about saintly intervention and could not believe that there was anything beneficial about bats or even more about bat fleas.

It got to be quite an animated discussion.

One of the men had been a part-time pastor in a protestant church, although of late he had taken a back seat, more or less retiring and no longer conducting services. Of all the group he was the most sceptical and argued that the whole business of dead saints doing miracles was Catholic brainwashing, although he had to admit that Kurt was not obviously anything like a Catholic.

His name was Pascal, and he had a tendency to get very loud and talk over everyone else.

Almost to dissolve the atmosphere, and perhaps to convince the naysayers, we offered to take them down to the caves so they could see them for themselves.

We trooped past Patrick's house where he was busy repairing his low rock wall. This seems to be an endless task in the village as the rocks keep falling off the walls every now and then. He is convinced the rocks have some kind of volition. Are there rock spirits?

He had to smile when I told him what was happening.

« Our caves are getting popular. I'll have to do wheelchair access soon.» he chortled.

Luckily there was no sign of Agathe.

We took a couple of torches and a rope to help with the decline to the bottom cave, but no-one wore any protection.

So we were totally unprepared for what happened as soon as we entered the first cave.

Once everyone was inside and looking around at the first cave, suddenly the bats, hundreds of them, came off their perches and flew around us in wild swirls, with their high-pitched squeals.

It was a classic horror movie scenario.

There was chaos as we all backed off and tried to get away from them, the entrance being so narrow. Kurt stood in the middle of the cave yelling and waving his arms while Erik tried to shepherd his guests away. Sally grabbed my arm and I pulled her down to the floor but the bats didn't seem to be interested in us, being so close to the ground and neither of us was holding a torch.

We lay there until everybody had made it out. The bats flew around for a little while then bit by bit they went back to their perches and stayed there in complete and eery silence.

«What was that?» Sally whispered.

I had no idea.

Once we all got out, it was obvious that almost all of Erik's guests had been severely bitten. Most of them had been bitten on their faces and they had red welts developing quite quickly.

What was weird, though, was the rest of us had nothing. Laetitia, Kurt, Erik, Didier and us, not one bite.

Back at Kurt's we found enough cream to lessen the stings, but you could see the victims were all quite shocked by it.

Naturally, Pascal who seemed to have been a particular target, had the most to say about the stupidity of what we had told him.

«Bats are bats and fleas bite. You are all deluded.»

He was threatening to get back on his Gold Wing and go home, but Erik persuaded him to stay at least for a few drinks.

The sun was strong enough for us to sit up on the terrace at the end of the afternoon, and the sunset offered us a gently pink spectacle to end the day. Bottles of Ricard and Lillet were demolished, we used up the last of the bug cream and everybody began to feel a bit better. Pascal had a livid face, but after quite a few Lillets he didn't seem to be so troubled.

Somehow no-one wanted to talk about what had happened so we got onto other things. Didier entertained everyone with a fantasy that he could open a three star restaurant downstairs. Or was it a fantasy? Fancy restaurants exist in small villages in France and he named some of the Michelin winners and where to find them.

Nonetheless, Sally and I wondered what was really behind the encounter in the cave, and when we finally retired we couldn't sleep trying to make sense of it. Why were these guys stung but not us? Why on all the other visits had the bats stayed quiet? What was different?

The next morning we were woken by banging on Kurt's door and we had some kind of answer.

Pascal stood there, white as a sheet, except for his red welts, with the two others who he was sharing one of the gites with.

When Kurt let them in, Pascal was almost incoherent.

«This is a mad village!» he was yelling.

One of the other guys explained, as Pascal stomped up the stairs, that he had had some kind of visions in the night and had been screaming.

Having woken us all up, we assembled in the lounge and Kurt poured everyone a Courvoisier, a somewhat unusual breakfast aperitif.

After two big ones Pascal tried to describe in frantic French, not all of which I caught, what had happened.

Sally and I looked at each other. We knew what was coming and so of course did Kurt and Laetitia.

«Pas juste un seule cauchemar, mais un avalanche des cauchemars.» Not just one nightmare, but a whole avalanche of nightmares.

«What was happening?» asked Erik.

«Torture. I was being tortured.»

«Who by?»

«Jesus Christ.»

«You mean the real Jesus Christ?»

«Of course.»

«Are you sure?»

«I have no doubt, and he was so angry with me. He was telling me that I had betrayed him and that I was never really worthy of being a pastor because I was a hypocrite. He said I was a fake Christian and that God was very angry with me. So he sent his fleas to punish me.»

«That's why you were attacked?»

«That's what he said, and there was another person there, another man who spoke in old French.»

Laetitia took out her phone and showed him a photo of the window in the church.

«Was it him?»

Pascal frowned and then nodded.

«Who is that?»

«Saint Livraque.» Several of us said it together.

«So maybe,» Laetitia said quietly, «maybe now you will believe what we said.»

«I don't know what to believe.»

We could see it was true.

«So maybe you are a hypocrite.» she said. I was wondering why she seemed to be enjoying his discomfort.

It shook him. He stared at her.

«You stopped being a pastor, did you not?»

«I did.»

«So you knew you were a hypocrite.» She said this like an unequivocal truth.

He sank down onto Kurt's couch and Kurt poured him another brandy. Three before breakfast.

We decided to get breakfast going, mostly to change the atmosphere and dilute the effect of the Cognac. Erik went out to round up the others, and Sally and I headed off down the valley in the Simca to buy a bulk load of croissants.

When we got back everyone had turned up. No-one else had been disturbed during the night, but there was definitely an atmosphere of disturbance in the room. It hung there as we ate together and it was obvious that they all felt a bit put out by their cave experience. Their red welts were still very obvious. The two Gold Wing wives had not been as bitten as much as their husbands but were both obviously upset about the whole business.

By the end of breakfast they had all decided to take off, even though Erik had booked them another night in the village gites.

There were mumbled apologies and promises to keep in touch, but you could see they were really keen to be gone.

Standing with them all arrayed in their fine leathers on their massive steeds, it did feel a bit strange, like we had missed something important.

Were they running away too soon?

Once they'd gone we retired upstairs and made some more of Jean-Pierre's son's coffee.

And then of course we wanted to check with Jean-Pierre himself to see if he had any insight into the cave events.

He wasn't there and the bookshop, which was always open, was shuttered.

That added an edge to our questioning, that was certain. Suddenly a negative turn of events in the cave and Jean-Pierre drops out of sight. What did it mean?

As so often happens, our fervid imaginations get us into trouble. At the end of the day we saw Jean-Pierre and Eloise trundling back into the village in their elderly Citroen Picasso. It was the third birthday of their grandson in Toulouse, and when we asked about the bat attack Jean-Pierre shrugged.

«It is the nature of bat fleas to bite. You know this.»

«But what does it mean?» pressed Sally.

He chuckled as he unloaded his car with several cartons of coffee. «Does everything have to have meaning?»

«So Saint Livraque hasn't said anything?»

«He did not put in appearance at a rather wild three year old's celebration in Toulouse, no.»

18.

And then things went quiet once again.

Winter set in and there was even a light dusting of snow on the terrace.

Didier went back to Bordeaux, and Erik dived into the rapidly advancing renovations on his little house.

He was close to moving in.

The weather being bleak, we didn't venture out much, and nobody felt drawn to revisiting the caves. Kurt and Laetitia happily tinkered away in the grange and the fleet of what used to be derelict bombs, the French call them «bagnoles», began to look surprisingly fancy.

There was no inclination to visit the caves. It was obviously a time to be patient.

Then Patrick noticed a change. Someone had built a fence blocking off the caves. The fence had metal stakes driven into the ground between the rocks and a wire gate with a padlock on it. The question was, who did it and why?

When we asked the Mayor he shook his head and didn't seem terribly interested. He suggested we scrutinise the cadastre to see who owned it. But anyway he added, whoever owns it has a perfect right to fence it off. Maybe they want to keep goats in there, he added, not without a trace of sarcasm.

With nothing else to keep us entertained, we perused the cadastre. The name on the lot that included the caves meant nothing to us and the address was for a resident of Toulouse. At least there was a phone number, so we asked Erik to call it and see what the story was.

The lady who answered said that she had no idea why there was a fence there and anyway, the property was owned by about ten different people all being descendants of a longstanding Livraquais family, none of whom now lived in the village. In a small stroke of genius Erik asked her if they were interested in selling. The lady had laughed and said in her family no-one could agree on anything so it was unlikely.

When he came back we talked it over. What did it mean and did we have to do something about it?

«Better ask the boss.» was Kurt's opinion, meaning our saint.

The trouble with that of course was that our saint was capricious when it came to communications. Jean-Pierre had nothing to add, saying if he heard anything he would pass it on.

Agathe turned out to be the guilty party, or at least probably the source of the change. Gwyn saw her at the decheterie one day and mentioned the new fence.

«Oh yes,» said Agathe, evidently with a malicious smile, «my brother-in-law's family are worried about trespassers.»

When Gwyn brought this news back it was obvious what was going on. Agathe was seeing the activity going on down there and she was not getting her cut. If her family had control then she could reap the benefits. Why else?

The next time we ran into her, we asked about it and she put on a surprised look that we were even interested. «It is just to keep good security.» she said.

« So if someone wants to go to the caves they have to ask you now?» asked Sally.

«Well,» she smiled, obviously enjoying herself, «I have no real say in what happens. The family who own that piece of land have to decide but my sister's husband, he is one of the owners, he was happy to put in the fence to protect it. If you like I could always talk to him about it.»

«But you would charge for anyone who wanted to go there?» I asked.

«Maybe,» she smiled. « we have not discussed it».

I had the distinct impression they certainly had.

«Anyway,» I decided to add, «it is probably not a good idea for people to go down there because some people went there a few days ago and they all got bitten.» I was not going to mention the other non-biting visits.

«I heard about that.» she said.

«So most likely there will not be too many requests for visits.»

«We will see. On verra.»

The fence seemed not just to block off the caves but also to quieten the whole saintly intervention atmosphere.

Was it symbolic or divinely ordained?

Whatever was behind it, life in the village was quiet and mundane. It was a kind of winter hibernation.

Then Erik announced he was ready to move into the new house and a large removals van arrived from Bordeaux.

We helped out and the little house was soon crammed with some very nice pieces of classic French furniture, some of which had been in his family for generations.

Once it was all set up and he had established himself, he decided we should have a «Pendre la Crémaillère» which is a French housewarming party. The expression comes from hanging a cooking pot over the fireplace for the first time.

Erik invited the Gold Wings crew, some of whom seemed a bit reluctant to come back. He also invited Jean-Pierre and Eloise as well as all the workers who had renovated his little house.

Having no garage, his Gold Wing would be housed in the grange. As he accepted Kurt's offer he cheekily observed that his bike would add a touch of sophistication.

It was a sunny but chilly December day and the event was a fully catered lunch firmly directed by Didier. We went off for another extensive shopping expedition.

The house is not all that big, but Erik still managed to find ways to accommodate everyone, although they tended to group themselves into homogeneous enclaves in different rooms in which Sally and I functioned as wait staff.

The village workers stuck together in the front room and there was not much interaction with the Gold Wingers, a kind of class divide that was very clear. The chosen drinks and even the subjects of discussion showed that. The workers drank Lillet and talked about local doings, family news, who was rumoured to be having an «affaire» with whom and who was playing in the local rugby team, as most of them were related to each other one way or the other.

The Gold Wingers drank some classy whites and champagne and mostly hung out in the kitchen. They talked about the caves and were interested about the fence. Some were keen to keep their bat flea grievances alive.

The most unusual conversation was between Laetitia and Pascal, although Sally and I only heard about it afterwards. It turns out that after he went back to Bordeaux he had almost constant religious dreams, or nightmares perhaps, where Jesus and our Saint harangued him. He couldn't bear to go to sleep for fear of them and he began drinking heavily. Then one night in desperation he threw himself on the floor and begged them to release him. And they agreed, which he reluctantly saw as divine compassion, but only as long as he promised to accept that they were real. By then he was convinced, although, as he told Laetitia, there was no way he was going back to pastoring because what he did before he now knew was complete nonsense. On the other hand he certainly had no intention of sermonising on his new relationship with God, based on his midnight visions and bat flea bites.

He had tears in his eyes, she said, when he told her that at last he could sleep. She gave him a hug.

He certainly looked rather different from the last time we saw him. If nothing else the bites had all healed. There was a peacefulness about him, and we both thought we were going to see a lot more of him in Saint Livraque.

The catering for the housewarming had fired up Didier's enthusiasm so, once Erik had been fully installed, he resurrected the idea of using Kurt's ground floor, if not for a fully catering restaurant, at least a bistro or a good coffee shop. The village had to have something he was certain.

After the housewarming he kept pacing around in the space, imagining how it could be configured. Where to place the bar, create a new kitchen, resurrect the big open fire place. He could see it.

I have to say that Sally and I loved all that. We are, after all, café people.

Kurt was not averse to it, he just didn't want to do it himself.

«You wanna flog coffee, go right ahead.» he said, mostly with his head under the bonnet of an elderly mode of transport.

How it could be done was a constant topic of discussion for the non-mechanics in our midst.

What are the rules and regulations for such a thing? Permits? The liqueur licence? Who could own it? How would it work? Who could work there?

Didier was our resident expert and loved our enthusiasm. «If you guys are serious about this, if you want to run it, then you will have to get proper visas, cartes de séjour.» he said «One of us French could be the owners of the business, but you can't work without the right paperwork.»

«We don't need to be paid.» I ventured.

«Nah!» grinned Kurt, « Cos they're my gentle slaves.»

Didier shrugged. «But still, you would have to have workers on your books or the authorities will get suspicious.»

So we kicked that around, and with it was the underlying question. Did Sally and I see ourselves as staying in Saint Livraque for the foreseeable future?

Kurt said as far as he was concerned he was happy to have us as long as we wanted. «You guys are part of the family.» he said, with just a trace of emotion. He likes having us around.

Then there was his own situation. Did he see himself as long term?

Laetitia was certain. «We have work to do.» she said, and reached up to rub his cheek which said more than she intended. She had a delightful way of making him colour up.

Sally and I talked about it and decided that maybe we were destined to be there for a while, so having cartes de séjour would be good.

Didier nodded. «In France,» he said, «with all things bureaucratic, the secret to success is who you know. The art of networking is at the very heart of the French savoir faire.» What he was referring to was that he and Erik knew a top Immigration Lawyer who could get anything in his field done with speed, as long as his large fees were paid.

This suggestion brought a subtle but strong change in our sense of what we were doing, a sense of destiny. There was a feeling of being more settled. We had a project, and we were appreciated.

Didier got us all the papers and stood over us as we filled them in and then he sent them off. We never actually got to meet the Lawyer.

In the meantime Didier moved into Erik's second bedroom in the little house and they began life as an odd couple. Sally and I wondered about what he was leaving behind in Bordeaux, but we decided not to probe.

For us, when we spoke to our families at home, we started talking about long term. They didn't seem surprised and it felt good. They even talked about future visits from Australia to check us out, France being high on the bucket lists for Aussies anyway.

Kurt was going to have to add a guest room or two. He had the space.

Thinking of ourselves as more permanent, Sally and I really put some effort into perfecting our French, taking full advantage of dear Jean-Pierre who was very generous with his time and his coffee. It became our regular morning ritual. I even made it through the book of Livraquais poetry, with lots if help. I couldn't read too much at once as it was too sad.

Our poet was a lyrical purveyor of despair.

While all this was happening, Didier and Erik began serious exploration into what it would take to turn Kurt's ground floor into a café. We sat round Kurt's coffee table doing drawings of what we imagined, what kind of flooring, how to heat it, what kind of decor. We talked to the Mayor about the liquor licence. Now that there were French people involved, Didier, naming himself as the owner of the future business, with Kurt's consent, the Mayor was all ears. He even came up with some archival photos of what the ground floor looked like way back when it was part of the Bat Hotel.

Obviously it had been quite classy in its time.

Christmas arrived without snow. We agreed that buying each other Christmas presents was pointless, but we did agree on a big feast. Erik and Didier were the chefs of course and we were dutiful subordinates. We were getting lots of experience.

The thought occurred to us that maybe our saint might put in an appearance, seeing we were celebrating his boss's supposed birthday, but he chose to ignore our subtle invitation.

Patrick and Gwyn joined us instead.

We had a prodigious feast with probably more alcohol than was healthy, and then both Erik and Didier took off to spend time with their children and grandchildren. Neither of them had said much about their families but evidently at Christmas there were obligations.

The village went quiet.

There was a Mass in the church but we didn't feel inclined to go. Certainly our saint had not extended any obvious invitations.

Then just after Christmas the two Alsacian girls came on their blue Kawasakis to see what Laetitia had been up to. She had called them often so they knew what had been going on but they wanted to come and see for themselves.

Christelle and Yvette rolled up together in time to join us for «le reveillon de Saint Sylvestre», New Years Eve. «Reveillon» means something like waking up, but maybe it is more like staying awake for the new year. I looked up Saint Sylvester but he was just some obscure pope from late Roman times so I don't think he has any relation to our saint.

Erik and Didier came back just in time and planned another big feast. It was our introduction to «Boudin blanc» which were powerful thick whitish sausages that went with the roasted goose. The girls had brought their best Alsacian whites in their saddle bags.

They had to hear about everything once again and the whole evening was a glorious loud mix of English and French.

Of course what they really wanted to do was to go down to the cave. They didn't think a fence with a lock would stop them, so the next morning was planned as a break and entry expedition.

However, our saint had other ideas.
Well I am convinced it was the saint and I think pretty well everyone else in the Bat Hotel came to the same conclusion.
We had an earthquake.
Just a little one, not much more than a window rattler. We had finally kissed each other rather a lot after quite a few champagnes and other intoxicants before tumbling into bed at around two in the morning.
A while later, boom.
It woke us up and Sally and I looked at each other. «What was that?»
When we staggered out for a late breakfast, everyone had felt the tremor. There seemed to be no damage in the house, although Kurt found shards of a large glass jar that had been on a shelf in his kitchen, scattered on the floor.
«Too much booze in the place.» he chuckled, but we all still wondered about it.
After a leisurely breakfast the girls were keen to visit the caves. We got into winter coats and hats and off we went in the new year's frost. That early we were pretty sure no-one was going to see us to break into the caves. Patrick and Gwyn joined us, Patrick coming armed with wirecutters plus his usual cave tools, rope and the big torch.
However, there was no need to trespass.
Nothing stood in our way.
There was no impediment.
A rock the size of a Renault Twingo had come loose from just above the cave mouth and had taken out the fence and a few fig trees below it, before rolling off down the embankment, taking Sumac bushes and gravel as it went, till it landed up blocking the road coming up from the valley.
We stared at the new hole where the rock had been, seeing that the cave now had a much wider entrance. It had been a bit of a squeeze before but now it was wide enough for two people at once.
We had to laugh.

The tangled remnants of the fence were way down the slope hanging off some blackberries.

The irony of it was delicious. Maybe Patrick's digging round the entrance had helped to dislodge the rock but we just knew who did the real shoving.

Anyway, in we went and showed the girls the bats, who did not acknowledge the «reveillons» at all and hung there serenely in the back of the first cave.

With the help of Patrick's rope, we slithered down to the lower cave where the pond is.

The water ran sweetly from the wall behind and we drank using our hands.

There was such calm in there.

We stayed for a while and no-one felt the need to say or do anything. I found myself wondering about our saint. What was his mission? If indeed he had one. He didn't seem to be intent on creating a following or if he did, it was something to do with a pair of mechanics and a few odd bodies none of whom looked like they were turning into disciples.

I promised myself I would have a good chat about that with Jean-Pierre.

It turns out it wasn't just me.

When we came out and looked down at the torn bushes and dislodged trees below the cave, we started talking about the saint, more or less all at once in a mix of English and French. It was if he had been there, quietly invading everyone's mind. As we clambered up the hill and headed back to Kurt's, we were talking animatedly about it and marvelling that we all had the same sensation. Even the two girls from Alsace had those thoughts.

What does he want with us?

Why us?

What is his purpose?

What was most obvious was that to all of us, that saint, whatever his motives, was very much alive for us.

We were a crowd of believers, if not budding disciples.

The girls stayed with us for one more day before taking their bikes back up north, choosing a day with unseasonably warm clear skies.

Laetitia told them she was not coming back and that she was selling her half of the mechanics business to her brother. This was the first we had heard of it but Kurt seemed to be already not only in the know, but rather happy about it.

They were now a couple, a couple of mechanics.

We kissed the girls off in bright early morning sunshine and the saint did nothing to impede their effortless journey. By the end of the day they called us from home, safe and sound.

The next day the local newspaper ran an article on the little earthquake which was small on the earthquake scale, but noteworthy in our little corner of France. There hadn't been a tremor for years. The paper included a photo of our blocked road below the walls, with a bulldozer clearing the rock and a statement from Monsieur Gaspard, the Mayor. The paper made no mention of where the rock came from, nor the destruction of a certain fence.

Sally and I took ourselves off to see Jean-Pierre, keen to know what he thought.

The coffee wafted towards us in delicious aromatic waves as we approached and he had the interior of his little shop toasty warm from his «poile a bois» in the corner, what we would call a pot belly stove. The cats had all taken up positions as close as possible.

«Of course I have been expecting you.» he smiled as he served the coffee. «And I expect you will be disappointed by what I have to tell you. Or more specifically what I cannot tell you.»

I nodded. «No saintly earth movements.»

«You have a tendency to attribute everything to our saint, now he has revealed himself but I have to tell you, just as in every religious path, the works of God take many forms and most are inscrutable.» I was impressed he knew that word.

«God works in miraculous ways and his saints do his bidding.»

«So you don't see any significance to the rock falling and taking out the fence and opening up the cave entrance?» asked Sally.

He smiled. «One can interpret of course. Man has free will to think as he wishes.»

«So,» I said «using your free will what do you think?»

«Well,» He had the ginger cat on his lap which was drawing warm purrs from its contented throat. «Like you, I am inclined to think the cave is opening up for some reason that will become apparent I am sure. As so often happens with our saint, we must be patient.»

We couldn't argue with that.

For her part Agathe seemed to be making a special effort to be friendly, and of course she had heard about the plans for Kurt's ground floor.

Maybe she was thinking it would bring her new customers and she didn't want to be left out. She walked into Kurt's one day and regaled us with the history of what had gone on in that building over the years. Much of it we knew, especially the more recent and seedy parts, but earlier on it had been a decent establishment with a restaurant that people travelled far to dine in. We had seen the photos. Now that a certain ex-Bordelais restaurateur was going to run it she was very excited about the prospect.

Of course we asked her about the fence.

«Maybe we don't need it.» she said with studied nonchalance.

When I asked her what had changed her mind, she shrugged. «It's a waste of money to make a new one.»

We let it go, but secretly wondered if our saint had dropped in on her.

Who knows?

19.

For the next few weeks there was a quiet sense of anticipation but no real action. There were no saintly interventions of any kind.

Plans for the renovation of Kurt's ground floor got going which involved setting up the usual crew of plumbers and electricians, but as it was all internal there was no need for permits. Obviously once it was done there would be inspections but Didier seemed to know all about that.

We went on excursions to showrooms full of potential equipment and visited various bistros and cafés, locally and further afield to see what other places were like. Of course we also sampled their wares, which varied from the excellent to the horribly mundane.

It was all very stimulating, and unlike the Crooked Nook it was not costing Sally or me one centime.

Then in mid-February, as the hyacinths began to appear in the village gardens, we got our invitations to attend the interviews for the cartes de séjour. Normally, according to the lawyer, it should have taken at least a year before that happened, but he had connections.

There were two days of bureaucratic events which involved health checks, language tests, written knowledge of France tests and compatability interviews, all on the first day and then a seminar on life in France on the second day.

We went into a concentrated phase of preparation, especially Kurt who had to endure daily sessions with Jean-Pierre to work on his French. Jean-Pierre actually seemed to enjoy torturing Kurt, pretending to be the interviewer for the language test and the «Life in France« conversation. The teacher in Jean-Pierre was having a field day.

To do the two days of the process we had to stay in Bordeaux, so we got to see where Erik lived. It was impressive. He has what is called a «Maison Bourgeois», a gentleman's house built in the eighteenth century. It nestles in a very genteel arboreal suburb close to a big formal park with manicured lawns and gazebos. His house even boasts a little turret with slate tiles on it. The rooms are replete with impressive period furniture under high ornate ceilings and there's a fountain with naked nymph statuettes in his front garden.

The house had been all closed up as he was in the process of getting ready to sell it, but he happily opened it up for us and a Portuguese lady came to clean and prepare. We felt most honoured.

The night before the tests and interviews Erik took us to Didier's old restaurant which had very successfully changed hands, now owned by the famous English chef. Erik assured us it was still very good and he was right. Nothing English about the menu.

Next morning, when we got to the place for the tests and interviews, it seemed like we were the only white-faced applicants, the others all appeared to be from Asia or Africa. Kurt was as nervous as a cat, given that his language skills were not as advanced as ours but he dived in. We were tested and interviewed separately but we all did OK as far as we could tell.

At the end of the day we dined at home as Erik had spent the day shopping and preparing.

The second day was the obligatory seminar on life in France and Kurt nearly fell asleep. It was interesting to see how much of the presentation was aimed primarily at showing Muslims that France had a different culture from Muslim countries. The hijab is banned in government buildings, men can only be legally married to one woman at a time, women can open their own bank accounts and conduct businesses without their husband's consent. If I was a Muslim I think I would be a bit insulted by the obvious focus.

Anyway we signed the papers to show we had attended and we filled in the written test at the end of the day to show we understood. Again Kurt struggled and I wondered how he would go, given that you have to get at least fifty percent of the questions correct. Hopefully, if needed, the expensive lawyer could do miracles. And the thought occurred to me that if our saint wanted his mechanic as an acolyte, then French papers would not prevent that.

When we got back to Saint Livraque, Laetitia had been hosting a guest. Pascal had turned up on his Gold Wing just after we left.
Even if our saint had been out of contact with us, he had evidently not been idle. I suppose saints can work wherever they want, once they aren't stuck with a physical body. They don't need a «Carte de Séjour».
Pascal had arrived, the day we left, in another of his states of anguish. Although he had stepped away from being a pastor and no longer played a rôle in the protestant church, still he was haunted. At least that's the way he described it.
«So maybe in the past,» he said «I was not really truthful. Maybe I was a hypocrite. I was saying what pastors are supposed to say. To be truthful, it was not my own personal experience. It was second hand and therefore utterly false. So I stopped. I had to stop, even before his fleas got me.»
I could see how difficult it was for him to admit this.
Then he shook his head and said: »But now he tells me I have to go back. He says I have to be truthful. He tells me I have to make amends for my falsehoods.»
«Do you know what that means?»
He shook his head. «J'ai aucune idée.» I have no idea.
«Maybe,» ventured Sally, who I was beginning to see had quite some intuitive powers, «maybe you have to become very quiet and he will show you what to do.»
«In that I must agree with you. I don't know any other way. I pray. I do know how to do that, but I have to admit that I am not sure to whom I am praying.»
«There's no-one at the other end?» I asked.
He shook his head, but he wasn't saying no. He just didn't know.
What he had been doing while we were away was going down to the cave and sitting there. Laetitia had more or less forced him to. What was driving him crazy was that he was getting nothing. Not even flea bites. Nothing. And it was cold.

Sally persisted. «I wonder if what you were saying, I mean when you were a preacher, maybe that might have been the truth in one way, but it wasn't your truth.»

He studied her for a long moment, then he nodded. «To be honest I was a good preacher. I enjoyed preaching. I was good at it. People liked what I said. I know that. But I preached only what I had heard, what I had been taught, what I read in religious books. It wasn't what I knew for certain was the truth. Now I have no idea.»

«But you have seen Jesus, haven't you?» asked Sally. Her French was really coming along and I was very proud of her.

He nodded.

«Maybe that is a start.» she said. «You know Jesus is real, you have seen him.»

He nodded.

«And you know our saint.» I added. «You have certainly seen him.»

He thought about all that, then he muttered. «I can't see myself preaching about fleas and a saint yelling at me.» His face was a mask of discomfort.

We all felt his pain, but what poor Pascal was supposed to do was a mystery.

Of course we checked in with Jean-Pierre but he had nothing to add.

«Sometimes», he said, «as you can see, you have to be very patient.»

Then I had a flash of inspiration. «Maybe the fact that Pascal rides a motor bike was a clue. After all if the saint had chosen Kurt and Laetitia to work for him, being mechanics, then he was part of the plan.

When I said that, I could see that everyone was giving it serious thought. We just didn't really understand what it meant and nobody had any idea about what the plan was.

We went with Jean-Pierre's advice.

Patience.

After a couple of days, Pascal took himself off back to Bordeaux, no closer to a solution than when he came.

We wondered what he was going back to.

20.

Moving on from trying to work out the divine plan for Pascal, we worked on creating the café.

Didier certainly knew how to move things along. The ground floor was stripped back to the raw basics, revealing the stone walls which needed patching here and there, the big oak beams got a good treatment of linseed oil and the ceiling between them which was horrible old plaster was stripped off and hauled away to the decheterie in several heavy cart loads.

Then Didier had an interior designer from Bordeaux come to work with us on how we saw the interior. It was a lively meeting over lunch and a very good Bordeaux red from the slopes of Saint Emilion.

Even Kurt had his opinions on how it should look. He insisted on keeping the open fire place which we all supported but were not quite so keen on his desire to have a space for a billiard table at the back. He insisted. Otherwise he let us have what we wanted. Didier was very generous with us and although he could see the whole thing in his mind, he gave us lots of space to say what we thought.

In the end it was all very amicable and the designer went off to begin drawings and estimates of material.

It was going to be a fancy café of proportions that would dwarf our dear old Crooked Nook, and certainly nothing like most of the local bistros that were more bars than restaurants.

The fun part was going off with Didier to buy a very sophisticated Italian espresso bar machine, top of the range. We bought matching café furniture in old style French café mode, wooden chairs with curved backs and round tables that we found in a café that had been closed for a few years but was totally intact.

Didier was big on tablecloths, the classic red and white check.

A couple of weeks went by where we immersed ourselves in café creation. It was the Crooked Nook for us all over again but on a much grander scale. Quite frankly such a fancy café was way overkill for an insignificant village like Saint Livraque, but that was the way it was going.

Then there was the question of what to call it. Because the building had been called the «Hotel des Chauves Souris», the Bat Hotel, we were tempted to just put Café on the front of « des Chauves Souris». Carry on the tradition.

Didier didn't like it. The whole idea of naming his café after bats was a diminution of his reputation. Or at least that's how he saw it.

That was until it was his turn to receive divine guidance.

We'd had a long alcohol-enhanced discussion the night before, but at breakfast he came over from Erik's house with a big grin on his face.

«You have too many good players in your team.» he said. We didn't get it till he said that our team had a saint who dropped into Didier's dreamscape and showed him what the outside of the «Café des Chauve Souris» should look like.

He didn't seem to mind too much and I think he felt rather honoured to be included in the elite of those who had a visitation.

«Did you see him?» I asked.

He shook his head. «No, no. But I heard his voice. «This is what my café looks like.» he said.»

«So how do you know it was Saint Livraque?» asked Sally.

He smiled. «I woke up convinced. What can I say?»

So that was that.

He went off up the valley to the bigger town twenty minutes away where there was a sign writer.

Then the interior designer came back with all his estimates and drawings. We studied them over the coffee we would be featuring, thanks to Jean-Pierre's son, and there was a wave of goodwill in Kurt's lounge. Even Laetitia seemed excited about the plans.

Then she said something that struck Sally and me.

«So many bikers will come. This will be Mecca for mechanics.»

Didier laughed but added that he hoped for more than just customers in leathers. His sense of style was not exactly biker hang-out mode. And certainly Honda Goldwings were not your regular biker's mount.

Kurt added that maybe he should think about turning the grange into a bike park. This led to talk of having a back entrance from the grange straight into the café, and a slight realignment in the design was made. A wider rear entrance going past the billiard table area became a reality replacing the existing little door out to the grange.

The work of installing the café interior started right away. The electricians and the plumbers completed their lines before the internal walls were built. Cafés need a lot of sockets.

Italian tiles were laid over the now level cement floor throughout the whole area so that the internal walls would go on top. The professional stainless steel and marble kitchen came in a set of flatpacks and was assembled in one furious morning by a team of Portuguese men in a big white van.

In less than a month we reached the point of decoration. Didier generously let Sally and me choose the colours, but he had a veto on anything that did not feel French. We did OK.

The sign came back ready to hang. It featured a dark red background with the black bats flying across the words «Café des Chauves Souris» in white. Raymond had turned up one day and begged Kurt for some work but Kurt had decided he was not going to indulge that charity any more.

One of the locals did a sterling job of securing the sign instead.

We did the cafe interior painting ourselves, although Didier was quite prepared to pay for it to be done professionally.

Somehow Sally and I wanted to put something of ourselves into this. Once we had that done, and both Didier and Kurt approved, the light fittings went in and the espresso machine was installed behind the new counter with a big glass display case for Sally's pastries.

We had to be trained on how to run the machine and it was quite complicated. The stove was a monsterous stainless steel work of art.

While all this was going on, Kurt and Laetitia tinkered away with their vehicular toys in the background and they seemed to be very content to let us get on with it. Their next big project was the installation of a vehicular hoist and the digging of a pit to go under it.

Every now and then we would go back to the grange to watch the proceedings as the contractors dug up the stones that made up the floor of the grange. They did discover a few old artifacts below ground but nothing that Agathe determined was worth analysing.

Once the pit was lined with a concrete wall, in went the hoist which Laetitia had found on «Bon Coin», the French website where they sell junk to each other. It came in a series of boxes on the back of a truck and there was more than a whiff of suspicion that maybe someone had stolen it from somewhere. How do you steal a vehicular hoist?

Once it was installed and Kurt worked on getting it going up and down. The first attempts saw a few inches of movement and then it got stuck. He and Laetitia spent a lot of energy and black grease before it began to cooperate.

Once it was going, he began to get requests from some of his neighbors to use it. It was the only one in the village. He refused payment but got some nice bottles.

Other than the hoist, it was as if the building of the café was the focus for now and nothing else was in prominence.

Through all this Erik came and went, often deciding to come and cook for us all.

Patrick and Gwyn monitored our progress and almost everyone in the village came to see how we were doing with the preparations for the cafe.

In general the Livraquais were amazed at how fancy it all was and there were a few who murmured that it looked to them like money going to waste, for such a minor hamlet, but nobody really complained. Quite a few put in suggestions as to what we should serve.

The Mayor was very happy to see a fine home being created for his liqueur licence.

Our saint said nothing.

Of course setting up a café meant bureaucracy had to have its rôle and Didier went about it like a warrior. We had to have all sorts of inspections covering health and safety, rodent prevention, asbestos checks, ventilation regulations, handicap access and regulation toilets, and all sorts of other things that we never had to face with the Crooked Nook. «C'est comme ça» Didier would say as he greeted officials. «That's the way it is.» In all this he seemed to be enjoying himself and he was a master at navigating the pathways of café bureaucracy.

By the middle of April we began to see the light at the end of the tunnel.

All the permits got processed and approved, all the fittings we ordered turned up, Kurt cleaned up one end of the grange for a bike park, installing a huge new door that opened at the push of a button, and we finished off the painting.

And then, best of all, we received our Cartes de Séjour, including Kurt who had somehow managed to get through the test.

We could stay in France as long as we liked and we could work.

It was time to think of a grand opening.

21.

May the 8th is a public holiday in France, commemorating the end of World War Two in Europe in 1945.

At the entrance to Saint Livraque there is a tall dark grey stone plinth with the names of all the Saint Livraquais who died in both wars and a few other French colonial military excursions. Every year on the 8th of May there is a wreath-laying ceremony, the Mayor reads a letter from the French President, and then everyone retires for drinks and aperitifs, usually in the Mairie.

It seemed like the perfect day to open the cafe and invite the village. Monsieur Gaspar was enthusiastic about the idea, although by tradition he was expected to host the post-ceremony events in the big reception room in the Mairie. The fact that we were offering it for free was a powerful persuasion. Of course he was invited to do the official ribbon-cutting and bid welcome home to his liqueur licence.

We printed up a little flier inviting the Livraquais(es) and the response was almost overwhelming. Everybody wanted to come and have a peek at what was coming. We spent half our time hosting tours of the ground floor. And no-one wanted to miss a free feast.

Days before the opening, we started trialing what we would offer. Although Didier's background was haute cuisine, there was no way that would work in our little hamlet so we had to think about our customer base and their budget. What would our villagers and visiting bike riders prefer?.

Sally reworked some of her Crooked Nook pastries and Didier approved. We tried pretty simple meals like most of the local restaurants offered as «Repas Ouvriers», workers' meals, and we got to be the guinea pigs. Some of the locals wanted us to do burgers, but that was just too low class for Didier and he refused.

It was all great fun.

Jean-Pierre's son Simon came up with the full range of his «torrefaction» coffee and our beverage machine did great service. It was the first time we had met Simon. He knew that we knew about his birth and he was very friendly.

For the opening day, we decided not to have sit down dining but a kind of buffet so the locals could mingle and sample what we were going to serve. We had tables and chairs along the walls for the older denizens of the village but it was mostly standing room.

Sally and I got matching cafe outfits: blue aprons over white T-shirts with little bat motifs.

We planned quite a generous spread. Erik and Didier had gone to town on the canapés while Sally had made dozens of her pastries in miniature. Patrick contributed a big bag of croissants from the nearest bakery which was going to supply our cafe on a regular basis. The smell of Simon's coffee added a suitably redolent aromatic authenticity to the atmosphere.

The Gold Wings crew all arrived early that morning and brought gifts of things to hang or decorate in the new establishment. Christel and Yvette descended on us and parked the Kawasakis with the assembled Gold Wings in the new parking space. They must have started out at the crack of dawn to get there in time. They brought two cartons of Rhine Riesling carefully protected in their saddle bags.

To honour the day at ten o'clock, having put on our best clothes, we all trooped down to the memorial where Monsieur Gaspar read the President's letter on a bright cloudless May day full of promise. Pigeons cooed and babies complained as the cliché-ridden communiqué wafted into the warm morning air. We all wore suitably sombre expressions until it was time to lay the wreath, and then the local brass ensemble struck up the Marseillaise and we marched off to open the Bat Café.

The obligatory welcome speech from our Mayor preceded the ribbon being scissored. Monsieur Gaspar talked about the history of the Bat Hotel and was now delighted that it was finding a new life for itself. He also accentuated his pleasure in seeing the liqueur licence find a good home and sure enough, with the ribbon severed, a lot of the locals headed straight to the bar.

To begin with Sally and I worked as servers and refillers, with Patrick and Gwyn helping out, but soon it seemed that everyone was quite happy to help themselves. This time everyone was beginning to integrate after the social sectionalising that took place at Erik's opening The Alsacian girls met the Gold Wingers and the locals seemed ready make them all welcome. Some of the older folk sat at the tables nursing glasses of whatever took their fancy. Jean-Pierre and Eloise chatted with some of their neighbourly contemporaries. There was an air of joyful celebration, and in the middle of it all Kurt could not stop grinning.

All sorts of cross-cultural conversations were happening, but the most interesting turned out to be Agathe finding out about Pascal's encounter with the saint. Somehow up till then she had not met anyone who had had an interaction with our saint. I don't think she was sure there really was an actual saint at all. And maybe our saint was making sure she was kept in the dark. After all Jean-Pierre had made it pretty clear that our saint was selective.

Up till then she had been using the occasion to peddle her wares, circulating, letting people, who were not Livraquais, know that she was the local historian and tour guide. She had a sheaf of little pamphlets to hand out. When she found out that Pascal was a pastor, although no longer preaching, she latched onto him, with her usual speil about our long and bloody village history. He in turn told her that he was very much taken with this village because it was here that he had had a «conversion».

Luckily I caught the edge of their discussion and observed from a distance. Her face was good to watch. She was fascinated and perhaps a little horrified. He was enthusiastically telling her about «our saint». I watched her mouth slowly open wider and her eyes did much the same. It appeared that she was somewhat religious but I couldn't tell if she was a Protestant.

«But you are sure about this? It was a vision?» She had leaned in close and was almost whispering.

«Oh yes, it was totally beyond doubt.»

«But you are Protestant.»

«Certainly.»

«But Saint Livraque I suppose must have been Catholic.»

Pascal put a gentle hand on her shoulder. «Oh I don't think that saints, real saints, care very much for such distinctions. A saint is a saint in God's eyes.»

«And, and..» I could see her trying to get a sense of how to talk about this. «Our saint spoke to you?»

«He has given me a very new sense of what I must do to fulfil the goal that my soul set for me.»

«And you know what that goal is?»

«I cannot say that I do. I think perhaps I have to wait for more revelations.»

It was then that Agathe caught my eye and realised that I had heard the conversation.

«You know about this?»

I nodded.

«Do you think it is real?»

«I have to admit that I have not had any vision of the saint myself, but there are other people who have.»

She narrowed her eyes. «Who?»

«The first one that I know of since I got here was Kurt.» I said, not wanting to betray Jean-Pierre's relationship with Saint Livraque.

«Kurt?» Her eyes were wide with amazement.

«Ask him.» I said.

Pascal and I smiled at each other and followed her across the room where she looked around for Kurt. Then following a few suggestions, she headed out to the back. As I passed Jean-Pierre's table he glanced up and gave me an enigmatic little smile, and I wondered if he had sensed anything.

Agathe tracked Kurt out into the grange where he was proudly showing a group of older French men the renovated Deux Chevaux. Kurt was using what battered French he had but the locals seemed to get it. He had generously alluded to Laetitia's expertise.

«Kurt,» Agathe said bustling up to him, «I must ask you something.»

He turned around and faced her. «What about?»

«Is it true that Saint Livraque has....» She seemed unsure about how to say it in English.

«What?» He clearly had no idea what she was getting at.

She pressed her lips together trying to work out what to say. Then she blurted out: «He talked to you?»

«Our little saint?» he said with a grin. «Sure. He talks to all sorts of people. But I think he's a bit choosy. Maybe you haven't been a good girl.»

She ignored the insult. «What did he say to you?».

I could see he was suddenly a little wary of her, maybe sensing that he had some responsibility to be judicious in what he said.

«Well not much. But he did fix my leg.» Then he told her the story of going into the cave. She listened carefully, only interjecting once to ask whether the fleas bit him. When he got to the part of falling to the bottom of the incline and the plaster falling off to reveal a fully healed leg, she stared at him.

«But you are certain it was him?»

«Clear as day,» he said.

She saw me standing close by with Pascal.

«So you believe this?»

«I saw it happen,» I said

She shook her head in amazement «And there are others?»

I nodded.

«Who are they?»

Then Pascal chipped in. «You know, I think each person's relationship with spiritual matters is very private. Perhaps each person will have his or her own willingness to say something or not say anything.»

«So you won't say.» Agathe glared at him.

«It would not be fair.»

The local men who had been standing with Kurt as he showcased the Deux Chevaux had lost the track of what was going on. Now one of them said: «What is she talking about?» He asked this in French and was looking at Pascal. As Kurt had talked in English to Agathe the men had not grasped the fixed leg story.

I wondered how Pascal was going to respond, seeing that he had been given a mission of a kind.

«Well,» he said, glancing sideways at Agathe. «You know how it is in France. We have our saints and some of them are very busy.»

«You mean Saint Livraque?» the man said. I recognised him as being local but not living in the village. He was most likely a farmer.

«Bien sûr.» replied Pascal.

«And you believe it is true?» asked the man. »I mean that Saint Livraque is a real saint and you can pray to him and he will answer your prayers?».

«That has been my experience.» said Pascal.

«So he is like Saint Bernadette in Lourdes?»

« I think so. Just not as well known.»

«I never heard that.» The man was genuinely impressed.

Then Agathe saw an opportunity. «Oh,» she said, «Many years ago people came to this village and went into the caves because they believed that our saint could cure them.»

He studied her for a second because up till then she had seemed antagonistic to the idea.

«And they were cured?»

«There were stories about that. How true they were I cannot say.»

«But they don't do that any more, do they? I mean I never heard of anyone going into our caves».

She looked at Pascal.

«Well it seems that maybe our saint has been sleeping for a while and he has woken up, come alive, and begun miracles like the leg of Kurt.» Then he did a short French version of what Kurt had said. Kurt even pulled up his trouser leg to illustrate the point.

«Good as new.» he said.

The man nodded. «My wife is a strong believer in saints and miracles. She's been to Lourdes so many times. I will have to tell her she doesn't have to go so far any more. I will save a fortune.»

This set off quite an animated discussion. Soon almost everyone in the café was talking about it. Several of the people were members of the families who owned the four different caves. They wanted to know which cave was the one where Kurt had been cured. Agathe set them straight, saying proudly that the cave where it all happened was owned by some of her family. She made it sound like she really was the custodian and would be happy to take people down there.

There was fascination that our saint was available for intervention. People began asking how to make contact. Were there visions? There was animated discussion about bats and fleas. Several of the Gold Wing riders told others that they had been in the cave but all they got were flea bites. They thought the whole thing was a hoax. Others like Didier and Erik were sharing their stories and people were nodding their heads while others were more sceptical. Nonetheless there was an air of fascination.

I watched Jean-Pierre as the conversations whirled around him. He had a gentle passive expression on his face, but I noticed that he and Eloise were holding hands.

Then Laetitia decided to set the record straight. By now, all over the place, people were talking about it. She jumped up onto a chair, as she was not exactly tall, and called out.

«Listen to me!» she called. «In this village, it is true we have a saint.»

Not everybody knew who she was and why she was talking about «our village.»

She ignored that and went on. «And that saint, when he feels inclined, will appear to people and he will help to cure what needs to be cured.»

«How do you know that?» someone yelled.

« I myself have had that experience and it is very real. I have changed my life because of this saint. And there are others who have had the same experience.»

Someone else shouted out: «What does the church say?»

«We are a small village.» she said. « The church does not know about our saint.»

«But if what you say is true than maybe many people will want to come here.»

The Mayor had watched all this with fascination, leaning on the bar with a refilled Ricard in his glass.

«Then this café will do very well.» he chuckled.

«So we just go down into the caves and there he is?» someone else asked.

«The fleas will bite you.» said one of the Gold Wingers.

Laetitia tried to regain control.

«It is true that those who have been into the cave have been bitten by the bat fleas but others have not. It seems that the fleas are the servants of the saint.»

«He must be the patron saint of bat fleas!» someone shouted.

Although this made everyone laugh, there was also a lot of quite serious talk.

Having made her point, Laetitia jumped off the chair and was then besieged by questioners.

Sally came up beside me and whispered: «The cat is out of the bag.»

I gave her a hug and said: «It's going to be fun to watch.» Then I quietly said: «I think Jean-Pierre knew this was coming.»

He saw us looking at him and he gave a little wave.

Gwyn joined us with a grin. «I sense a business opportunity.»

Neither of us got what she meant.

«Flea-proof outfits for sale or rent. Could be a gold mine.»

And of course Agathe had something of the same thought. She let it be known that she would be available to do tours to the caves if anyone was brave enough.

Then she and Gwyn went into a huddle.

Sally whispered. «Let's see what our saint has to say about that.»

22.

As the afternoon wore on most of the locals wandered off leaving us with the detritus of a successful opening, the Gold Wingers and the Alsacian girls.

We all adjourned to the roof to sample some of the white wine the girls had brought. Everyone agreed the opening had been a great success.

Of course the big subject was the revelation of saintly potential. We still had Gold Winger sceptics, although bit by bit they were beginning to accept that maybe there was something going on. Pascal was a persuasive convert.

We all agreed that now the village was aware of the cave there was certainly the possibility of some kind of holy site potential. We speculated on how this could affect our new venture, after all after a cave visit everyone would want coffee. Even lunch.

We began discussing how the day to day running of the café was going to work, especially if word got around.

Sally and I had already offered to be the core staff but Didier was of the opinion that we should run the business as a business and we should also employ at least a few locals. It was important in his eyes to keep good community relations. He was also very optimistic about the café's prospects and could see us being open every day. It was The Crooked Nook in a new hemisphere.

In the middle of all that we heard shouting and when we looked over the parapet of Kurt's terrace we saw two young men yelling. They wanted to see Laetitia.

She went off downstairs and we watched from above.

It didn't take long to work out what had happened. They were both covered in flea bites. Laetitia gave them some bug cream which calmed them down. However, they were both convinced the whole saint thing was a complete hoax and their experience had just proved it.

When Laetitia came back up to the roof and told us what they had said, it led to some interesting discussion. When she had asked them why they went, they said they were just curious. They had never heard of the bats or the fleas before or that Saint Livraque was actually a real saint. They just wanted to have a look.

Remembering what Jean-Pierre had told us, it occurred to me that maybe the way the bats and their fleas responded might have something to do with the attitude of whoever goes into the cave.

«No doubt about it. Our little saint is a tad choosy.» said Kurt with a grin.

«Maybe it's a bit of both.» said Sally.

«How do you mean?» asked Kurt.

«Well,» she said still thinking about it, «It could be our attitude and also what the saint wants. If it isn't the right combination then in go the fleas. If it's the right combination then the fleas do their work. Their bites are beneficial for those who deserve it and nasty for everyone else.

We found ourselves nodding. She was onto something.

«Bat radar,» said Kurt. «We already knew they can see things that we can't see. Now I reckon they have more than just sonar.»

«It's what is in your heart that matters.» said Pascal.

It sounded like they both agreed with Sally.

And somehow that shifted something for all of us, as if we felt we had some kind of responsibility. We had brought the saint out into the public, unlike Jean-Pierre's generation, so now we felt implicated in what might happen.

The question of course was what was the saint expecting us to do. Especially his mechanics.

In the days that followed, while we opened up the café and did a gently growing trade, not much happened in or around the caves. Or if it did, we didn't get to hear about it.

After the girls went back to Alsace and the Gold Wingers went back to Bordeaux, we dropped into a comfortable routine. Sally and I felt no great urgency to train up anyone else for the moment. It was like old times for us. We organised daily deliveries of «viennoiseries» from the bakery up the valley, croissants, chocolatines, pains au raisins, and a variety of other pastries that are the staples of every café in France. Every day a little white van would chug up the hill with the fresh delivery. Whatever didn't sell we ate. Sally made her own specialities.

Every morning we would open up at about 9.00 and soon there were several of the locals - mostly retired men - who became our «habitueés». We had the wifi router installed, and soon we had more than one regular customer with a laptop.

The coffee was universally praised and the patisseries sold like hot cakes. I tried to explain that to some of our bilingual customers but it was beyond them. When they tried word play jokes with me I never got those either.

The question of starting to offer meals arose, but we decided to start small, not much more than warmed up snack food. We did a daily soup, various quiches and a few other hot dishes. We could build up after a while, maybe for when the long summer vacation sets in. France devotes two whole months to that. Didier was not altogether happy about this, but he could see that it was going to take a while to build a clientele so he let it go for now.

Gwyn and Agathe had been putting their heads together about cave tourism but so far there wasn't much call for it. Maybe the two guys who been bitten had spread the word. We heard of a few folk who had ventured down and several of them went back a second time with water bottles to draw water from the spring. Some had been bitten but others not.

In the meantime Gwyn had come out with a simple and easy to put on outfit with a wide Chinese kind of hat, mosquito proof cloth hanging down and long gloves. She decided that the rest of the body would be dealt with by the clothes her prospective clients would wear. She decided five euros was a good rental price and she set up a table outside her house with a sign detailing the deal.

She also became something of a chronicler of what took place. When people returned her outfits she would ask them what had happened. Some said there was nothing there and the whole thing was a just a myth and accused her of being out to trick the locals. She refused to refund their five euros. Others talked in hushed awe about the atmosphere and those who had been to other holy sites said it felt like Lourdes or Fatima. Some ventured down without her outfit and the results were mixed. It was obvious pretty quickly that somehow the bats knew what each person was carrying inside themselves. The curious and the sceptical got bitten, the believers and the seekers did not, although it was never as clear as that. Gwyn reported that most of the non-bitten seemed to be women and some of them had begun to go almost daily, taking their water bottles to draw from the «holy» spring. Although no-one reported any miracles exactly, those who went regularly swore that they could feel the benefits.

Patrick had decided he was something of the custodian of the caves and spent days in there making it easier to descend to the lower areas. He installed metal spikes on the downslope and ran a rope between them. Visitations were steady and he often met people inside. The bats never bothered him. Agathe went down there, always with protective gear of her own devising, and she was now more than happy to see Patrick's improvements.

This all went on for a few weeks while we worked on our cafe.

Now and then we would venture down there ourselves and it was clear that it was changing. The well beaten path down to the cave entrance was easier to use and Patrick had ensured that even the elderly and infirm could get down to the lower chamber. No wheelchair access, though. Patrick had talked to the Mayor about installing some kind of lighting but that would bring in a whole bureaucratic process. Anyway who was going to pay for it?

Not everyone had been as respectful as others and there was rubbish left behind. For us though, it was a bit strange to find it now so public. Sally and I both felt that, especially when we sat together by the pool in the middle of the lower cave. Somehow the feeling that we had when we first went in there was not quite there any more. In a way we both regretted that it was no longer our little secret.

Then the local newspaper got hold of it.

Until the article appeared, no-one seemed to have been aware of the presence of either the journalist or the photographer, but when it came out, it was obvious who was behind it. Agathe had decided her little enterprise would benefit mightily from a bit of promotion. She was quoted liberally and not without a whiff of self-promotion. Even the journalist who wrote the piece made a veiled reference to her motives. The person who really suffered in the article though was Gwyn. The paper described her as a foreign profiteer, making euros out of the gullible locals. Was that Agathe? Gwyn was convinced it was and darkly suggested that Agathe was trying to run a monopoly.

Agathe had obviously warned the newspaper people about the danger of being bitten and they had come prepared. There was a photo of the journalist just outside the cave in her outfit. There was another photo taken inside, done with a flash, that showed the bats hanging there. A third photo was taken from a distance of Gwyn and her stand. She didn't know they had taken it and certainly they did not get her permission. She muttered darkly about suing the paper.

The effect of that kind of publicity was mixed and fascinating. We couldn't complain because we benefitted, at least from the Bat Cafe perspective.

The curious came from far and wide, the whole spectrum from the devout to idly curious to the darkly sceptic. We ran out of pastries on several days and the coffee was doing fabulous business.

Gwyn decided she was not going to be intimidated and went right on renting her outfits, right until a very pushy young woman from whatever French department oversaw small enterprises arrived and shut her down with threats of arrest. What she was doing, she was sternly informed, was completely unhealthy, immoral and certainly illegal. So that was the end of that.

Agathe on the other hand was in fulltime tour guide mode. She set herself up in one of the abandoned shop fronts two doors down from the Bat Cafe and announced with big posters that she was the local tourist office. She was running several tours per day. She also offered a version of Gwyn's protection for the same five euros and nobody seemed to think that was at all inappropriate. After all she was the registered local historian. It was not a subject we could discuss with Gwyn whose deep anger was a sight to behold. She saw herself as a classic victim of anglophobia.

A couple of days after the newspaper item appeared we encountered the first religious intervention. The Catholic church came to check.

We got the first sight of them when they dropped in for coffee. Two young men in very smart suits carrying briefcases were accompanied by a rotund figure who we later found out was a Bishop, although he came somewhat disguised. They ordered some of Sally's best homemade pastries and coffee and were very complimentary.

They were waiting to be joined by the local priest. Oddly enough, although we knew vaguely about him, we had never set eyes on him. Most likely our little village was the least of his workload, except the occasional birth, death and marriage. And Christmas mass.

Now he had been summoned.

When he arrived several of our regular patrons got up and shook hands with him. He was a small man, probably in his fifties, with a greyish complexion and eyes that darted around as if he wasn't sure who his friends were. I suspect he knew he was in for a grilling, although as far as we knew he had never said or done anything about the caves or Saint Livraque himself. Quite possibly, although he must have heard about it and certainly seen the newspaper article, he had hoped it would all blow over and leave him and his little rural parish in peace.

He joined the Catholic group at their table, nervously shaking hands with each one, then ordered a Ricard. In the space of the next half hour he ordered two more. He needed fortification.

Agathe came in and joined them She had a very purposeful stride, markedly different from the priestly approach. It turned out she was Catholic. She kissed the Bishop's ring so she must have been.

It was hard to tell exactly what the conversation was but we could imagine. Agathe did all the talking but she leaned in conspiratorially, glancing now and then in my and Sally's direction.

Then finally they got up, one of the young men paid for everything and Agathe took them off to her «Tourist Office» to get kitted up. The reluctance of the local priest was palpable.

An hour later they were back and ordered lunch. The priest had left but Agathe stayed with the visitors. As she took her seat, she looked at me with a superior smile. I couldn't tell what it meant, except that she liked being in the limelight.

After lunch, with more of Simon's coffee served, one of the young men came over to me and asked in very good English if I could introduce the person with the broken leg. Kurt had not put in an appearance that morning, maybe aware of who was dining on his premises.

I took the young man out to the grange and there was Kurt with Laetitia, both with greasy hands, in the pit under the hoist doing something to the undersides of the Peugeot 203. The Panhard was almost ready to hit the road so the Peugeot was their new challenge.

The young man introduced himself and told Kurt that he worked for the Catholic church. Laetitia frowned and quietly slipped out of the pit.

«You want to convert me?» grinned Kurt as he clambered out. Then he apologised for not shaking hands.

The young man smiled. «I can assure you that conversion is not my intention.» he said. «I work for the church in a department that is entrusted with saintly investigations.»

«So you heard about our saint, did you?»

«The news has reached us, yes.»

«Do you believe it?» Kurt was showing no sign of being intimidated at all.

«For us, it is not a matter of belief. We are, if you like, detectives. In our archives we have found some references to Saint Livraque from many years ago, but our church has not proceeded with any movement towards acknowledged sainthood.»

«So you don't think he really was a saint?»

«Do you mean whether he was a real person, or was he a saintly person?»

«Either way. Why else does the village have that name?»

«I am sure the answer to that is lost in history. Maybe your historienne can give you the answer.»

«Yeah, dear old Agathe knows lots of stories. True or not, who knows.»

«For us, the question is whether there is evidence, clear evidence of saintly intervention. We must distinguish between myth and reality.»

«What does it take for our guy to get the nod?»

«You mean to be granted sainthood? For the church to recognise a saint, there must be clear and irrefutable evidence of miraculous healing. Intervention.»

I was very impressed with his vocabulary.

Kurt chuckled. «You want to know about my leg I suppose.» Then he winked. «Do I get a reward?»

The young man smiled. «Maybe in heaven.» Then he added: «but perhaps you have already received your reward, if it is indeed a miracle from a saint.»

«I thought it was pretty miraculous.» said Kurt, then went on to tell his story. He started with the dream and what he heard. The young man asked if the instructions were in French. Kurt wasn't too sure, admitting his French wasn't great.

The young man smiled and said that he was sure that Kurt's French must be improving. I notice that with the French. Whenever you apologise for your level of language skill, they always politely assure you that you are doing OK. I think they like the fact that you are at least trying your best. I have become very used to apologising almost every time I talk to a new French person. It always seems to set a good tone.

So Kurt described going down into the cave with me and Patrick. The young man looked at me for confirmation and I nodded.

«I was a witness.» I said,

Then Kurt told him how we lowered him down and how the rope gave way.

«I hit the bottom, the plaster fell off and bingo, busted leg in one piece.»

The young man nodded. «But it could also have been that your leg was already healed before the plaster fell off. Don't you think?»

«Coulda been.» agreed Kurt. «Not being anything of an expert on miracles, I can't say more than I told you. You might be right.»

The young man nodded and looked like he was about to go back to the café.

«I tell you one thing, though,» added Kurt. «I knew it was him.»

The young man stopped «How?»

Kurt shrugged. «I just knew.»

«OK,» said the young man. »But we hear there are others.»

«Oh yeah. I'm not the only one.»

«Yes,» said the young man. There was no doubt Agathe had talked about what she knew, but probably not nearly as much as Kurt.

He had a small kind of tablet device and was making notes on it as Kurt told him about Laetitia, Erik, Pascal and the motor bike boy from Gordon, but you could see that the young man was less than impressed.

«I am thinking we need something a bit more, shall we say dramatic. Curing of a deadly disease, or resurrrection after apparent death. And usually the miracle happens after someone prays to the saint.»

«I think you might be out of luck there.» said Kurt, « I certainly didn't do any praying. I don't think any of the others did either, but if I hear of any Lazaruses I'll let you know.»

The young man thanked Kurt and went back to the Bishop to report. The Bishop sat back in his chair and nodded.

They got up and thanked us for lunch and off they went.

Once she had waved them off, I asked Agathe whether she thought, they might go any further and she shrugged.

«I am not so hopeful. They hear stories all the time and they need to be sure. They need serious miracles.»

«Our miracles weren't up to standard?»

«Not so far.»

«You must be sorry,» I said. «It could have been a good deal for you.»

She nodded, then she looked at me sharply. «You think I am doing this to make money?»

I hastened to assure her that I was thinking no such thing.

After the lunch shift was over Sally and went round to see Jean-Pierre.

He had the coffee on, although these days we were drinking much more than we should be in the Bat Café.

When we asked for his opinion on the church investigation, he smiled. «Oh I don't think our saint is looking for too much publicity of that kind. He has always been, how you might say, low key.»

«So no big miracles then?»

«He will do what is miraculous, when he feels inclined. I don't think he wishes to be a spectacle.»

That kind of made sense to us and in a way I was glad. I was beginning to be very fond of our little saint and rather liked having him more or less to ourselves. Just us, the holy mechanics and the simple folk that he wanted to help.

It felt rather good.

23.

Once word got around about the church investigation, the village enthusiastically talked about the possibility of becoming a holy site, at least in the eyes of the church. There was more than a hint that some of them saw some lucrative opportunity, but as time went on and nothing much happened, the speculation died off. The gites did steady business but not much more than usual.

Visitors kept coming though, and Agathe did quite well with her outfits and her guided tours. She had even branched out into souvenirs, most probably breaking various French laws to do it, but nobody seemed to care. She had taken unauthorised photos of the stained glass window of our saint and had them reproduced in posters, one size fits all T-shirts and mugs. She had a brand new glass-topped counter installed in her tourist office and I think she did pretty well out of it.

Those visitors who were true believers had no need of her assistance and went down on their own unprotected, filling up their water bottles and leaving feeling blessed. We'd often see them in our café, sitting with their water bottles and talking about our saint in soft voices.

Others went down into the caves, not wanting to pay for a guide or protection and got thoroughly bitten. Quite a few others came with their own versions of protection.

And our little enterprise did a very steady trade.

Sometimes the ones who ventured in without protection and got bitten ended up in the Bat Café, so we bought a good supply of mosquito bite ointment, offered at no charge.

Summer holidays were approaching. In France this means all of July and August. The French are very particular about «les vacances» and they even have names for those who choose which month: «Juilletistes» in July and «Aoûtiens» in August.

All the gites in the village were booked solid and we got lots of enquiries as to whether we would rent rooms like the hotel used to.

Kurt was very clear about that. No way.

As all this went on there was a steady stream of anecdotes that showed that our saint was still in the business. Now and then one or other of our customers would tell us that they had benefitted in some way or heard a story about it. There were no major miraculous resurrections or death defying recoveries, but, as someone would tell what they had received or heard, most of them were convinced that Saint Livraque was responsible. It felt like there was a deep desire for something like that to exist.

The French do like having their own saints.

There was a general air of both gratitude and local pride.

Our village didn't have too many babies born, but two new pregnancies were joyfully attributed to divine assistance. Both Mothers swore they had prayed.

One young man who had been arrested for drug possession got his case dismissed and his mother was totally convinced that her daily visitations to the cave and ingestions of the spring water had been the reason. She also was a strong practioner of prayer. The one time she brought him to the Bat Café he sat with his head down and wouldn't make eye contact. I'm not sure he believed in miracles.

Laetitia would often take herself out on the Harley, sometimes in tandem with Kurt on his Ducati, sometimes on her own. Now and then Erik would go with her. And every now and then she would come back with some kind of two-wheeled entourage. A couple of them went with her into the cave.

Although none of them talked directly to us, it seemed that she was good at finding bikers who had problems, a few with drug challenges, others with marital problems, and one who was about to be deported.

Maybe some of them benefitted from saintly benevolence but it was hard to tell. Most left without saying anything to us, but we were pretty sure they had told Laetitia.

It was clear that she took her rôle seriously.

When Pascal came to stay with Erik, he went down into the cave every day.

Pascal was a changed man. He sat with us in the café often and it was fascinating to see what he was wrestling with. He was discovering a whole new relationship with God, with Jesus, and with our saint. What he was most challenged by was how to align what he was discovering inside himself with the established religion that he still felt he belonged to.

Kurt joked that maybe he had to start a new religion of his own but Pascal said he had no intention of doing that.

«Imagine the work it takes to run a religion.»

«Oh, I dunno,» chuckled Kurt. «You could make a lot of money doing that.»

«Or get crucified.»

«Look at the Americans.» said Kurt, obviously enjoying himself. «Guys there set themselves up in mega churches and then tootle around with private jets. Looks like a good career move.»

«No,» Pascal said, not really offended by Kurt, «I don't think that what I am going through could be turned into a church. It is just something inside me.»

«So you don't think you can still be a pastor?» asked Sally.

He shrugged. «Who knows?»

This took a fascinating turn when the local priest came to Saint Livraque for the baptism of one of the, possibly miraculous, babies. After the baptism in the church the party came to the Bat Cafe to celebrate and the priest was invited.

He ordered his Ricard and was sitting with the proud new parents and grandparents when Pascal came in.

I didn't see how it happened, but somehow Pascal and the priest ended up sitting at a table in a quiet corner with their heads together.

When the priest finally got up to leave, he and Pascal gave each other a very long hug and I had to ask what happened.

«He had a secret.» said Pascal. «He knows all about Saint Livraque. He has known about him since he was a very young man, but Saint Livraque told him not to tell anyone. Saint Livraque prefers to work in the shadows.»

«Did the saint do something special for him?»

Pascal nodded. «He doesn't want anyone to know so I can only guess about the details. He did say he went down to the caves very often when he was young and did not keep good company at that time. I think maybe he had some friends who were, shall we say, not very well behaved.»

«And they used to hang out in the caves?»

«I think so.»

«What did they do in there?»

«He didn't say but I don't think it was anything his parents would have approved of.»

«But our saint changed that?» asked Sally

«I think so.»

Then I had to smile. «Maybe I can give him back his Bic lighter.» I then had to explain how Patrick and I had found one on our first ventures into the cave.

Pascal shrugged. «Maybe so.»

«Is it because of our saint that he became a priest?» asked Sally.

Pascal nodded.

«This much he did say. He became a priest to say sorry and because the saint told him he had work to do and being a priest would be the best way to do it.»

«Jean-Pierre must know about this,» said Sally.

Pascal nodded. «Probably.»

«What else did you talk about?»

«Oh we have a lot in common. He has an Indian motor bike. He has a Royal Enfield.»

Then Sally and I had to laugh. What was it about this saint and motor bikes?

Sally asked: «So I suppose you told him about Kurt and Laetitia? The saint's mechanics?».

Pascal nodded. «He knew already.»

Sally and I talked about all that at the end of the day, sitting in bed after closing up the cafe for the day. There were probably so many more stories about our saint. Maybe there were all sorts of people who had some connection but had kept it secret.

We wondered just how much Jean-Pierre and Eloise knew.

The mystery of how saints work and why they seem to come and go, do a bit of good and then disappear, intrigued us both. And here we were, neither of us directly affected by the saint but somehow connected to it all.

What did it mean?

We both agreed, in the end, that it was just the way it was and that trying to rationalise didn't do any good.

24.

Then suddenly it was all over. Not that the events in Saint Livraque stopped happening, they probably never will, but for us, it did.

The first sign of that was when Sally woke up one morning and said: «I think we are going home.»

That was a total surprise to me. Up till then I had felt that maybe we would live out our days holed up in our little village, selling coffee and enjoying the mystical doings of our own local saint.

Sally said it was just a strong feeling she had. I was getting quite used to her intuitive side and I trusted it a lot.

I had called my parents now and then and they seemed to be fine. My mother did most of the talking and my father would add a few words here and there. It turns out however that they had been shielding me from the truth. My father was rapidly descending into Alzheimers.

My Mother had agonised over how and when to tell me. However once the police found my father walking down the street in nothing but his dressing gown in the middle of the night, my mother freaked out and told me.

That was just a few days after Sally's intuitive feeling.

It was clear to us that my mother was terrified to face this on her own and we knew we had to go.

Kurt put up mild resistance, muttering that he had invested in us and hadn't got his money's worth yet but it was not real. He understood.

The thought did cross our minds about our saint. Could he do something?

We asked Jean-Pierre.

«Sometimes,» he said, with a cat on his lap, «when a soul gets towards the end of its time on earth, it has to face things that are just too difficult, so it retreats into a state of what you might call not-knowing, to shelter it from what it cannot face. The saints understand this as compassion for that soul and so they would not want to reverse it. Of course it is a challenge for those who have loved and need to look after this person.»

«So there is nothing for us to do?»

«Oh yes, there is something to do. It is good that you will go and be with your mother, but before you go you can spend some time in preparation.»

«In the cave?» asked Sally, and he nodded.

«You may not even be aware but you can be sure that you have received his blessing.»

I think, even if Jean Pierre had not suggested it, we would have gone down there anyway.

For the week before we left, we trained Gwyn in every aspect of how to run the cafe and she was on fire with enthusiasm. Didier insisted she be salaried and she was chuffed, as she said. He set it all up with the right paperwork. France loves its paperwork. He himself decided to become more physically present. They were going to be a dynamic duo.

While Gwyn stepped into her rôle, Sally and I went down every morning to the caves. Sometimes other people would come and go but mostly we were alone.

Kurt and Laetitia did not come with us, nor any of the others. They knew it was our time to be there on our own.

What happened I can only describe as deep peace. We would sit there, drink some of the water, and close our eyes.

There was such a sense of being supported, buoyed, comforted.

That was his blessing.

Saint Livraque himself never appeared to either of us, nor gave us any direct instructions, but he is certainly and always will be our saint.

And we went home.

Authorial Note

As mentioned up front, this is a work entirely of fiction. Of course some readers who have visited the bastide alluded to in the foreword will recognise the genesis of the tale. There are bats in the caves under the walls and they do have fleas, although I have never been brave enough to venture in. I hasten to claim that none of the characters are based on citizens of said village but of course, as all fiction writers do, I have borrowed and hybridised all sorts of elements. Now whether this village ever had a saint, well anything is possible.

Once again I am grateful for the discerning eye of Susie L, even when she and I disagree about how to use commas.

Thank you Pip D for the cover photo.

And thank you for choosing to dive into the life of Saint Livraque.

I am always happy to hear from readers at rudra.sharp@gmail.com

www.ingramcontent.com/pod-product-compliance
Lightning Source LLC
LaVergne TN
LVHW041702070526
838199LV00045B/1160